A million things could go wrong, but they had to go in anyway.

The helicopter touched down and Bolan was the first one out. He dropped into a crouch and watched for any threats while the others disembarked.

The carnage was striking. The soldier counted two helicopters, their twisted and charred remains at ten o'clock and three o'clock. Fire ate the frames and pumped thick black columns of smoke into the sky. A quick sweep of the terrain revealed five dead uniformed guards. A couple of the corpses bobbed facedown in the swimming pool, the water around them clouded with blood. The bodies of two other men, both in black, were sprawled on the ground. Bolan assumed they were part of Geiger's crew.

He also saw the bodies of at least a half dozen men and women in khaki pants and dark green polo shirts. They seemed to be e~~~~~~~ ~~~~~ magazines and hand~~~~~ ground near a couple ~~~~~ been a fight; it had be~~~~~

Other titles available
in this series:

Silent Running
Stolen Arrows
Zero Option
Predator Paradise
Circle of Deception
Devil's Bargain
False Front
Lethal Tribute
Season of Slaughter
Point of Betrayal
Ballistic Force
Renegade
Survival Reflex
Path to War
Blood Dynasty
Ultimate Stakes
State of Evil
Force Lines
Contagion Option
Hellfire Code
War Drums
Ripple Effect
Devil's Playground
The Killing Rule
Patriot Play
Appointment in Baghdad
Havana Five
The Judas Project
Plains of Fire
Colony of Evil
Hard Passage
Interception
Cold War Reprise
Mission: Apocalypse
Altered State

Killing Game
Diplomacy Directive
Betrayed
Sabotage
Conflict Zone
Blood Play
Desert Fallout
Extraordinary Rendition
Devil's Mark
Savage Rule
Infiltration
Resurgence
Kill Shot
Stealth Sweep
Grave Mercy
Treason Play
Assassin's Code
Shadow Strike
Decision Point
Road of Bones
Radical Edge
Fireburst
Oblivion Pact
Enemy Arsenal
State of War
Ballistic
Escalation Tactic
Crisis Diplomacy
Apocalypse Ark
Lethal Stakes
Illicit Supply
Explosive Demand
Jungle Firestorm
Terror Ballot
Death Metal

Don Pendleton's Mack Bolan®

Justice Run

A GOLD EAGLE BOOK FROM
WORLDWIDE®

TORONTO • NEW YORK • LONDON
AMSTERDAM • PARIS • SYDNEY • HAMBURG
STOCKHOLM • ATHENS • TOKYO • MILAN
MADRID • WARSAW • BUDAPEST • AUCKLAND

Recycling programs
for this product may
not exist in your area.

First edition June 2014

ISBN-13: 978-0-373-61569-8

Special thanks and acknowledgment to
Tim Tresslar for his contribution to this work.

JUSTICE RUN

Printed in U.S.A.

Justice is justly represented blind, because she sees no difference in the parties concerned. She has but one scale and weight, for rich and poor, great and small.

—William Penn
Some Fruits of Solitude

Justice may be blind, but I am her eyes, forever seeking out those who would escape punishment.

—Mack Bolan

PROLOGUE

Monaco
Three months earlier

He had to get out of there.

The elevator doors parted and Fred Gruber burst from the confined space. He found himself surrounded by the sounds of meat sizzling, knives striking cutting boards and people shouting at one another in French. He looked around and saw men and women dressed in white chef hats and stained aprons standing at cooking stations, cutting vegetables or cooking meat on large griddles. On any other day, the amateur chef would've considered this a gift from heaven, a chance to watch skilled cooks make five-star French cuisine.

This night he couldn't have cared less.

He just wanted to stay alive.

At first he tried walking fast through the kitchen, hoping to pass through with a minimum of fuss. He had covered maybe ten paces when one of the chefs, a heavyset man with a handlebar mustache, spotted him. Without setting down his utensils, the guy turned toward Gruber.

"What are you doing?" the chef demanded in French. "You can't come in here."

Without breaking his pace, Gruber forced a smile on his face and closed the distance between them.

"Sorry," Gruber, an American, replied in the same language. "I am lost."

Gruber brushed past the man, who was offering to help him find his way, but Gruber tried to ignore the man. On the other side of the kitchen, he saw an exit door. He wanted to get through it, step into the warm Monaco evening and run like hell to his car.

He wore blue suit pants, black wingtips and a white broadcloth dress shirt. The tails of the shirt were pulled out of his waistband. His tie was where he'd left it, looped over the back of a mahogany chair. His Glock was stuffed into his waistband.

Before he could take another step, he felt a hand clamp heavily on his left shoulder. His stomach plummeted and he whirled. His right hand slipped up under his shirt, fingers curling around the pistol's grip, while his other one slapped the man's hand away. In a heartbeat the chef's expression went from mildly irritated to surprise. Gruber took a step back from the guy, ready to order him to back off, when he heard the elevator ding followed by the whoosh of the opening doors.

Gruber yanked the Glock from his waistband and displayed it so the chef could see it. The guy's face paled and he stepped back. Gruber wheeled and resumed his sprint for the door, shoving other members of the kitchen staff from his path. Judging by the screams, the slap of footsteps against the floor and the clatter of dishes breaking, pandemonium had broken out behind him. Though his pursuers likely were armed, he doubted they'd try shooting at him in this crowd or, for that matter, in this building. The hotel catered to the rich and powerful, which included police chiefs and military generals. The last thing the people chasing him wanted was official attention. They had been operating in the shadows for years. Gruber had no doubt they wanted to keep it that way.

That's why they wanted to stop him. He'd spent a couple of weeks in Berlin, rooting around for information.

What he'd found had knocked him on his ass. Enough so that he'd considered contacting his old cronies in Washington. He'd dismissed the idea outright. What he knew just seemed too fantastic. If he called his friends at the Bureau, they might not believe him. They might even assume he was bored in retirement and trying to drum up excitement and relive his glory days.

He wouldn't have blamed them.

Then he'd come to Monaco, to put some final pieces together. Gruber knew their plans; he knew the players. He finally had some proof. Now all he needed was to share what he knew.

When Gruber reached the exit, he pushed down on the release bar, shoved the door open and ran outside, barely slowing at all. The night was warm, with a light breeze. But the stench of rotting food rising up from the garbage bins hung in the air. He'd put several yards between himself and the kitchen by the time he heard the door slam closed behind him. Arms and legs pumping hard, he tried to gather speed as he put some distance between himself and the building.

He hadn't expected to end up in this situation, running for his life. A former FBI agent, he figured he'd left all the dangerous stuff behind when he had retired from the Bureau, got his PI license and started chasing wayward spouses for a daily fee plus expenses. Then he'd gotten a call from an old man offering incredible money. What did he have to do to earn it? The old man sat on a corporate board with another guy who as of late had been disappearing for days on end. Money had been disappearing from the company's coffers, too. Could Gruber look into it? The old man was willing to pay a retainer, put him up in sweet hotels and make sure he ate like a damn king.

Hell, yeah, Gruber could look into it.

Idiot.

He'd be lucky if he lived to spend his retainer.

When he reached the sprawling parking lot at the back of the hotel, he heard footsteps pounding against the pavement behind him. Pumping his arms and legs harder, he darted between a pair of parked cars.

His first inclination was to turn and fire on his pursuers. A warning shot over their heads might make them back off. He dismissed the idea. If he was still a U.S. federal agent, he'd do it and hope he could avoid any legal problems. As a private detective he had no authority, including the authority to carry or discharge a pistol in a foreign city. He'd bought the gun from a contact here in Monaco. When he asked the guy whether the gun was hot, the man had just smiled, knocked fifty dollars off the price and told Gruber to stow the questions.

Gruber heard something slap against one of the cars. He glanced down and saw a spiderweb had formed on the rear window of the vehicle, followed a heartbeat later by second bullet sparking off the car's roof and zipping into the darkness.

They had sound suppressors.

Gruber dropped to one knee an instant before a storm of bullets pounded into the cars on either side of him, drilling holes in the bodywork. Slugs pierced tires, flattening them, as other rounds lanced through the windows.

Jesus, if he didn't fight back, they were going to kill him right here. He hadn't expected this. But either he was dealing with true believers willing to go to jail for their cause or they had enough money to buy their way out of trouble.

From what Gruber knew, it was a little of both. He was dealing with fanatics and they had money.

Moving in a crouch, he backed away from the shooters, sticking as close as possible to the silver Mercedes to his right. The cars were parked nose-in, so the bullets were piercing the trunk lids, the rear quarter panels and the roofs.

When Gruber reached the Mercedes' front bumper, he saw it was parked a couple of feet from the front bumper of another luxury sedan. Rounding the car's front end, he sandwiched himself between the two vehicles and popped his head up in time to see one of his pursuers—a guy built like a pro wrestler with the long, bleached hair to match— closing in on the car. He had his pistol extended forward in a two-handed grip, and Gruber could see a wisp of smoke coming out of the sound suppressor.

The guy was so intent on looking at where he'd last seen Gruber that he failed to see the former federal agent from his new position. Resting both arms on the car's hood, Gruber drew down on the man, exhaled and squeezed off a shot.

The Glock roared and the shooter jerked back, as though hit by an invisible baseball bat. Releasing the pistol from his hands, he grabbed at his throat and collapsed to the ground.

To the former Fed's right, a second thug togged in a loud Hawaiian shirt popped up from behind a parked car and squeezed off a couple of shots. The PI felt one of the bullets zing past his left ear. He folded down between the cars again, grinding his teeth as slugs pelted the Mercedes.

After a couple of seconds the shooting ceased and Gruber guessed his opponent was reloading. Rising slightly, he peered over the Mercedes' pocked hood and saw the guy had dropped out of sight.

It also occurred to him that three guys had followed him from the hotel.

In the distance he heard sirens wailing and, out of reflex, he felt relief wash over him.

Yeah, he hadn't wanted any legal entanglements. But that was before these bastards showed just how determined they were. Plus, the FBI agent and lawyer in him balked at running from a dead body, especially when he was the killer. Maybe he'd be safer in police custody. They'd contact his embassy, he'd tell them what he knew and Washington would, hopefully, swoop in to help.

They'd have to do something. Even if they didn't help him, they had to stop the hell that was going to unfold across Europe.

He peered over the hood again and saw Mr. Hawaiian Shirt creeping across the parking lot toward him. Gruber raised the Glock and snapped off a couple of shots at the guy. The gunner flinched and darted out of sight.

The sirens were louder and closer.

Gruber heard the rustle of cloth behind him. He wheeled. A shoe sole hit him in the jaw and knocked him on his side. The coppery taste of blood filled his mouth.

Another man, the third guy who'd disappeared, stood over him, his sound-suppressed weapon aimed at Gruber.

"Please to drop the weapon," the man said.

Gruber loosened his grip and the weapon clattered to the ground.

The guy grinned.

"You can't stop this," he said. "It's gone too far."

The gun whispered once. A bullet slammed into Gruber's forehead and thrust him into blackness.

THE ALARM ON Reinhard Vogelsgang's wristwatch beeped three times, interrupting his train of thought as he pored over the most recent profit-and-loss statements.

Clicking off the alarm, he removed his wire-framed reading glasses, set them on his desk blotter and rose from his chair.

Crossing the office, he moved to a rectangular panel built into the wall and surrounded on all four sides by wood molding. He pressed a small stud and the panel slid away, only the slight hum of a motor audible from behind the wall. Behind the panel was a recessed area that contained a large video monitor. He snagged a remote from inside the compartment, switched on the monitor and thumbed the button that turned on the screen.

The phone call had come twelve hours ago. The news he received had left a knot in his stomach and had forced him to make a decision. Considering the stakes, it'd been an easy one. Even so, the ramifications could bring all sorts of hell crashing down on his head if he didn't handle it correctly.

The screen was separated into four boxes. In the far right corner sat an elderly man in a dark blue suit. In a box beneath him, the image of a woman was visible. The meeting's third participant was late, as usual, joining the call two minutes after the start time.

"I guess we can begin now," Vogelsgang said as the latest participant, Werner Nacht, a construction-industry magnate, seated himself.

"So sorry," Nacht said.

"It's nothing," Vogelsgang replied.

"I was caught in a meeting."

"Of course. No doubt it was more important."

Nacht laced his fingers and leaned toward the camera.

"Tremendously important," he said. "Shall I share?"

Vogelsgang shook his head.

"I think we've lost enough time," he said.

"No, really. This has more than a little relationship to our work here."

"Oh?"

"It's about Monaco. I think everyone wants to know about that. Wouldn't you agree?"

Vogelsgang forced a smile. "Of course. Please update everyone."

"A private detective was killed tonight, shot down in

the streets by a couple of thugs. They accosted him in his hotel and chased him into the street. Awful business."

"Awful," Vogelsgang agreed.

"Would you like to tell the rest of the story, or shall I?"

Vogelsgang swallowed hard. His forced smile fading, he shrugged and leaned into the camera. "We had a problem," he said. "Someone sent a private detective after me. The man was better than we anticipated. He figured a few things out. I had him eliminated."

The woman leaned forward.

"You what?" she asked. "You had him killed? Without discussing it with us?"

The executive's smile faded. "Let me assure you, it needed to be taken care of. I had no time to consult you. Frankly, I saw no reason. The decision was painfully obvious."

Anger flashed in the woman's eyes, but she stayed silent.

"What did he know?" asked the elderly man, a media mogul who owned two newspapers, three television stations and a book publishing operation.

Shrugging, Vogelsgang backed away from the large monitor and lowered himself into a leather chair. He knew what was coming and he wanted the best view possible. He responded to the old man's question with silence.

After several seconds the old man's face reddened. "Damn it," he said, his voice growing louder, "what did he know? Did he know everything?"

Another shrug from Vogelsgang, who busied himself staring at his drink.

"He knew a few things," Vogelsgang said finally. "He knew a surprising number of things for someone who'd come out of nowhere, a foreigner, in fact. He had credentials and experience, of course, but could barely speak the language."

Vogelsgang turned his eyes up from his drink.

"He could barely speak German or French. Yet he pieced together so much information. He even started to tie me to the United Front. It was amazing, as though someone was feeding him information." He paused and let his words sink in. "An insider, I mean."

The woman, Katharina Rothschild, leaned away from the camera and licked her lips. "Do you know who hired him?" she asked, her voice husky.

"I have some ideas," Vogelsgang said. "A hypothesis, really. Nothing more."

He dipped an index finger into his drink and stirred it.

"It's a bit early for a drink, I suppose. Still, I'm feeling good, feeling as though things are moving forward. A drink seems in order. I digress, though, Katharina. You'd asked me a question and I owe you an answer. No, I don't know who hired our dead friend. My thought— My theory, if you will, is someone close to me hired him. Maybe someone who's getting cold feet, someone who's lost her sense of vision."

He saw fear flicker in Rothschild's eyes. "'Her'?" she asked.

"Excuse me?"

"Her. You said 'her.' Surely you don't think I hired the man, do you?"

He made a dismissive gesture.

"Just a theory," he said. "Okay, a little more than a theory, actually. We grabbed his cell phone and his laptop and scoured the hell out of those things. So it's a theory based on evidence."

The old man leaned toward his camera. "Katharina? Katharina, did you do as he says? Why would you do this?"

"I did no such thing!"

"Please, everyone, please calm down," Vogelsgang said.

"Let's pull it together. Katharina, I admit it was a bit of a shock at first. However, now I want to thank you."

Nacht, the construction executive, laughed derisively.

"Thank her?" he asked. "For betraying us? Have you lost your mind?"

Vogelsgang shook his head slowly. "Lost my mind? Quite the contrary. I feel as though I've gained it. For the first time in years, since I first began all the hard work on this, I'm really seeing how this works. See, I don't... No, I can't trust you people. I've suspected that for some time. And now you've proved me right. This thing I want to accomplish, this thing Europe and the world needs so badly, I must accomplish it by myself."

"You're throwing us out?" It was Nacht again. "Damn you, I've sunk millions into this! You can't just toss us aside like this."

"I appreciate your passion, Werner. It's a business decision. Surely you of all people can appreciate that. Rest assured I'm not going to toss you aside or dissolve the partnership."

"Well, what the devil are you talking about then?"

"It's a liquidation."

Nacht continued to protest as did the others. Vogelsgang pressed the mute button on his remote control and blissful silence fell over the room. He felt the anticipation building, a ticklish sensation in his stomach that spread to his groin.

The woman suddenly whipped her head to the side and appeared to gasp. She slapped a hand over her chest, as if to keep her heart from jumping out. Vogelsgang turned the volume back up just in time to hear a scream burst from her lips. From off screen, gunshots sounded and one slapped into her forehead, knocking her from her chair. His team would make sure it looked like a robbery, just as they'd made the detective's murder look like a mugging.

Vogelsgang sat transfixed as the others died on-screen,

one right after the next. A man togged in black, his face covered by a ski mask, jabbed a needle into the old man's neck. His heart problems were common knowledge among friends, politicians and the financial press. Though he was ninety-three, he'd placed himself on a transplant list for a new heart.

He needn't have bothered.

The syringe's contents would result in a heart attack and be virtually undetectable in an autopsy.

In the other screen, Werner's head was tilted to the right. Dead eyes stared at the camera, but his body was still. A black-suited figure stood behind the executive, still pulling on the rope looped around his neck. Vogelsgang's mercenaries would make Werner's death look like a suicide. A couple of his high-profile deals had gone south in the past few months, which would make suicide plausible.

Vogelsgang clicked a button on the remote control and the monitor went black.

The brush with the detective had been too close. He'd devoted too much time and money bringing this plan together to have it fall apart because of betrayal. There was too much at stake.

Looking up at the monitor, he focused on the image of the old man. Vogelsgang had known the man for decades. But looking at him now, he just felt cold. Vogelsgang knew he'd kill 100—hell, 1,000 more—just like this man to realize his vision.

Let the bloodletting begin.

CHAPTER ONE

Monaco
Present day

Jacques Dumond lived on an estate on the outskirts of Monte Carlo. A stone security wall surrounded the property, obscuring the grounds from passersby.

Mack Bolan, aka the Executioner, was at the wheel of a black Jaguar sedan. He guided the vehicle past the front gate. Peering through the windshield, he studied a pair of men standing outside a wrought-iron gate that led into the estate.

Though he could see no weapons, Bolan assumed the grim-faced men were guards because they seemed more focused on their surroundings than interacting with each other. And the smaller of the two, a slim guy decked out in a black suit, was holding what appeared to be a two-way radio in his right hand. The other guy—dressed in jeans, a white shirt and an ill-fitting blue sport coat, his bald head glinting under the streetlights—fixed his gaze on Bolan's car as it glided past. The Jaguar was outfitted with black-tinted windows that prevented the big man from seeing anything other than his reflection as Bolan wheeled by.

Leo Turrin was in the front passenger's seat. He nodded at the man watching their car.

"The big guy is yours," Turrin said. "I'll take the little one."

"Thanks."

Bolan drove three more blocks, making sure he was well out of the guards' sight before he turned right. He drove another two blocks before making another right and maneuvering around the rear of the estate.

Pulling the car up to a curb, the soldier's mind reeled through key facts about his target.

Before falling from grace, Dumond had been a high-level French soldier who specialized in counterterrorism operations. After a decade he'd moved to the dark side. His business card read "security expert," but in truth he worked as a mercenary and enforcer for some of the world's most vicious regimes. He'd led death squads in Sudan and Sierra Leone, trained antigovernment killers in Colombia and provided muscle for Mexican drug cartels. A scrape in that country had cost him his left eye. Apparently, once he moved into his mid-forties, he'd decided it was easier to sell guns than wield them. He began selling arms to some of the same criminal regimes he'd once worked for. The experts back in Washington disagreed on his exact body count, but knew it was significant, at least two-thirds of it being women and children murdered in the world's conflict zones.

So, yeah, Bolan was hunting a jackal this night. The bastard's blood-drenched résumé was more than enough to make him a legitimate target, but Dumond also had made the mistake of grabbing Jennifer Rodriguez, an American federal agent, which kicked him up a few more notches on the soldier's hit parade.

Bolan and Turrin had arrived there ready to take on the Frenchman and his crew of gunners. Beneath a light black windbreaker, Bolan carried a pair of Beretta 93-R pistols in a double shoulder harness. The pistols were able to fire either single rounds or in 3-round bursts of 9 mm Parabellum ammo. With a foregrip in front of the trigger guard, the pistol could to fire 1,100 rounds per minute.

The soldier also had procured another of his old stand-bys. The 44 Magnum Desert Eagle Mark VII rode on his left hip in a cross-draw position. Outfitted with the six-inch barrel, the hand cannon's magazine carried eight rounds.

Bolan's other tools of war were sealed in the trunk. There he had stashed a Heckler & Koch MP-5 fitted with a sound suppressor, and a small duffel bag loaded with additional magazines for the submachine gun as well as an assortment of fragmentation, flash-bang and smoke grenades.

Turrin, on the other hand, had opted for a Benelli M-4 Super 90 shotgun. Manufactured by Benelli Armi SPA, an Italian company, the shotgun could be loaded with one 12-gauge round in the chamber and seven more in the tube. Like Bolan, Turrin was carrying a Beretta 93-R. He wanted the weapon because of its sound suppressor and its ability to fire multiple rounds with a single trigger pull. But he also was armed with a .38-caliber Colt Cobra that was holstered in the small of his back. The short-barreled pistol's aluminum-alloy frame made it light to carry and it was easily concealed.

Bolan eased the Jaguar to the curb, turned off the lights and killed the engine. He popped open the door and stepped into the warm night. Turrin had stepped out of the passenger's side and both men made their way to the trunk.

Bolan raised the lid, reached in, hefted the duffel bag and slid its strap over his shoulder. The bag's weight caused its strap to pull taut until he could feel it dig into the muscles of his left shoulder. Next he pulled out the MP-5 and checked its load. Turrin had pulled out the Benelli and was looping the strap over his right shoulder.

Reaching back into the compartment, Bolan pulled a rope with a grappling hook.

"You realize it'd be easier to go through the front gate," Turrin said.

"Sure," Bolan replied. "No one would notice two guys shooting two other guys and then busting through a wrought-iron fence."

"I'm just making a point."

"Rope climbing a little too strenuous for you, Leo?"

"No comment."

Grinning, Bolan turned and looked back at the wall surrounding the estate. Inside the wall, Dumond usually had anywhere between four and six gunners patrolling the grounds, especially when he was entertaining high-end clients, most of whom also were prone to violence. And, according to his dossier, the arms dealer also sampled some of his own wares, carrying a pair of Detonics .45-caliber pistols beneath his well-tailored jackets and at least one combat blade.

Bolan keyed his throat mike.

"Striker to Base," he said.

"Go, Striker," a female voice replied. It was Barbara Price, the mission controller for Stony Man Farm. Bolan and Turrin were connected with the Farm's ultrasecret facility thanks to satellite links.

"We're EVA," he said, "and ready to hit the town."

"You're clear," Price told him.

"Did they crash the party?"

"They" was the Farm's cyber team, which had been working to hack into the computers that controlled Dumond's lighting, security system and other critical infrastructure ever since Bolan and Turrin had left the United States.

"Party crashed. Once we saw you stop outside the target, we set the outside surveillance cameras on a loop. If anyone's monitoring the cameras, all they'll see is the same empty street they saw three minutes ago."

"Which is fine," Bolan said, "until they realize they've

seen the same car or dog walker pass by eight times in the last couple of minutes."

"Guess you'll have to move faster than they can think," Price replied.

"Are you getting any good intel otherwise?"

"Satellites indicate four guys walking the grounds inside the wall," Price said. "Two smaller animals, probably dogs, moving separately from them. That's all in addition to the thugs at the gate. Looks like another moving around on the rooftop."

"Okay," Bolan replied.

He returned to the trunk and popped the lid again. Pulling aside a blanket, he revealed a rectangular box, covered in faux leather, which was about four inches thick.

He opened the box and from its interior removed a CO_2-powered dart pistol. Breaking the weapon open, he slid a tranquilizer dart into the barrel and snapped it closed. He slipped a smaller box filled with extra darts into his jacket pocket."

"Still won't shoot dogs, huh?" Turrin asked.

Bolan turned toward him and shook his head. "The dogs don't know what they're doing," he said. "They just do as their told."

Turrin nodded his understanding. "You always did like your rules."

"It's what separates me from Dumond," Bolan said.

"Yeah, that and his massive bank account in the Cayman Islands."

Bolan allowed himself a grin. "There's that."

Shutting the trunk for a second time, the soldier slid the dart pistol into the duffel bag and moved toward the fence. If the cyber team had done its job, the motion detectors and other security devices should be disabled without actually registering on Dumond's IT systems.

They had considered shutting down the electricity remotely, but had decided against it.

Dumond had to expect someone would come for the missing federal agent, even if he'd done his best to move her around. If they shut down electric power to the estate, it would alert Dumond that something was about to happen. His security teams probably would retreat to the house and form an iron ring around Dumond and Rodriguez, making them harder to reach. Besides, it was a safe bet the facility was outfitted with backup generators that would fire to life shortly after the power went out.

Bolan figured it was better for them to take out as many of the exterior guards as quickly and quietly as possible. They still had surprise on their side, and the neighborhood around them had no idea of the mayhem about to erupt. The longer the Stony Man warriors could maintain their advantage, the better.

Bolan scaled the wall. The muscles of his arms, shoulders and thighs bunched and released, starting to burn as he reached the top ledge and pulled himself onto it. He lay across the top of the wall, MP-5 clutched in his right fist, ice-blue eyes scanning for threats, while he waited for Turrin to finish his ascent.

The little Fed reached the top of the wall, his breath coming in labored gasps, sweat pouring down his face.

"Jesus," he muttered.

Bolan held up a finger to silence him, then jerked his head slightly to the left. Two of Dumond's hardmen had fallen across his line of sight. The submachine-gun-wielding thugs were less than thirty yards from the Americans, walking a few yards apart from each other.

Bolan raised himself onto his elbows, like a cobra lifting its head from the ground. He lined up a shot on the closer hardman.

Turrin had filled his hand with his sound-suppressed

Beretta and was maneuvering his body so he could put a shot into the second guard.

The Executioner caressed the MP-5's trigger. The weapon coughed out a burst. Bolan had tried to catch the guy in the chest. In the instant the soldier squeezed the trigger, the man turned. The bullets ripped into his right shoulder and lanced into his ribs, caused him to yelp in pain and shock. As he stumbled back, his partner spun toward the commotion and was searching for a target with the muzzle of his SMG. Before he could trigger his weapon, Turrin cut loose with a triburst. The Parabellum manglers ripped a ragged line across the guy's chest. He stumbled back a couple of steps before falling to the ground in a boneless heap.

Repositioning the grappling hook, Bolan dropped the rope down the wall. Letting the MP-5 fall loose on the strap, he gathered the rope in both hands and rappelled to the ground while Turrin covered him. When he touched down, the soldier dropped into a crouch and scanned the area for more attackers while Turrin made his way down the rope. Holding the MP-5 in his right hand, Bolan unzipped the duffel bag and withdrew the dart pistol. In the meantime, Turrin was kneeling next to one of the dead men. He plucked a bud from the dead man's ear and, reaching under the guy's coat, pulled the cord, tracing its length until he found the radio.

Bolan watched as Turrin slipped the bud into his own ear and listened for several seconds.

"They keep calling out names," he said, speaking in a whisper. "I assume it's these chuckleheads."

The soldier nodded and slowly rose into a crouch. As Turrin began to uncoil from the ground, Bolan looked just over his old friend's shoulder and spotted a shadow emerging from a copse.

Bolan's hand snaked out and he struck Turrin in the

right biceps. The impact knocked the man sideways. At the same time Bolan was able to aim the pistol's barrel at the shape launching itself from the ground. He could see the German shepherd dog's black face, jaws open, saliva-soaked fangs bared and gleaming as it hurtled toward him. The soldier triggered dart gun. The missile buried into the muscle of the animal's shoulder. If the sting of the dart registered with the dog, it gave no outward signs. Bolan whipped to the side, the animal's body hurtling past him, striking the ground, rolling once before springing up from the earth and turning back toward the humans.

A growl escaping its throat, the animal raced toward the Stony Man warriors. It leaped at Bolan, who was closer. Its jaws snapped at empty air. The soldier shoved his forearm out, and the dog's jaws clamped down on it. Bolts of pain radiated from Bolan's forearm, but he ignored it. The force of the dog striking him hammered Bolan from his feet and knocked him onto his back. He felt the animal's jaws loosen and by the time he hit the ground, the soldier was able to push the dog away with a hard shove. It wheeled back in his direction. Mouth open, it stared at Bolan, but its stance had grown unsteady and it seemed to stare at Bolan without focusing on him. Whimpering, its legs grew rubbery and it dropped to the ground, panting.

Bolan turned away from the animal, certain it would be all right once the tranquilizer wore off. A quick scan of the sleeve of his windbreaker revealed torn fabric and punctured flesh, but nothing he couldn't tolerate.

Turrin gathered the dart pistol from the ground and handed it to the soldier. Bolan took the pistol, broke it open, slid another dart into the breech and snapped the weapon closed.

"Bullets," Turrin said. "Faster, more effective."

"No," Bolan replied.

"Figured as much."

The Executioner gestured in the direction of the house with his chin.

"This way."

He brushed past Turrin and moved in a crouch toward the mansion. A long expanse of land, much of it covered by a well-manicured lawn, lay between them and the massive structure. Several large oak trees rose from the ground, each of which would provide decent cover in a firefight. A driveway wound in from the front gate and carved out a semicircle in front of the house. A large circular pool stood in front of the building. In the center of the pool stood a statue of a woman dressed in flowing robes, a pitcher gripped in both hands. Water spurted from a hole in the pitcher and arced into the pool.

After a few seconds Bolan spotted three more guards moving in a ragged line in his direction. He shot Turrin a look. With a nod the little Fed acknowledged that he saw them. One of the towering oak trees stood several yards away. Bolan gestured for Turrin to circle it and catch the guards from the side while Bolan moved head-on at them. He nodded once to signal his understanding and headed toward the trees.

Bolan had returned the dart pistol to his combat bag. A group of halogen outdoor lights bathed the yard in white light. The lights had caused the trees' canopies of leaves to cast fairly big shadows over the sprawling lawn, which provided them with additional cover.

The soldier knelt and brought the MP-5 to his shoulder. He flicked his gaze to the right and could see Turrin's shadow melt into a nearby tree. The man's location would position him within a couple dozen yards of the approaching hardmen.

"You have a clear shot?" Bolan asked.

"Yeah," Turrin replied.

"On three," the soldier said.

He whispered the three-count into his throat mike. When he reached the final number, he squeezed the trigger on the subgun. The volley of rounds sliced through the air between him and his targets as he dragged the SMG in a tight arc. At the same time, Turrin began firing the Beretta from Bolan's right. The sustained volley tore through the guards, whipsawing them as both fighters unloaded their weapons.

Within seconds all three guards lay on the ground, dead.

Getting to his feet, Bolan ejected the H&K's magazine, slammed a new one home and kept moving.

TWO DAYS EARLIER Bolan had walked into the War Room, part of the Stony Man Farm facility in Virginia, and taken in the activity buzzing around him.

Hal Brognola, the director of the Sensitive Operations Group, was seated at the large briefing table. A stack of folders stood at his right elbow. One was fanned open and its contents—papers and photos—spread in front of him on the tabletop. His tie was pulled loose from his throat and his shirt unbuttoned at the collar.

Barbara Price was seated next to Brognola, studying the contents of one of the folders.

"There he is," a voice called to his right.

Bolan turned and saw his old friend, Jack Grimaldi, grinning at him. The pilot, his slim frame togged in olive-drab coveralls, stood at the coffeemaker, a carafe clutched in his right hand. The other two hadn't noticed Bolan until Grimaldi spoke. They lifted their eyes from the files.

Brognola greeted Bolan with a tight smile and a nod. "Striker," he said, using Bolan's code name.

Price flashed Bolan a warm smile, the curve of her full lips telegraphing a hint of invitation. When the soldier stayed at the Farm, he often shared a bed with Price. Though they had mutual respect for each other, their physi-

cal relationship revolved around satisfying a mutual need
and not a deeper emotional commitment.

"Glad you're back," Price said.

"But don't unpack the toothbrush," Brognola added.
"We have a priority mission that's cropped up. You don't
have to take it, but you're the best option we have."

"No pressure," Bolan said.

"Your country needs you," Grimaldi said. "But don't
let that sway you, you goldbricker. Let me pour you some
coffee so you can relax."

"Did you ever think of becoming a military recruiter?"
Bolan asked.

He looked at Brognola and nodded at the color photo
the man held. "So, is she the problem?"

"Yes," Brognola said, "and no."

"Now we're getting somewhere," Bolan replied.

Brognola grinned. "What I mean is, she's the reason
you're here. But she's one of the good ones. Jennifer Rodriguez has been with the FBI for a decade. Lots of arrests.
She worked counterintelligence for a long time. More recently, though, the Bureau put her undercover tracking
weapons dealers. Does a damn good job of it, too, from
what I can tell." Brognola paused and sipped at his coffee.
"Unfortunately we lost track of her a couple of days ago.
She was supposed to check in with her handler. She didn't
make the contact. By itself that's not a big deal. They had
a backup time in place, just in case she got waylaid. But
that time came and went—"

"And still no word from Rodriguez," Bolan said.

"Right."

"Where was she?"

"Monaco," Price said.

"Because?"

"She was tracking someone for the Bureau," Price told
him. "Ever hear of Jacques Dumond?"

Bolan thought about it for a few seconds before the name clicked with him.

"Weapons dealer," he said. "French."

"Right," Price said. "He's got a pretty impressive record. Sells a lot of weapons in the Middle East and Asia. His semiofficial client list includes North Korea, Iran and Venezuela. The non-state groups include Hezbollah as well as a couple of minor al Qaeda-inspired groups."

Brognola leaned forward and rested his elbows on the table. "Obviously we're interested in all those clients," the big Fed said. "With the large countries, it was at least a little easier to track the purchases. Not easy, but easier. Plus, those countries are a little more cautious about how they use those weapons."

"A little," Bolan agreed.

"But the radical Islamist groups? The U.S. had almost no information about Dumond's transactions with them. We knew he was selling weapons. But what types of weapons was he selling them? In what quantities? We had no idea. You can imagine how happy that made us."

"And Rodriguez was checking into this."

"Right," Brognola replied. "It was supposed to be low-impact. She wasn't supposed to infiltrate too deeply. She was supposed to set up a couple of purchases, make a few contacts, pass along what she found and move on. The FBI set up a front company for her a few years ago to give her cover for some of her activities. It's really just a shell. But it gives her some kind of base to use when she knocks on doors."

Crossing his arms over his chest, Bolan leaned back in his chair. Grimaldi slid into the seat next to him.

Brognola continued. "A lot of the work she does is monitoring the sales of high-tech weapons and large military weapons systems. Since she was involved in counterintelligence, she's usually looking for Americans who are sell-ing bad stuff to other countries or terrorist organizations."

"But," Price interjected, "Dumond likes the ladies, so the U.S. figured it might be good to have a pretty woman with lots of cash knocking on Dumond's door. He might be a little more receptive. And it never hurts to cloud a target's judgment with a little sex."

"A French guy's who's also a skirt chaser?" Grimaldi said. "What are the odds of that?"

"Did she learn anything?" Bolan asked.

Brognola shook his head slowly. "We don't know for sure, but considering how little time she was there, it's highly unlikely."

"We think Dumond had made her as an FBI agent be-fore she ever arrived. We're not sure how he did that. She's worked in deep-cover operations for years, under another name. It's all in the dossier we gave you. But anything she knew, she had learned from existing FBI files."

"Maybe Dumond has a mole in the FBI," Bolan said.

Brognola, who'd been digging in his pants' pocket for a packet of antacids, heaved a sigh. "It's possible," he said. "The Bureau is investigating, just to make sure they didn't miss anything on that front."

Bolan leaned forward in his chair and fixed his gaze on Brognola. "I assume we aren't just shooting the bull here?"

The big Fed was peeling the foil away from the roll of antacids. He glanced up at Bolan and shook his head.

"I don't remember a time when I didn't have stomach problems. You know that?"

"At least you quit smoking."

"Well, I suppose chewing on a cigar doesn't count."

"To each his own."

"To answer your question, no, we're not just shoot-ing the bull. This whole thing's got the attorney general spooked. Unfortunately, FBI agents go missing sometimes.

It's not that. It's the fact that someone apparently had outed her before she ever stepped foot in Monaco. Also, she has a head full of secrets. A lot of them concern Dumond's competitors and our country's efforts to curb illegal weapons trafficking. She also has an expertise in al Qaeda, Hezbollah and some Pakistani Jihadist groups. It was something she developed as part of her undercover work. Unfortunately, for her and us, that's valuable information, information a lot of bad people would pay for."

"He could use her like a Pez dispenser full of classified information," Grimaldi said.

"Not the image I was expecting, Jack, but thanks for that," Brognola said. "Bottom line is I'm asking you to swoop into Monaco, find the lady and get her the hell out of there. Or, God forbid, if she's dead, find out who killed her and burn them down. I'm a big believer in letting the underworld know messing with American agents will only get you dead. I know you feel the same way."

Bolan nodded his agreement, but stayed silent. He kept an arm's-length relationship with the U.S. government. That meant he undertook missions on behalf of his country, but only the ones he agreed with. As much as he loved his country, he wasn't an employee of its government, its military or its intelligence services. He rarely turned down Brognola's requests for help, though he had a few times when something about the mission didn't feel right.

This was not one of those times, though.

"I'm in," he said.

The flight from Washington, D.C., to Monte Carlo, Monaco, took about nine hours. Bolan slept the first six hours while Grimaldi piloted the aircraft, a Gulfstream executive jet. On paper, the jet was owned by an import/export company with its headquarters in Alexandria, Virginia. In reality, the DEA had seized the aircraft from a Colombian

drug kingpin, given it a new tail number and registration
and put it back into service for undercover operations.

After he woke up, the soldier downed a cup of coffee
and pulled a brown valise from the seat next to his. Setting the case in his lap, he popped it open and withdrew
a sealed mission folder that Brognola and Price had prepared for him.

Tearing open the seal, he pulled out a handful of papers
and began leafing through them. He found a biography on
Jennifer Rodriguez first. The picture of the FBI agent that
Bolan had seen in the War Room was pinned to the front
of the packet. The woman was a stunner. Her black hair
spilled well past her shoulders in loose waves. Her eyes
were a deep brown, and bore a striking intensity. She obviously was a beautiful woman, but Bolan had no trouble
imagining a man twice her size squirming under her gaze.

The soldier removed the paperclip holding the papers
and the picture together. He set aside the picture and studied the file. Rodriguez was a first-generation American,
the daughter of a Mexican couple who had moved to the
United States a year before her birth. Her father, Vidal,
had moved to the U.S. to take a high-level job as an industrial chemist while her mother worked as an accountant
for the same company.

As Rodriguez grew up, she proved to be a natural ath-
lete and highly intelligent. She ran track while also making dean's list as a pre-law student. Once she was accepted
to law school, she quit competitive sports and focused on
her studies.

Her parents had hoped she'd focus on corporate law.
Instead she'd joined the FBI. With her ability to speak
English and Spanish, she'd been assigned to the Los Angeles office, where she was mentored by Fred Gruber,
that office's special agent in charge. Gruber, who was on
the cusp of retirement, and his wife, Kate, had taken the

young woman under their respective wings and provided her with a surrogate family. The report noted that Gruber, who'd retired a few years later and started a second career as a private detective, had been killed in Monaco three months ago in a mugging.

Bolan didn't believe in coincidences, especially in his line of work. He guessed that Gruber's death had, on some level, played a role in Rodriguez volunteering for her latest undercover assignment. The soldier didn't necessarily believe she'd come here looking to avenge Gruber's death. Judging by her record, the woman was a pro and focused like a laser on her mission. There was always the chance, though, she'd visited the location of Gruber's murder or some other landmark associated with his last case so she could connect with him, some way, one last time. It was a very human thing to do. Had it been the thing that had tripped her up and betrayed her identity? It was possible. Maybe Bolan would have a chance to ask Dumond.

Right before she'd gone off the grid, Rodriguez had contacted her mission controller. The guy, a Fed named Peter Kellogg, said she'd used her secure phone to call him from her hotel a few hours after she'd arrived in Monte Carlo. It was twenty-four hours before she'd been set to meet with Dumond for the first time. She'd planned to get some sleep and then have a look around Monte Carlo, maybe hit the beaches, since she wasn't a gambler.

When she missed her next check-in call, Kellogg had gotten worried and eventually realized she'd disappeared.

Bolan set down the papers and drank more coffee. It was possible, he supposed, that Dumond hadn't been involved in her disappearance. Maybe she'd fallen victim to a random crime, a robbery or rape turned to murder, for instance. It was also possible, the soldier realized, that she'd turned on her government. Those theories were plausible. The way Bolan saw it, though, the smart money still was on her being nabbed by Dumond for some reason. That made finding the Frenchman Bolan's first priority once they hit the ground.

The guy apparently had done well for himself. According to a CIA file, he had not one but three houses sprinkled throughout Monaco. Two agency psychologists had labeled him as moderately paranoid, which explained why he moved between the various houses on almost a daily basis, never sleeping under the same roof more than a single night. It also might mean the guy had become suspicious of Rodriguez with little reason other than a chronic short circuit in his brain that made everyone look like an enemy.

Shifting in his chair, Bolan again pushed aside his questions about why Dumond did anything. Getting into the arms merchant's head and understanding his behavior only benefitted Bolan to the extent it helped him find the missing FBI agent. Anything beyond that was distraction, one that could lead him down a wrong path and cost Rodriguez her life.

Price had checked with some of her former colleagues at the NSA. Dumond and his lieutenants apparently had gone silent within the past twenty-four hours. No calls or emails via the guy's known numbers or email addresses. The key word, Bolan knew, was "known." If he had an encrypted line the various intelligence agencies didn't know about, it was possible he'd circumvented their surveillance.

Bolan skimmed the rest of the intelligence report. Dumond's organization apparently was fairly big. In Monaco alone, he kept a fairly large contingent of muscle, at least a couple dozen.

The arms dealer had maintained enough contacts in the French government to buy himself a pass with the authorities in Monaco.

The French connection didn't surprise Bolan much.

Nearly half the population of that country, located on
the Mediterranean Sea on the southern coast of France,
was French and French was the official language. Bolan
guessed Dumond was greasing palms in the French and
Monacan governments. That was a key to building a criminal empire—put the government in one pocket and the
business community in the other, and pillage at will.

Bolan noticed what he was thinking and a smile ghosted
his lips. At times, he had to remind himself that most people were decent and honest, good people trying to get by.
He spent so much time hunting the savages of the world—
mobsters, rogue spies, corrupt dictators—it was easy to
forget who he was fighting for.

He didn't consider himself an idealist. But he was a
soldier, a defender. As such, he needed to know he was
fighting for a just cause. Otherwise he became a hired
gun, a violent man, running from fight to fight, without
reason. He would become a murderer instead of a soldier
and Bolan couldn't stomach that.

The soldier believed in what he did. He made no apolo-
gies for his methods. In his experience, brute force needed
to be met with brute force. He needed to find the arms
trafficker and free Rodriguez. The numbers were falling
fast; hours had slipped away.

So he'd hit Monaco with a vengeance and accomplish
his mission. Or go home in a body bag. In his life, in
his War Everlasting, those were the only two options for
Bolan.

When Bolan arrived at the safehouse, he found Agent
Peter Kellogg waiting for him.

Bolan had met a lot of FBI agents and none looked like
the man who answered the door. By the soldier's reck-
oning, the guy stood a few inches under six feet tall and
looked wiry. However, he answered the door clad in torn

jeans, a black T-shirt and cowboy boots. His long silver hair was pulled back from his face in a ponytail, and his salt-and-pepper beard was long and unkempt. The handle of a Glock 19 peeked above the waistband of his jeans.

Before Bolan could ask, Kellogg showed him his FBI credentials. The soldier flipped open a leather wallet containing a forged Justice Department ID featuring his Matt Cooper alias. Grimaldi, who was traveling as Jack Williamson, also showed the guy an alias ID.

Kellogg nodded, stepped back from the door and gestured for the men to enter the house.

"Well," Kellogg said, "now that we're done sniffing each others' ass, you guys want some coffee?"

Both men said they did. Kellogg gestured with his chin at a door. "There's the living room. Your buddy is here already if you want to hang out with him. Coffee's in there. Let me get two more cups."

The living room was huge, with polished hardwood floors, a fireplace and luxurious furniture. They found Leo Turrin standing at a shelf full of books, apparently reading the titles. He turned to them as they entered and made a face.

"Some tightass must buy all the Bureau's books," he said. "There's nothing but international law texts and some history books about France and Monaco."

Grimaldi snorted.

"Wow, did you read the titles all by yourself?"

"Screw you, fly boy," Leo Turrin said.

"Got a headache from all that reading? Need to lie down?"

"Be careful," Turrin said, "I have friends in low places. One phone call and I can have you rubbed out."

Kellogg entered the room, a coffee mug in each hand. He looked at Bolan who'd been silent. "They carry on like this all the time?"

"Yeah," Bolan said.

"Jesus, I ask Washington for help and they send me this."

"Look, Easy Rider," Turrin said. "No need to be a jerk."

Kellogg smiled coldly. "Son, when I'm being a jerk, you'll know it. I just want to make sure I have some people who can do the job. As for the clothes, they're part of my cover."

"As what? A clerk in a gay porn shop?" Turrin asked. "Son of a…"

Kellogg took a step forward.

Bolan put a hand on his shoulder and said, "At ease." He turned to Turrin. "He's been working deep cover in an American motorcycle gang. It's been branching out overseas, looking to set up shop in Paris and Berlin. Agent Kellogg is here to help the gang get a foothold in Europe. He's also been funneling the information back to the FBI. Am I right, Agent Kellogg?"

"Well, at least one of you isn't a damn buffoon," Kellogg replied. "Yeah, that's the short version of my cover. The guy who should've been running Rodriguez's operation retired three months ago. I was filling in for him. Needless to say, I wish they'd had someone else do it." He slurped some coffee. "Okay, is that enough about yours truly?"

"It is," Bolan said. "We need to focus."

Kellogg had set the mugs on an end table next to a carafe of coffee. Bolan poured himself some coffee, put the stopper back in the carafe and sipped the brew. Kellogg backed into an armchair and looked at Bolan.

"Let me say right up front, I feel shitty how this whole thing went down," Kellogg said. "My team and I were planning to back her up every step of the way. She was going to wear a wire. That prick Dumond has a penthouse in Monte Carlo, and the meeting was scheduled for there. We had, um, appropriated some maintenance uniforms so our agents could put themselves within striking distance just in case things went south. I ran operations like this for years before I went deep cover. My people are pros. I—we—were going to have her back every step of the way."

The guy's eyes were bloodshot and rimmed by dark half circles.

"No doubt," Bolan said. "Obviously someone figured out her identity beforehand, though, and nabbed her."

"Yeah."

"Which raises the question—was there a leak?"

Bolan had expected the guy to get defensive. Instead he shook his head wearily.

"I've asked myself the same question a few dozen times. I've gone over everyone's file. If there's a leak here, I can't spot it."

"Maybe you're too close," Bolan said.

"Maybe. I'd like to think you're wrong. But, yeah, maybe. That's why I asked Washington to shadow me on this. Headquarters has people going through the files of every agent and tech involved in this. If they say my team's clean, they're clean."

Bolan sipped more coffee and set the mug on a table. His gut was telling him Kellogg was right; there wasn't a mole in the guy's organization. If that was true, it only made finding Rodriguez harder.

"A former FBI agent was killed here three months ago," Bolan said.

"Yeah, Fred Gruber. Did you know him?"

"No, but Rodriguez did."

"So what's your point?"

"Not sure I have a point," the soldier replied. "But it's something to think about."

"He died from a random mugging," Kellogg said. "I read the reports myself."

Bolan responded with a noncommittal shrug. Chances

were Kellogg was right and there were no links between Gruber's death and Rodriguez's disappearance, though it still nagged at him.

"You don't look convinced," Turrin said.

"I'm not."

"Shit," Kellogg muttered. Pulling a notebook and a pen from his jeans, he scribbled something in the notebook.

"I'll have someone look into it."

"Thanks," Bolan said.

"I'm not sure what we'll find, though," Kellogg added. "Last I heard, he had his laptop with him when the mugging happened. The SOBs who killed him made off with his computer, his wallet and his phone."

"You'll probably find nothing," Bolan conceded. "But it doesn't hurt to check."

"Fair enough. Without the hardware, it may take a while to find anything, unless he backed stuff up somewhere else."

"Understood."

"Okay," Kellogg said. "Now that you've added to my to-do list, what's next? Do you need weapons?"

Bolan shook his head. "We brought some."

"Good," Kellogg said.

The phone clipped to the agent's belt began trilling so he answered it.

"What?" he said. He went silent for several seconds, occasionally nodding. The caller spoke loudly enough that Bolan could hear the voice, but couldn't understand what he was saying.

"How sure are you about the information?" Kellogg asked. "Reasonably sure? What the hell does that mean? Fifty-fifty? Seventy-thirty?" The caller responded and Kellogg went back to listening and nodding for another minute or so. "Okay," he said. "Put some people on the house. Keep track of every vehicle coming in and out of the estate. Try to be discreet, though. Good job."

He ended the call, set the phone on top of his right thigh and looked at Bolan.

"Okay," he said, "I think we caught a break. Dumond has three residences in Monaco. One of our sources knows which one."

"Knows or believes he knows?"

"My agent is 'reasonably certain,'" Kellogg said. He gestured air quotes when he spoke the last two words.

"Wow," Turrin said.

"Man, you're getting on my nerves."

"Just trying to make you think," Turrin stated. "The last thing we want is to bust into the wrong house and let Dumond know we're here. Once that happens, he'll disappear and take Rodriguez with him."

"News flash," Kellogg replied. "He already has disappeared."

"I'm talking 'leave the country' disappear. You ready to deal with that?"

Kellogg glared at Turrin for a few seconds. Finally he heaved a sigh and nodded slowly.

"Fair enough," he said.

"So, do you have an address?" Bolan asked.

"Yeah."

"Get us some floor plans," the soldier said. "We need to figure out our next move."

CHAPTER TWO

Jennifer Rodriguez knew she needed a miracle.

She paced her makeshift cell and wondered about her next move. Her captors had taken away her watch and, obviously, her smartphone, and her cell contained no clocks. Combine that with the fact she was apparently in a basement of some kind, with no windows, and she really had no idea how long she'd been down here. She guessed it'd been twenty-four hours, but she couldn't be sure.

She did know she was losing precious time. She'd come to Monaco to find answers. In the past several months, there'd been murmurs in the underworld about Dumond's gunrunning operation expanding. A lot of the talk had been troubling because the Frenchman supposedly had begun acquiring large quantities of weapons from rogue military generals, particularly in the Middle East, where the U.S. supplied weapons to friendly nations. Dumond had a record for selling weapons to anyone willing to pay the price.

Initially, some had worried he'd sell arms to China so it could study the technology. Working undercover, Rodriguez had learned the weapons weren't advanced enough to pique China's interest. She'd also learned the tools of the death trade that were being trafficked also were coming from countries at odds with the U.S., such as Libya.

Once they crossed espionage threats off the list, at least as far as major powers were concerned, the problem became identifying the buyer. Was Dumond going to sell weapons to al Qaeda, Hezbollah or another major terrorist organization? They'd tried for months to get an answer, but kept coming up empty. While Dumond wasn't discerning about his clientele, he did fret over security.

U.S. intelligence had found it damn near impossible to hack his computer. He switched phones regularly, handing the old ones to his lieutenants to carry and use. This confounded the intelligence agencies trying to track him and often kept him a step or two ahead of authorities.

That was why Washington had decided to send Rodriguez after him. She'd spent months infiltrating another arms-smuggling ring, had made lots of contacts, many of them mutual "friends" of Dumond and her. She'd put out the word she wanted to meet with him. The wheels had started turning, albeit slowly, and it had taken weeks before she got an audience with him.

She thought she'd gotten a break. Instead she'd walked into a trap.

Dumond's people had overpowered her and searched her for a wire. The absence of one hadn't improved her situation. They'd knocked her out and transported her from the meeting site to here, wherever that was. She had no idea whether she'd been moved across town or across the globe.

The whole thing had taken a weird turn when they'd started asking her about Fred, her first boss with the FBI. She'd tried to play stupid. That strategy had fallen apart when Dumond had held out a smartphone to her.

"Take this," he said. "Look at the screen."

She'd hesitated, then taken the phone from the outstretched hand and looked at the screen. Though she'd tried to keep her best poker face, she doubted she'd succeeded. The single image had triggered a flood of conflicting emotions—shock, grief, anger and fear being just a few. It had been a photo of Gruber, his wife, Kate, and Rodriguez, at Gruber's retirement party. He stood in the middle of them, clad in khakis and a polo shirt, a tight grin on his lips, an arm around each of the two women. His successor, Donna Goldman, had shot the photo for him.

Rodriguez had noted the slight glaze of alcohol in his eyes and remembered how drunk he'd gotten that night, singing "Love Me Tender" with the karaoke machine, a record nine times. Aside from fueling his bad attempts at impersonating the King, the drinking had been notable for another reason. Gruber rarely drank and then in moderation. However, he'd arrived for his own party, seeming sullen and withdrawn. Kate later had confided that he hadn't wanted to retire and that she was worried how it would affect his health. The alcohol had dissipated the black cloud around him and he'd loosened up, at least for the evening. The following day, though, he'd sunk back into his depression and remained there until he'd hung out a shingle as a private detective. Having a job had restored his sense of purpose and made him feel useful again.

He'd always sworn the PI gig had saved his life.

Since his death, she'd thought back on the bitter irony of those statements.

The photo had delivered a punch right to her heart.

Had she stared too long? Had her eyes glistened with tears? She didn't think so. But, when it came to emotions, she knew the mind played tricks and the face sometimes could reveal too much information.

With little time to think, she'd made up the best story she could. She said she vaguely remembered meeting the couple at a party, but didn't know them beyond that. Why did he have the photo on his phone? She'd shrugged and said maybe the guy was a pervert and liked looking at the picture. Her stomach had clenched as she'd uttered the words about Gruber, though she knew he'd understand.

It hadn't taken Dumond long to shoot holes in her story.

After more interrogation, he'd slapped his thighs, stood and given her a halfhearted smile.

"I don't believe you," he had said. "I will give you some time to consider your situation. Then I will come back and see you again. If you don't offer a better explanation—" he shrugged "——I will use more aggressive methods of securing answers." He turned the phone screen back in her direction. "I have friends in America. They would be happy to pay this woman a visit."

His security chief, a man named Bellew, stood to his right. Dumond turned and looked over his shoulder at him. "What was her name again?"

"Kate," Bellew said. "Kate Gruber."

"Yes," Dumond said. His lips split into a wider smile. "She's a widow. Perhaps she would like the company."

Rodriguez had tried her best to feign apathy and maintain her cover. When she'd spoken, her throat had felt tight and pushing out the words took effort.

"Hope those thoughts give your limp Johnson a little lift," she'd said. "While we're swinging things, you might want to think about what you're doing here. I came here, with references, to transact business. If something happens to me…"

She let the sentence trail off. Dumond's smile faltered for a moment before he caught himself and let out a dismissive laugh.

"See you in a few hours," he said.

Dumond had left. She had no doubt things could get worse for her.

The arms dealer already had taken the leap of kidnapping someone he at least suspected to be a U.S. federal agent. He had to know he'd passed a point of no return, one where he couldn't let her walk away alive. Either way, the U.S. government was going to hunt him down for this.

From his standpoint, there was no incentive to leave behind a witness.

A chill raced through her, causing her to shiver even though the room was warm and stuffy. Without thinking, she stopped walking and hugged herself.

The weight of her situation hit her hard. There is no way out, she thought. They are going to kill me.

Her head suddenly felt light and her heart began to pound faster, speeding up in spite of the emotional and physical fatigue that gripped her.

Her chest tightened and she struggled to drag in a full breath. Jesus, she was going to die here. And she wasn't even sure where "here" was.

She moved to the single bed, the room's sole piece of furniture, and dropped onto the edge of the mattress.

Pull yourself together, she chided herself. If you give up, you will die. If you fight, at least you have a chance.

Granted, it was a small chance, but it beat the hell out of waiting for somebody to walk in and put a bullet in her head.

She looked around the room for the umpteenth time. Dumond's people had removed everything from it except the bed. She could see impressions in the carpet, where there'd been shelving units standing against the wall, a small table and two chairs, a dresser. They'd stripped the mattress of its sheets. The bolts holding the metal frame in place were too tight to be removed with her bare hands. The bed's frame also was bolted to the floor and couldn't be moved.

They'd even stripped her belt and her shoe laces, presumably so she wouldn't hang herself out of desperation.

Bringing her hands to her face, she massaged her temples with her fingertips. She'd been racking her brain for a solution for so long, she felt as though her thoughts just kept going in circles.

Yeah, she finally decided. She needed a miracle.

She again dismissed the thought. She'd spent too many years in law enforcement, seeing firsthand the pain and misery humans heaped on one another, mostly to steal a few bucks or to get their rocks off, to believe in miracles.

She heard a muffled sound emanating through the floor. Seconds later, it came again. Just a couple of pops in rapid succession.

Gunshots? Had somebody come to help her? Maybe she'd get her damn miracle after all.

CHAPTER THREE

"The crazy bitch has told you nothing?"

The statement from his security chief prompted Dumond to turn and give the guy a dirty look. Jean-Luc Bellew held his boss's stare for a couple of beats before casting his eyes to the floor. Dumond turned away and walked to his desk.

"Is she secure?" the arms dealer asked.

"As secure as possible," Bellew replied. "We aren't set up as a prison. But she's secure in that storage room. It has a heavy wood door and a couple of locks. She won't be going anywhere."

"She'd better not," Dumond said.

Bellew's cell phone began to buzz before he could make a further comment.

Irritated, the arms merchant turned to Bellew, who was digging in his pocket for his phone.

A couple of seconds later Dumond's own phone began vibrating on his hip. He pulled it from the holder on his belt, saw he'd received a text message and began pressing buttons to access it. When he opened the text, he felt a cold sensation travel down his spine. BREECH, the message read.

He wheeled toward Bellew, his fear quickly turning to anger. The security chief had his phone pressed against his ear and was reaching under his jacket for something with his free hand.

"Don't worry about the how," Bellew said. "Just make

sure they don't get to the building. Send out the dogs!" He paused for a few seconds. "If you sent them out, where are they? Gone? What do you mean gone? Damn it. What? Call the police! We cannot call the police here, you idiot."

Bellew pulled a Walther pistol from beneath his jacket and flicked his gaze at Dumond.

"I have him right here," Bellew said. "Yes, I think you're right. Let me call you back."

By now, Dumond had returned his phone to its belt holder. He opened the lap drawer of his desk, withdrew a holstered Beretta and, pulling aside the tail of his jacket, attached it to his belt. He fished a couple of magazines from the same drawer and slipped them into his pocket. When he looked up, he saw Bellew staring at him.

"We should get you out of here," Bellew said.

Dumond shook his head.

"We need to get the woman first."

"There's no time," the security chief replied. "We had half a dozen men patrolling the grounds—"

"Had? What the hell?"

"We've lost contact with them."

Dumond's hands clenched into fists. "Lost contact? Are they dead?"

"I have no idea," Bellew replied. "I just know we can't reach them and there are no technical problems with the radios. We have the capability, but no one is answering us."

"Son of a bitch!"

"We need to go," Bellew repeated.

"I can't leave her here," Dumond said. "She knows things. If I leave her here, there will be problems."

"Problems? You mean from the Germans?"

"Mind your place," the other man said.

"My place is to evacuate you."

"We try to get the woman first," Dumond replied. "Otherwise, I lose everything."

"And what if we come across these intruders?"

"Then we damn well better kill them."

BOLAN CLIMBED THE steps to Dumond's mansion, the MP-5 held at the ready. Turrin hung back a couple of yards so he could cover Bolan's six. The soldier moved up to the door. He tried to work the handle, but it wouldn't budge.

Feeling someone moving up behind him, Bolan looked over his shoulder and saw Turrin there.

"Don't worry," the little Fed said, patting the shotgun. "I brought a key."

Bolan nodded and stepped back from the door. He watched as Turrin swung the shotgun's barrel toward the lock. The soldier knew the weapon was loaded with slugs capable of pounding through a steel lock. Unlike ceramic rounds, though, the slugs wouldn't disintegrate before pierced their target. Bolan figured it was worth the risk.

The shotgun boomed once. The slug mangled the lock and shoved it through the door, leaving behind a ragged hole. As the door swung inward, Turrin moved through it first, followed by Bolan.

The door led into a foyer with high ceilings. Paintings covered the walls and several busts stood on pedestals. Bolan guessed the items were expensive, paid for with the blood of innocents shed on the world's killing fields.

Movement to Bolan's right caught his attention. He turned and saw a pair of Dumond's gunners step into view. The man in the lead, dressed in a gray suit, his hair shellacked with gel, swung the barrel of a machine pistol toward Bolan. The Executioner's MP-5 coughed a fast line of bullets that pummeled the guy's center mass. Even as the gunner crumpled to the floor, the second guard had marked Bolan's chest with the red dot of a laser sight. Before the soldier could react, the hardman's head suddenly snapped back in a spray of crimson.

Bolan threw Turrin a glance. The former undercover mobster had slung the shotgun and unleathered one of his Berettas. Bolan nodded his thanks, turned to the left and crossed the room, making his way to one of the exits, which opened into a long corridor. He'd taken a half dozen or so steps when he heard voices, accompanied by shoe soles clicking against the floor tiles. He held up a hand for Turrin to stop, but he had already halted. An instant later, a heavyset man with a shotgun stepped into the corridor. His eyes lighted on Bolan and he swung the shotgun in his direction. The soldier had the guy by a microsecond. He tapped the MP-5's trigger and stitched a line across the new arrival's torso. The shotgun clattered to the floor, but fortunately didn't discharge. A second shooter appeared around the door frame, his hand filled with a submachine gun.

The hardman squeezed off a fast burst. The bullets sliced through the air just to Bolan's left, missing him by several inches.

The Executioner responded by firing a burst at the shooter. The fusillade missed the shooter, but came close enough that it forced him to jerk back out of sight. The soldier edged down the hallway, hugging the wall. When he got close to the door, he snagged a flash-bang grenade from his web gear, pulled the pin and tossed the bomb into the room where the man was hiding. An instant later it exploded with a loud crack and a flash of light visible to Bolan even in the hallway.

As the noise died down, he went through the door low and found the guy standing near the doorway, disoriented. A burst from the MP-5 took the man down.

BELLEW DESCENDED the stairs, his eyes sweeping the area as he searched for the intruders, his submachine gun leveled and leading the way. His heart slammed in his chest and blood thundered his ears. It had been years since he'd been in a live-fire situation. That had been back in Africa, where he'd been surrounded by a dozen or more well-armed and well-trained mercenaries. Over the past few years, he'd spent more time sending other people into harm's way while he sat back and planned.

Who the hell could have broken through their defenses? he wondered. For a residential area, the estate had been as secure as possible. They'd deployed sensors, cameras, armed guards, dogs. That someone had gotten past all that told him he wasn't dealing with a run-of-the-mill burglary or home invasion. Besides, most of the underworld in the city, right down to the low-level thieves, knew better than to break into Dumond's property.

That he couldn't reach his mercenaries only heightened his anxiety. He obviously was dealing with at least one combat professional, if not more.

When he reached the bottom of the stairs, Bellew paused and listened hard. Somehow all the cameras had gotten fried. He'd tried to reach the monitor room, but they hadn't responded. There was no way for him to know how many people he was up against or their location.

That left him to handle it the old-fashioned way—rely on his instincts and his senses.

To his right, he heard something. It was muffled, but unmistakable to anyone who'd spent any time at all in his deadly trade. Someone had just fired a weapon, and he heard the clank of brass hitting the marble tiles.

Bellew crossed the entryway, making his way to a door that would lead him deeper into the mansion's first floor. Coming up on the door, he paused, chancing a look around the door frame. Down the hall, he spotted three men. He recognized one—a guy sprawled on the floor—as one of his guards. Arms and legs splayed out, his midsection was dark red.

Two men stood over the corpse. One was short with a

medium frame. The second guy was tall with broad shoulders and jet-black hair. Bellew recognized the gun in the taller man's hands as a Heckler & Koch MP-5.

Chancing another look, he saw the men were moving in his direction. Fear gripped him, and for a moment he considered bolting out the door. Maybe he could take these two by surprise. But it would be a damn sight easier without backup just to run out the door, flee the estate and get away with his skin intact. He guessed they'd already taken down nearly a dozen men. It wouldn't be easy for him alone to take them down.

But if he ran? He'd get away with his skin, but it'd come back to haunt him.

He'd lose his reputation. Once word spread that he'd bolted on a client, he'd end up blacklisted. While he'd never bought into the notion of death before dishonor, he'd sure as hell choose death before poverty.

To hell with it. He'd try to take them.

Coming around the door frame, he entered the room, ready to take down his opponents.

CHAPTER FOUR

People who'd never been in combat didn't understand what it did to the mind and the senses. How it changed a person, enhancing some perceptions and subduing others. Bolan understood the transformation all too well, though. He'd spent his entire adult life as a warrior—first as a U.S. Army soldier, then in his war against the Mafia and more recently his war against terrorism.

He'd spent his life honing his skills as a warrior. At the same time, he'd honed his senses. It was something he couldn't turn off now, even if he wanted to.

When something nagged at him, alerting him to a threat, he couldn't ignore it.

Acting on gut instinct, he turned just in time to spot a man coming through the door. The guy's SMG was lining up on Turrin's back. The soldier lunged, wrapped his arms around his old friend's midsection and drove his right shoulder into his middle.

Turrin lost his footing and dropped to the floor. The bullets sliced through the air above them, missing them by a few feet. A microsecond of hesitation on Bolan's part and Turrin likely would have been dead. Just as they hit the tiles, Bolan heard his friend grunt from the impact. The Executioner rolled away, brought up the MP-5 and squeezed off a burst at their attacker.

The bullets flew wide, though the onslaught was enough to make Bolan's adversary dart from the doorway.

The soldier glanced at his friend. Turrin was already

pushing up from the floor and appeared to be okay. Bolan was on his feet and moving slowly down the hallway, hugging the wall and waiting for his opponent to come back into view.

The guy was going to bolt or risk another shot at the Americans. Either way, Bolan needed to prepare himself to react.

He saw a blur of motion at the doorway. The gunner had popped back into view, the barrel of his SMG hunting for a target. In addition to his gun, half of his face and one of his shoulders was visible.

A burst of gunfire screamed down the hallway, but again left Bolan and Turrin unharmed.

The H&K churned out a short burst. The bullets drilled into the gunner's exposed shoulder. A cry of pain burst from the guy's mouth. His weapon fell from his hand and clattered to the floor.

Surging to the doorway, Bolan caught the guy on his knees. The fabric covering the man's left shoulder was ripped and darkened with blood. His hand was under his jacket as he struggled to pull something free.

Bolan's right foot lashed out and caught the man in the chin. The kick knocked the guy backward and caused him to land on his injured shoulder, eliciting another yelp from him.

Bolan moved through the door and locked the H&K's barrel on the man's chest.

The hardman froze and then tried to raise both hands. The move apparently sent bolts of pain coursing through him because he inhaled sharply and grimaced. Prying his eyes open, he raised his good hand.

Bolan reached down, grabbed a handful of the guy's jacket and yanked him to his feet. He spun the guy and shoved him face-first against a wall.

Looking at Turrin, he said, "You do the pat-down."

"Jesus, why do I always have to frisk these guys?"

"Nimble fingers."

Scowling, Turrin stepped forward and searched the man. His hand disappeared under the guy's jacket and came out with a Walther .380. Handing it to Bolan, he continued the frisk, ultimately turning up a couple of magazines for the Walther and a folding knife.

He pocketed the knife.

Bolan ejected the magazine from the Walther and tossed it aside. He then threw the empty pistol in the opposite direction.

Bolan turned the guy around.

The soldier pulled a field dressing from his pocket. Unwrapping it, he handed it to the man, who took it and gingerly placed it on his wound.

"You speak English?" Bolan asked.

"Yes."

"Where's the woman?"

The man hesitated. Bolan reached out and pushed down on the hand the man was using to hold the dressing in place. The man grimaced and moaned, bending slightly at the knees.

The captive cursed in French.

"Let me ask again," Bolan said. "Where is she?"

The guy pushed himself up to his full height. He leaned against the wall for support, but glared at Bolan.

"Downstairs," he said, forcing the word through clenched teeth.

"Downstairs where? And how do I get down there?"

The hardman opened his mouth to speak, hesitated, and clamped his eyes closed for a couple of seconds, apparently riding out another wave of pain.

"Downstairs where?" Bolan repeated.

With some effort, the guy opened his eyes, turned his head left and gestured with his chin. Even that much movement seemed excruciating to the man. A double door stood a few yards away.

"Go through there," he said. "Follow the hallway. There's a freight elevator at the end of it…"

"Go on."

"Hit the B2 button. Get off and…"

The hardman's voice trailed off again. He looked pale and Bolan guessed the blood loss was weakening the guy.

"Get off on B2."

"Three doors," the guy said. "You want the second one."

"Locked?"

The guy nodded. "Security card."

"The one around your neck?"

Another nod.

Bolan took hold of the card and pulled up, drawing the lanyard over the other man's head.

"How many guards down there?"

"How many have you killed?"

"Ten."

"Two, maybe. They might have gone elsewhere."

"Where's Dumond?"

"Look, I already told you where the lady is. Isn't that enough?"

"Answer the question."

"I sent him away. I knew this was a lost cause," Bellew said, licking his lips, "so I told him to go."

"Where would he go?"

The guy's eyes looked heavy and he was unsteady. Bolan guessed the effects of shock and blood loss were overtaking him.

"I don't know. There's Paris. There's Africa."

"Where in Africa?"

"Evergreen. Monet…." His voice was barely audible.

His eyes slammed shut and his body sagged. Bolan let him slide to the floor.

"Not much to go on," Turrin said.

Bolan shrugged. "You look for Dumond," he said. "I'll find Rodriguez."

CHAPTER FIVE

Turrin bolted up the stairs to the second floor in search of Dumond. He wanted to capture or kill the guy. If Dumond was in the house, Turrin guessed putting him down was going to require blasting through a line of well-armed thugs.

And maybe he wouldn't make it. It was something he always knew yet tried not to think about. When his old friend Mack Bolan called on him for help, it almost always required putting his life on the line. Turrin expected it. It was one of the few things in life he'd made peace with.

Before he could reach the top of the stairs, a hardman rushed into view. The guy was lining up a shot at Turrin with his Steyr AUG. His mind and body conditioned by countless near-death experiences, Turrin triggered his Beretta. The handgun coughed discreetly and a 3-round burst of 9 mm bullets drilled into his adversary's chest. Surprise flashed on the man's features an instant before his body dropped to the floor at the head of the stairs.

Turrin stepped over the corpse, moved onto the second floor and ran his gaze over his surroundings. The stairs led into a semicircular landing. Ornate tiles covered the floor and crystal chandeliers lit the upstairs. Railed walkways ran on either side of the stairway, and across the landing a door opened into another corridor. Since the walkways were empty, Turrin crossed the landing and moved into the corridor. Three doors lined the right side and four stood on the opposite side.

The first two doors on Turrin's right were open. He checked the first room quickly and found nothing. Inside the second room, he found an oak desk with a computer monitor on top of it. As he moved around the desk, he spotted the computer tower on the floor. The side was cracked open and fragments of circuit boards and other electronic guts were strewed over the floor. Apparently the PC had contained something of value. He made a mental note to check with the cyber team at the Farm to see whether he should try to recover it.

Slipping back through the door, he caught a fast-moving dark shape in his peripheral vision.

He spun in time to see a rangy man hurtling at him, his right arm pulled back, his hand clutching a gleaming knife. The guy was on him quickly. Turrin didn't have time to swing the Beretta toward his attacker and squeeze off a shot. He saw the knife plunge at him and stepped sideways, letting the blade cut through empty air. As the knife slashed downward, the guy's torso leaned forward, putting him slightly off balance. With his left hand, Turrin grabbed a handful of his attacker's shirt and jerked him forward, hoping to send him hurtling into a wall. At the same time, Turrin used the extra space to bring the Beretta into play.

Unfortunately the guy caught his footing. His hand snaked out and, grabbing the wrist of Turrin's gun hand, pushed it away so the little Fed couldn't get a decent shot at him.

Balling his other hand into a fist, Turrin lashed out and flattened his adversary's nose, causing the guy to moan. Turrin pressed the attack, thrusting an open hand up at the tip of the man's nose and driving the broken cartilage into his brain. The guy's fingers uncurled from Turrin's wrist and he backpedaled a couple of steps before sinking to the floor.

The Stony Man warrior leaned against the wall, taking

a moment to catch his breath as he watched a last shudder pass through the man at his feet.

Two down. How many to go?

Hell, it was time to find out.

Turrin quickly searched the rest of the second floor, but found no one. Figuring he'd check the third floor next, he headed down the corridor. As he hurried forward, he heard footsteps pounding down the stairway, then spotted three men.

The hardman in the lead saw Turrin and reacted. In the blink of an eye he fired off a shot from a handgun. The weapon's report echoed through the enclosed space as Turrin dived to his right just a bullet passed through the air where he'd stood only a microsecond before.

His body hit the hard tile floor, and sent bolts of pain through his chest and right shoulder. However, he kept a firm hold on his pistol and rolled away from his opponents.

Raising his pistol, he spotted the same thug trying to get another bead on him. The Beretta churned out a triburst. Two of the rounds missed the guy by inches while the third bit into his biceps. Through a haze of pain, the guy fired off two more rounds, both of which slapped against the floor just in front of Turrin's face.

Turrin adjusted the aim on the Beretta and squeezed off another triburst, the rounds sinking into the man's stomach and doubling him over. Turrin had spotted Dumond and was swinging his gun toward the arms dealer when the second hardman stepped between them. The Beretta's Parabellum rounds drilled into the man's torso. He teetered on unsteady legs but was still able to fire off a single round that zinged over Turrin's head. Another trio of bullets from the Beretta hit the teetering thug's chest and he pitched forward, his body tumbling over the stairway railing.

Dumond was gone, and Turrin could hear rapid footsteps on the stairs. He had been so hyper-focused on the two guards he'd missed his target sprinting away. From outside the building, the little Fed could hear the whipping of helicopter blades.

Dropping the magazine from the Beretta and reloading, Turrin got to his feet, cursing, then sprinted for the steps. By the time he reached them, he could hear Dumond running across the floor below. He surged downstairs but found that his target had disappeared. Hearing a heavy door slam shut to his right, Turrin spun in the direction of the noise and raced toward it.

Passing through a luxuriously appointed sitting room, the former undercover mobster found a heavy wooden door. He grabbed the knob and twisted, but the door wouldn't budge. A dead bolt installed above the knob explained why the door was holding fast.

From the other side of the door, he could hear glass breaking. Muttering a curse, he holstered the Beretta, stepped back, unslung his shotgun and blasted through the shiny new lock. The dead bolt gave way in a shower of metal fragments and chunks of wood, and the door swung inward. The room in front of him was an office of some kind, outfitted with a desk, book shelves and filing cabinets.

Beyond the desk, Turrin saw the window had been broken out. The growl of a helicopter's engines and the thrumming of its blades grew louder.

Turrin sprinted to the window and peered outside. A helicopter hovered overhead, the rotor wash causing tree branches and leaves to whip around as though caught in a monsoon. A rope ladder swung from the bottom of the aircraft. His eyes followed the length of the ladder. At the top, he saw Dumond, just a couple of feet from climbing into the craft.

Turrin aimed at the fleeing man. Before he could fire

off a shot, though, two of Dumond's ground thugs began
unloading their automatic weapons at Turrin.

The sudden hail of bullets forced him to dive away
from the window and land on the floor on his belly. Turrin rose, slinging the shotgun and unleathering his Beretta. He flattened against the wall and eased back to the
window. Bullets speared through the opening, chewing
holes in the large desk, shattering a set of crystal liquor
bottles and glasses that stood on top of the desk, and ripping pockmarks in the walls.

Turrin remained just to the side of the window until the
shooting subsided before he took a chance to peer around
the frame. Dumond had disappeared inside the helicopter.
One of the guards had slung his machine pistol over his
shoulder and was climbing the rope up to the helicopter.

The other shooter, who was reloading his machine
pistol, spotted Turrin in the window. The thug's mouth
dropped open. If he said anything, the noise was swallowed up by the helicopter. A burst from Turrin's Beretta
hit the man in the chest and knocked him to the ground.

The whine of the helicopter's engines intensified, telling Turrin it was about to grab some altitude. He swung
the Beretta, aimed at the aircraft and drew a bead on the
second hardman on the ladder.

Before he could squeeze off a shot, though, the ladder
came loose from its moorings and fell away from the helicopter. The man holding on to the ladder uttered a short
cry before his body slapped hard against the ground.

Turrin climbed through the window. He ran a few
yards before he stopped, raised the Beretta and tried to
line up a shot at Dumond who was visible in the door
of the retreating helicopter for a brief instant. Then he
withdrew into the craft and slammed the door closed.
Turrin let the pistol fall. There was no reason for him to
waste another shot.

THE ELEVATOR CARRIED Bolan to the cellar. When the doors slid open, he stood to one side, holding the MP-5 in his right hand by its pistol grip. With his other hand, he kept a finger pressed into the Open Door button.

Light from the elevator spilled into the darkened hallway, illuminating several yards. Bolan saw shadows moving in the darkness.

The soldier took a flash-bang grenade from the pocket of his windbreaker, jerked out the pin and tossed the bomb through the doorway. He covered his ears as best he could, with one hand holding his pistol, and opened his mouth slightly. The grenade unleashed a white flash of light and a disorienting peal of thunder. The soldier went around the doorway in a crouch. One of Dumond's hardmen had been knocked to the ground by the device's concussive force. The other man was aiming his submachine gun at an angle, well past Bolan.

The Executioner swept the MP-5 in a wide horizontal arc as the weapon churned through the contents of its magazine. When he let off the trigger, the hardmen were sprawled on the floor in their own blood.

The soldier reloaded as he moved along the hallway. All the doors were locked. The soldier rolled one of the guards onto his back and searched through the pockets of the guy's expensive suit. When he came away empty, he searched the second man and found a set of keys.

Bolan knocked once on the nearest door.

"Jennifer Rodriguez, are you in there? My name's Matt Cooper. I'm from the Justice Department. I'm here to get you out."

"Yes, I'm here," the FBI agent replied.

The soldier tried a few keys and finally one unlocked the door. He pushed it inward.

Rodriguez had stepped back from the door and stood in the center of the room, staring at Bolan. The soldier was struck by her height first. Even at a distance, he could tell she was just under six feet tall and she still had a trim, athletic build. Her eyes were dark brown and Bolan could see the distrust beaming from them. After what she'd been through the past several days, he could hardly blame her.

She looked over Bolan's shoulder. "Where's the rest of the team?"

"The other half is upstairs."

"Other half? There are two of you?"

Bolan nodded. As she moved to the door, he stepped back from the room and started walking toward the elevator. "Are you okay?"

"I haven't eaten or showered in forever. But otherwise, I'm okay, yes."

"Good," Bolan said. "Let's get you out of here."

Bolan ushered her into the elevator, then followed her inside and they returned to the first floor. When the doors opened, Bolan gestured for her to remain inside and he left the car.

A ragged line of hardmen was scrambling to head Bolan off. The soldier scythed them down with a barrage of 9 mm rounds just as the MP-5 clicked dry. Ejecting the magazine, he slipped his last fresh one into the weapon and called for Rodriguez to come out of the elevator.

They made a beeline for the front door with Bolan still in the lead. As they stepped into the warm evening, the soldier heard sirens screaming. Keying the throat mike, he called for Turrin.

"Yeah?"

"Meet me at the Jag," Bolan said.

"Roger that," the retired Fed replied.

"Jag?" Rodriguez asked. "You have a Jaguar? What department are you with again?"

"It's complicated," Bolan said.

When they reached the car, Turrin was already there, tossing some of his gear into the trunk.

The Stony Man warriors claimed the front seats, with Bolan behind the wheel. Rodriguez slipped into the backseat as Bolan stomped on the Jaguar's accelerator. The car's engine responded with a growl and the vehicle lurched ahead, barreling toward the gates of Dumond's estate. Rodriguez twisted at the waist and stared through the rear window.

Bolan looked into the rearview mirror and saw a couple of muzzle-flashes wink in the darkness. A bullet struck the trunk lid, sparked against the steel and angled off into the darkness.

As the Jaguar neared the gate, another of Dumond's shooters ran into the vehicle's path, a machine pistol tucked in close to his body.

Turrin stuck an arm through his side window to fire on the guy. Even over the roar of the engine, Bolan heard the dry crackle of autofire and saw jagged flames lash out from the shooter's weapon. The bullet went low. The Executioner heard something thunk against the vehicle and he guessed the round had hammered into the vehicle's engine block.

Turrin's Beretta roared twice, just as the Jaguar rolled over a speed bump. The car shuddered. Bolan clenched his teeth and fought to keep control of the steering wheel, which wanted to jerk to the right.

The bullets from Turrin's weapon went wild, leaving the guard untouched.

Headlights bathed the hardman in their white glow, making his face look deathly pale.

His mouth dropped open and he threw up an arm to protect himself. The vehicle's right front fender smacked into the shooter, the force spinning his body and heaving it into the air all at once.

"Bull's-eye," Turrin muttered.

THEY'D DRIVEN LESS than a half mile when Bolan caught a whiff of the distinctive odor from a busted radiator. The needle on the temperature gauge was rising to the red quickly. The vehicle probably would overheat in a matter of minutes. Bolan knew they needed to do something.

He glanced at Turrin. "We're going to have to ditch," he said.

Turrin nodded.

"Ditch?" the woman said. "If Dumond sends his people after us, we can't outrun them on foot."

Bolan looked up into the rearview mirror and saw a reflection of her staring at him.

"We also can't outrun them in a dead car," he said. "Trust me. We'll get you out of here."

She opened her mouth to reply, but hesitated, seeming to consider his words. "Okay," she said with a nod.

"Up there," Turrin said, pointing at something beyond the windshield. Bolan followed where he was pointing and saw the mouth of an alley up ahead. The smell of antifreeze intermingled with overheated plastic, metal and oil had grown stronger. The soldier acknowledged Turrin with a nod.

A couple of seconds later when they reached their destination, he cut the wheel to the right and guided the car into the narrow alley. He killed the engine but left the headlights burning. "Wait here," he growled.

Popping open the door, he stepped from the vehicle and walked up to the front end and checked the damage. Bullet holes pockmarked the grille in a ragged line.

Another slug had taken out one of the running lights. White plumes of steam curled up from around the edges of the hood. The car definitely was damaged goods.

Moving back to the driver's door, Bolan leaned inside, pulled up on a floor switch that opened the trunk and switched off the headlights.

"Let's go," he said.

Turrin nodded and exited the car. The woman climbed from the backseat and, eyeing the two men cautiously, approached them. She stopped several feet away from them.

"We need another car," she said.

"We'll get one," Bolan replied.

"What, are you going to steal one?" she asked, her voice incredulous.

"Yeah."

"Wait! What?"

Turrin looked at her. "Don't worry," he said. "The big guy does this shit all the time."

"He's a federal agent!"

"Not exactly."

"What do you mean 'not exactly'?"

"No time," Bolan said.

The Executioner glided past her and moved to the trunk. He slid his fingertips into the seam between the edge of the trunk lid and the car and pulled. The lid sprang open. He tossed the MP-5 into the trunk. When Turrin saw what Bolan was doing, he reached into the car, pulled out his shotgun and tossed it into the compartment. Bolan slammed the lid.

He hated to leave the weapons behind, but he had little choice. They could conceal their sidearms under their jackets. But walking around a foreign city with shotguns and submachine guns would probably attract all the wrong kinds of attention.

For all intents and purposes, John "Cowboy" Kissinger, Stony Man Farm's armorer, had rendered the weapons untraceable. If someone ran the prints on the weapons, they'd find nothing. Any prints the soldier had left behind as Mack Samuel Bolan or under his aliases Matt Cooper or, before that, Mike Belasko, had been scrubbed. Whenever he had any brushes with the authorities, the Farm's cyber team hacked into the computers after the fact and erased any mug shots or fingerprints that might have been taken. As far as the world was concerned, Bolan was dead and had been for years. It was a fiction that Stony Man Farm went to great lengths to maintain.

From the corner of his eye he saw Rodriguez standing there, watching them. Bolan raised his right foot, set it on the bumper and pulled up the cuff of his pant leg. A small Glock pistol rode on his ankle in a holster. He drew the pistol. He sensed Rodriguez tensing, saw her back away a step. Turning toward her, he extended his hand and offered the weapon.

"You need a little something," he said.

Nodding, she took the pistol from him, pulled back the slide and looked to see whether a round was in the chamber. Satisfied, she let the slide snap forward and slipped the pistol into her waistband.

"Thanks," she said.

Spinning away from the car, the Executioner strode toward the mouth of the alley. When he reached it, he paused for a couple of heartbeats and glanced in both directions to see whether Dumond's men had followed them. Men and women, tanned and fit, walked up and down the sidewalk, smiling and laughing.

Bolan slid the Beretta into the shoulder holster under his jacket and stepped from the alley, with the others moving behind him. As they moved up the street, he glanced at Rodriguez. The woman had plastered a smile on her face and was walking with a steady, confident gait, all of which took attention from her mussed hair and ripped jacket. In the distance, Bolan could hear sirens. He assumed police and emergency vehicles were speeding to Dumond's estate. Once they arrived, they'd find the place littered with bodies.

And, if prowl cars weren't already sweeping the area

for Turrin and him, they soon would be. Once the police found the Jaguar, they'd realize whoever had driven the car had moved away on foot. They'd establish a perimeter that would make it harder for Bolan and the others to get away quickly.

They needed to move fast before that happened.

They'd put a couple of blocks between themselves and the Jaguar when Bolan spotted a police car halted at the intersection just ahead of them. The officer driving the car stared at them. Had Dumond or his people given the police a physical description? Bolan doubted it, but he felt himself tense up just the same.

"Is he looking at us?" Turrin asked, his voice low.

"Seems like it," Bolan replied.

Rodriguez cast a glance at the soldier. "What if he is looking at us?" she asked.

"Let him look," Bolan replied with a slight shrug.

"We can't fight him."

"You're right. We can't. And we won't."

One of the few rules Bolan had in his War Everlasting was that he never would draw his weapon on a police officer, even if the cop was about to shoot him. A second later, the traffic light changed and the squad car lurched forward and turned onto the street Bolan and the others were walking along. The officer at the wheel gave them one last look as he drove past, but kept going.

"Thank God," Rodriguez said quietly.

"Yes and no," Bolan said. "We just gained a couple of minutes. But if the guy's instincts nag at him enough, he may turn around and want to talk to us. Look at us. We don't exactly look like rich, carefree tourists."

"True."

When they reached the intersection, Bolan veered right down a side street and followed it away from the main drag for three blocks. An older-model blue Citroën parked along the curb caught the warrior's eye. He walked up to it, peered through a side window, looking for blinking red lights that might signal an alarm, but saw nothing. Pulling his arm back, he shot forward and drove the point of his elbow into the glass. The window shattered on impact, glittering shards falling to the ground and into the car.

Bolan reached through the window, unlocked the door and within seconds was seated inside the vehicle, working to hotwire the starter while Turrin watched their surroundings. Once the engine growled to life, Turrin opened the passenger-side door and gestured for Rodriguez to climb into the backseat. As she settled inside, he stuck one leg into the car before the sound of yelling caught his attention. He turned and saw an elderly man, silver hair contrasting against deeply tanned skin, running down the street, yelling in French and shaking his fist.

Turrin folded himself into the car and slammed the door just as Bolan began wheeling it from its parking space. He gunned the engine. The Citroën gained speed as it hurtled away from its owner who was now standing in the street, shaking a fist at the thieves stealing his car. The soldier navigated the car out of the neighborhood and aimed it toward the safehouse.

CHAPTER SIX

"How did you screw this up?" the voice on the phone asked.

Seated in the helicopter, Dumond bit down on an angry reply and squelched a desire to heave his phone across the floor. He hated the son of a bitch on the other end of the line. He didn't even know his name. Not his real name, anyway. But he knew he'd love to put a bullet in the bastard's head.

"It's complicated," the Frenchman replied, regretting the words instantly.

"Perhaps you need an easier job," the other man said.

"No."

"You lost the woman."

"We've been over this."

"You lost her."

Dumond heaved a sigh. "She got away. Yes."

"Was she looking for me?"

"No."

"No?"

Dumond squeezed his eyes closed. "I don't know."

"Neither do I."

"She never asked about you."

"Which means nothing."

"I told you someone attacked us. I lost eighteen people today."

"How many did they lose?"

"You bastard!"

"Well?"

"None," he said.

"And how many men were there?"

"You know the answer!"

"I want to hear it from you."

"Two. It was just two men."

The other man fell silent. Dumond thought he heard a lighter being worked, followed seconds later by the sound of a slow exhale. The pause only heightened Dumond's anxiety.

After several seconds the voice said, "Go to Tunisia."

The line went dead.

VOGELSGANG SLAMMED DOWN the receiver of his secure phone. The sound of someone chuckling to his right caught his attention and prompted him to spin his chair in that direction. Friedhelm Geiger was leaning against a wall, his arms crossed over his chest, staring at him. No, more to the point, Geiger was smirking at him.

"What the hell are you laughing at?" Vogelsgang demanded.

"The Frenchman screwed it up, right?" Geiger said. "Did I not say this would happen?"

Vogelsgang ignored the question and instead studied the smoke curling up from the end of his cigarette. After several seconds he nodded slowly.

"You were right," he said. "The Frenchman was a complete washout."

Vogelsgang quickly repeated Dumond's account of what had happened, breaking off occasionally to puff from his cigarette. When he finished, he looked over at Geiger, who was rubbing his clean-shaved chin with his thumb and forefinger. The smirk had morphed into a scowl and his brow furrowed.

"Two men took out eighteen of Dumond's people?"

"That's what Dumond said. What? You don't believe it?"

Geiger pushed himself off the wall and started across the office toward a small bar located in the corner. Opening a bottle of spiced rum, he poured some into a short glass, sealed the bottle and, drink in hand, headed back to Vogelsgang.

"Dumond's a pussy," Geiger said. "But his security team's another matter entirely. I can't believe two men took out the whole team."

"You think he's lying?"

"Not necessarily," Geiger replied, shaking his head. "He may have counted wrong. Fog of war and all that bullshit. Dumond's not a soldier. Perhaps he's been shot at before. I don't know. But under that sort of stress, it's easy to get things wrong."

Vogelsgang nodded once. "But we still have eighteen men dead. That much we can be sure of."

"Yes."

"Let me ask the obvious question, then," Vogelsgang said. "What if he got it right? What if it was just two people?"

Geiger drank more rum. Staring into the glass, he swirled the liquid around. "They'd have to be damn capable," he said.

"Indeed."

"Especially to do this with little or no visible support. No special vehicles. Nothing but small arms. I'd say Dumond was lucky to escape with his skin intact."

"How many people in the world could do this?"

Geiger considered the question and shrugged. "Not many. I could do it. Not too many others. A handful, maybe."

"Exactly. That means we've drawn the attention of someone quite formidable. And now we should assume they're following Dumond. They won't let him just walk away from all this. They'll want to arrest him."

"That wouldn't be so bad as long as Dumond would keep his mouth shut. But we know better. If it'd buy him another ten seconds of breathing, he'd blurt out everything he knows."

"So deal with him. And, if someone's tracking him, take them out, too."

"With pleasure," Geiger said.

He set his empty glass on a nearby table, turned and headed for the door.

VOGELSGANG WAITED UNTIL the other man had exited the room before allowing himself a small chuckle and a pitying shake of his head. Geiger was a good soldier, a true believer, resourceful and smart. His mistake was in believing they were in this thing together.

He was wrong. Geiger indeed was a formidable soldier. The former intelligence officer was, at best, a pawn, an attack dog. Like any dog, he could be useful and loyal. But, if Geiger forgot his place, Vogelsgang had people available who could deal with him.

Vogelsgang had a small army waiting in the wings and he was sitting on a storehouse of cash. That made him unstoppable.

His thoughts went back to the situation in Monaco. Whether it was two people or four who attacked Dumond was an interesting question. The more important question was their identity. Vogelsgang had to assume it was the Americans coming to help one of their own, or another country working on behalf of the United States, an ally such as Britain.

Either way it now meant they'd attracted unwanted attention. Or, more to the point, Dumond had attracted attention.

Geiger had been right. The man was a clown. Vogelsgang had hoped to use the Frenchman's greed and stupidity to an advantage. Even so, he'd also been careful to build firewalls between Dumond and himself. Dumond didn't know his real name or his location. Vogelsgang spoke letter-perfect English with no trace of an accent, and his secure phone processed his voice through a distortion device. He was sure the man had no idea of his nationality. Vogelsgang also paid the man with funds from a bank in the British Virgin Islands. Though Geiger had helped pick several members of Dumond's security team, the two men had never met directly. Even if someone hunted down Dumond, chances were slim he could betray Vogelsgang and his associates. Just to be on the safe side, though, Vogelsgang would feel better once Geiger killed the man and closed that hole.

Vogelsgang didn't need the distractions.

Not now.

He was on the edge of changing history. He'd spent a life working hard. A son of working-class parents, he'd never been satisfied when he'd looked at their way of life, stressing over mortgage payments and other bills. Vogelsgang had started work in the same machine shop that had once employed his parents. Unlike them, he'd had a head for numbers and a willingness to stick a knife in someone else's back. Within a few years he was working on the administrative side of the business. In another ten years he'd bought the place from its original owner, using blackmail to force the owner to sell for next to nothing. From there Vogelsgang had begun the slow process of building an industrial empire, one with its roots in Germany, but with factories in India, Bangladesh and other developing countries.

He'd succeeded in every way. Still, he hadn't been satisfied, not completely. Things were happening in his homeland, things that disturbed him. Each day, he saw foreigners invading his country. They weren't attacking in a traditional way, in fighter jets, tanks or troop formations, of course. In some ways, he would consider that preferable.

Instead the immigrants who made his blood boil looked harmless to most people, even though they wore strange clothes and had dark skin. They mewled about coming to Europe for a chance to earn a decent wage or to escape the religious or political persecution fostered by their dysfunctional governments. As best he could tell, all they really did was leech off Germany's prosperity, steal its industrial secrets, send money back to relatives, dilute his country's culture yet again. His homeland already had been through so much—the unfortunate failure of Hitler's Third Reich, the cleaving in two of the country after World War II, the allies and the Communists squashing the country's proud, independent heritage under booted heels.

The latest indignity was Germany allowing itself to be bound to the European Union, which was a front for freeloaders and incompetent bureaucrats. For decades his people had been forced to crawl when they should have soared. The Spaniards, the Greeks, with their limited intellects and their almost pathological laziness, were little more than anchors dragging down his homeland into a morass of mediocrity.

Crossing the office, he made his way to the bar where he splashed some whiskey into a glass. Bringing the glass to his lips, he tipped it and let the alcohol fill his mouth, savoring the taste for a moment before allowing it to travel down his throat. A burning sensation ignited in his stomach. It wasn't the alcohol. It was a byproduct of the rage he felt whenever he considered the slow disintegration of his homeland. And, truthfully, he considered Germany's leaders complicit in allowing the whole thing to happen. They pandered to minorities and foreigners. They wel-

comed Muslims with open arms, allowing them to practice
their religion with the same freedom as his own people.
Such permissiveness, he knew, was tantamount to suicide.
Yet he had watched them do it over and over again until
he swore he was about to lose his mind.

But it was the exact opposite, he later came to realize.
He'd been regaining his sanity, not losing it. He was seeing
things with a clarity he'd never before experienced. Finally
he'd realized the people in charge weren't going to change
things. For whatever reason, they'd decided it was better to
let Germany plummet into hell than to take the hard steps
necessary to save it. Faced with that realization, it became
clear that Vogelsgang had only one recourse.

He'd have to change things. Not by himself, of course.
He'd found other like-minded men and women throughout the years. Some had money, others had special skills.
A rare few had both. Vetting and recruiting these people
had been a long, expensive process.

Mistakes had been made. Occasionally he, Geiger or
other key members of the United Front had recruited the
wrong person, someone without the foresight and courage necessary to understand that occasionally the greatest
act of patriotism was to overthrow the government. Fortunately those people had been identified and killed quickly
before they could derail the Front's goals.

He was pacing now. Twelve paces forward, twelve back.
A smile ghosted his lips. His country—his damn country—was about to undergo a rebirth. It stood at the edge of
greatness, the dawn of unparalleled prosperity and power.
Sure, it'd go through a long, dark night first. Blood would
be spilled. Gallons of blood. The weaklings in Germany
and around the world would despise him for the fire he
was about to ignite. He cared little about them. They'd be
the first ones to take a bullet. He'd burn their bodies to
fuel the purifying fires his country so desperately needed.

So, yes, he'd kill his own countrymen. They wouldn't be the first to die. Far from it.

Long before sweet revolution swept through Germany and other parts of Europe, blood would rush through the gutters in another part of the world.

But, first, it would happen in America.

AN HOUR LATER Rodriguez, Grimaldi, Turrin and Bolan had made it back to the FBI safehouse.

Kellogg was waiting for them. He threw his arms around Rodriguez and gave her a quick hug.

"Damn, lady," he said, "it's sure good to see you. What the hell happened out there?"

She gave him a tight smile. "It's a long story," she said. "I'll fill you in a little later. First, I need a shower and some food. And some coffee. I feel like my head's in a vise."

"You got it," Kellogg said.

He turned and headed for the kitchen. Turrin stared after him for a second. "Hands down, that guy is the nicest biker I have ever met."

Forty-five minutes later, they convened in a secure conference room. A cup of coffee and a turkey sandwich were waiting on the table for Rodriguez. She ate ravenously at the sandwich, downing half of it before trying the coffee. Additionally she had procured a pack of cigarettes from Kellogg. She was seated at the table. The cigarettes clasped in her left hand, she stared down at the pack and peeled away at the foil wrapper with the nail of her right index finger.

Bolan stood next to the table, his arms crossed over his chest, and studied the woman as she raised the canary-yellow plastic lighter to the cigarette she'd put between her lips. Applying the flame to the end of the cigarette, she puffed a couple of times until the end of the cigarette turned bright orange and a small wisp of smoke curled up from the tip. He noticed her hands were steady as she worked the lighter. Her voice sounded calm, almost flat, other than the sarcastic edge when she spoke.

"You seem to be recovering," he began.

"From my near-death experience?" She shrugged. "I'm fine. Really. I was going to swoon, but I didn't have a fainting couch to fall on."

"I didn't mean it that way," he said.

Her eyes slightly narrowed, she showed him a thin smile. "Really? How did you mean it?"

Leaning forward, he set his palms on the table and locked his gaze on her.

"You went missing twenty-four hours ago," he said. "From everything I've heard, Dumond is unstable and a little masochistic. He held you prisoner for a whole day. Yet you seem to be in damn good shape. That's unusual. Almost as though you'd never been at risk in the first place."

Her cheeks flushed scarlet. "You son of a bitch," she snapped. "He planned to kill me. I'm lucky I got out of there before he did something really awful."

Bolan held her gaze for a couple of seconds before he finally nodded slowly a couple of times.

"How did he know you were with the FBI?"

"I had a friend," she said. "Actually he was more than that."

"Gruber? The SAC from Los Angeles?"

She looked up, the surprise evident in her eyes.

"How did you know about that?" she asked.

"I read your file," Bolan said.

She nodded. "Of course you did," she replied. "You probably wanted to see whether I'd gone rogue."

"I had to consider all the possibilities," Bolan stated.

"Of course," she said. "I would've done the same thing."

"So how did Dumond make the connection?"

"Somehow, he had Fred's phone. The phone had a picture of Fred, his wife and me on it. I have no idea why he had the phone."

Bolan uncrossed his arms and pressed his palms to his eyes for a couple of seconds.

Instinct told him Rodriguez was clean and just had been in the wrong place at the wrong time.

That Dumond had turned on her so quickly bothered him. But he decided to let it ride, at least for now.

"So what's Dumond's story?" Bolan asked.

"What do you mean?"

"What did you find out?"

"Look Mr. Cooper—Matt," she said. "I appreciate you pulling me out of there. I really do. But this is a sensitive investigation. I can't just blurt out everything. How do I know you're authorized to hear this stuff."

"I am," Bolan replied. Reaching inside his jacket, he withdrew a letter-size envelope and tossed it onto the table.

Placing her hand on it, she pulled it to herself. "What's this?" she asked.

"Authorization papers from the attorney general," Bolan replied. "Feel free to go through them. In the meantime, I have a phone call I need to make."

The soldier turned and left the room.

IN THE CORRIDOR outside the conference room, Bolan took out his sat phone and punched in some numbers. Several seconds passed as the call traveled through a series of cutout numbers, a precaution to keep the call from being traced. The phone rang a couple of times before someone answered.

"Striker, do you have a status report?" Brognola asked.

"We recovered Rodriguez. She's safe."

"Good job. I figured it wouldn't take you long to handle this," the big Fed stated.

"Thanks."

"Okay. I've known you a long time, and I've heard that tone of voice before. What's eating you, Striker?" Brognola growled. "Spit it out."

"It bothers me that she got nabbed," the soldier said. "How did Dumond know she was a Fed?"

"She mess up?"

Bolan shook his head no, even though Brognola couldn't see him. "She says no. My gut tells to believe her. She seems like a pro."

"That's the book on her. Tough and honest. Good in the field."

"That leaves a couple other options, neither good. Maybe they just had dumb luck. Dumond or one of his guys spotted her doing something, meeting with someone when she didn't know they were looking. That's one scenario."

"It's plausible," Brognola said.

"There's another scenario."

"I think I know where you're going," Brognola told him. "And I don't like it. You think there's a mole in the FBI?"

"Makes the most sense. Unless there's another agency with access to her dossier."

Brognola said nothing. The soldier stayed quiet and let his old friend ponder what he was saying. Brognola was high up in the Justice Department, and Bolan knew the guy hated it when one of his people turned out to be dirty. Brognola wasn't naïve, and he'd seen several supposed good guys turn out to be anything but over the years. But he also was committed enough to justice that it bothered him.

"Well, damn," Brognola muttered finally. "I'll bet you're right."

"We'll see," Bolan replied.

"I'll rattle some cages at Justice to see what I can dig up."

"Forget that," Bolan said. "Have the cyber team handle

it. It may take a little longer, but at least then you know you won't have to deal with any leaks."

"Fine. Any other joy you'd like to share?"

Bolan told him about the abandoned Jag, the lost weapons and the stolen car.

"We can have someone recover the weapons," Brognola said. "I'm sure Langley has someone on the ground who could get them for us. Stories about the firefight have already started surfacing on the cable news networks. Barbara showed me a clip of an interview with Monte Carlo's police chief. I don't speak French. He looked pissed. And, judging from his tone of voice, he's not a fan of yours."

"Shocking," Bolan said. "I usually score big with the local authorities. Hey, one other thing."

"Yeah?"

"Rodriguez didn't want to share what she knows. She needs a little downward pressure. Either you can apply it, or I can do it."

"Give me five minutes," Brognola said.

FOUR MINUTES AND thirty seconds later, Bolan returned to the secure conference room. He found Grimaldi pacing the room and scowling. Turrin was seated, his feet propped up on the table. He flashed Bolan a tight smile when the soldier entered the room.

Rodriguez greeted Bolan with a glare. He noted that one of the guys' sat phones lay on the table in front of her.

Bolan jerked his head at the door. "Why don't you two go for coffee?"

Grimaldi and Turrin exchanged a look. "By your command," the Stony Man pilot said agreeably.

After they left Bolan rolled a chair away from the table and sat.

"I take it you heard from Washington," he said.

"Yes," Rodriguez replied. She gave Bolan a curt nod.

"So what's Dumond up to? How did you get caught?"

"He's an arms dealer. I track arms dealers." She paused.

"I already know that," Bolan said. "What is he doing?"

Leaning forward, she laced her fingers together and rested her forearms on the table. "I want a piece of this."

Bolan shook his head no. "I work alone."

"What do you call Frick and Frack out there?" she asked, pointing at the door.

"Why do you want to stay in this? You almost got killed."

"So? You think I should hop a plane back to the States? Maybe take some time to meditate, eat tofu and find myself while you go hunt the bad guys?"

"I have no idea what you're talking about."

"Here's what I'm talking about. I'm not a damsel in distress. I can continue on this case."

"And?"

A puzzled look spread over her features.

"And? What do you mean 'and'?"

"And when we find Dumond? What then?"

"Arrest him, of course."

Bolan shook his head slowly.

"How many people did I arrest at Dumond's place?"

She hesitated.

"None," she said finally.

Bolan nodded once.

"Getting warmer," he said. "Those guys were Dumond's flunkies, a bunch of mercenaries with more guns than brains."

"And you shot them. Sure, I understand that. They drew down on you and you had to shoot them."

"No," Bolan said. "Those are your rules. We were there to free you. I also was after Dumond. And I suspect that I wouldn't be stuffing him into an airplane and bringing him back to the United States."

"You were going to kill him?"

"If I had to."

"But why not interrogate him?"

"I would have."

"You would have questioned him and then killed him?"

"He'd have a chance to fight back. Scum like that usually don't give up."

"So you'd kill a suspect? A prisoner? That's murder!"

"Not a suspect. An enemy. I was there to help you, but I also was there to decapitate his network. Obviously, I still have unfinished business to handle."

"Since when does the Justice Department sanction this sort of thing?"

When Bolan said nothing for several seconds, she broke the silence. "You're not Justice, are you? Are you Langley? The Pentagon?"

"Don't go there," he said.

The creases in her forehead deepened and her lips pursed into a bloodless line.

"Our government sanctions this?"

"Don't go there, either."

"Damn it! So I'm out of this completely? I'm just supposed to walk away and pick up another case somewhere?" Rodriguez asked.

"Yes."

"You are a piece of work."

"When necessary. See why I work alone?"

"I still want to be part of this."

"I don't think you heard me."

"Yes," she said, "I did."

"Just tell me what you know. We'll go from there."

"Bullshit."

Bolan spread his hands. "Best deal you're going to get."

She seemed to think about it for a few seconds before heaving a sigh. "Fine."

"I'll tell you what I know. Once you hear it, you'll understand why you need my help."

"I'm listening," Bolan said.

Rodriguez shut her eyes and chewed on her lower lip, as though gathering her thoughts. After a couple of moments she heaved another sigh and snapped her eyes open.

"I think Dumond's involved in something bigger than running guns to the usual bad guys," she said. "I think in a weird way he's the least of our worries."

"Explain," Bolan replied.

"You know I've been tracking him for months, right? I spent months in Washington studying his network and trying to figure out who he supplies and who supplies him. And this whole effort didn't start with me. Another team of agents was looking at him for a year before that. I thought we were being relentless. Turns out we don't have a clue as to how this guy was operating."

A bottle of water stood on the table in front of her. She picked it up and took a long swallow from it.

"We thought he was the top of the heap," she continued. "He bought the guns from one lowlife, sold them to another lowlife and laundered his money through a bunch of shell companies."

"He doesn't do that?"

"He's into all that crap. I thought that was the worst of it. But I think there's a lot more going on that we didn't realize. From what I picked up, he's shipping weapons to the United States. Not just handguns and rifles, but something larger. I just don't know exactly where he's sending the weapons or why."

CHAPTER SEVEN

Johann Krakoc stared at the sky, his eyes searching for
Dumond's airplane. Even though its approach had been
tracked by radar and radio communications, Krakoc
wanted to view the craft with his own eyes to know for
certain Dumond was going to arrive in one piece.

Things had gone wrong in Monaco. In spite of that,
the situation remained salvageable for the moment. But
they had to change their course. The stakes were too high
to do otherwise. Geiger told him to kill Dumond, so Dumond would die.

In the distance he finally could see a small black dot
on the horizon and knew it had to be Dumond's airplane.
They hadn't seen any other aircraft coming this way. The
tightness in Krakoc's chest loosened a little and he exhaled with relief.

Krakoc looked over the desert facility. It was situated
outside the city, separated by miles of scrub-covered desert
floor. It had a single airstrip and a large hangar for storing
and maintaining the airplanes. Another half dozen buildings dotted the property. Three were used for storing Dumond's weapons inventory. Another building housed the
radar and communications equipment while the final two
contained living quarters, offices and storage.

Krakoc hated the place. It was hot and flat. He couldn't
recall the last time rain had fallen. For a man raised on
a farm in rural Germany, every day in the Tunisian desert—the hot sun beating down on his bald head and thick

neck, his arms and legs covered in bug bites—felt like
another day in Hell.

That alone should've been enough to make him hate
his current surroundings. However, the place had additional significance. His grandfather had been a captain in
the German army's Panzer division, serving under Field
Marshall Erwin Rommel. The so-called Desert Fox had
drawn blood on U.S. forces at the Kasserine Pass in this
god-forsaken country and went on to fight the British yet
again. The Nazis ultimately had lost North Africa, with a
new commander surrendering to the Allies.

Krakoc's grandfather had respected Rommel's intellect
and his aptitude for battle. He'd later confided, however,
the man's unwillingness to follow Hitler's orders to the letter, his unwillingness to kill Jews and his distrust of Hitler explained the Axis Powers' defeat in Africa. Krakoc's
grandfather had been so concerned about Rommel that,
according to family lore, he'd fed information back to Berlin in the hope they'd remove him from command sooner.

For Krakoc's grandfather, those defeats turned into life-
altering experiences. He'd been captured when Axis forces
surrendered to the Allies and spent the rest of the war as a
POW. His captivity hadn't broken him. Instead he'd considered it an indignity and a source of righteous rage that
he'd carried for the rest of his life and also passed down
to future generations. The war had left the old man so fi-
nancially and spiritually impoverished that rage was the
only legacy he conceivably could leave behind.

So living in North Africa had been almost too much for
Krakoc to stomach. Geiger had encouraged him to look
at the bigger picture, one where his homeland rose to lead
the world. While that had been an attractive notion, he
also knew he had little choice but to obey. Krakoc would
do as his employers wished. Or, like the Nazis, they'd kill

him and find someone else to do the job. He really had no options.

By now the airplane was swooping toward the airstrip. The whine of the engines drowned out all the other sounds. The plane touched down, its tires screeching against the pavement and setting the German's teeth on edge. As he closed in on the strip, he felt small bits of swirling sand bite into his cheeks and heard them tap against his sunglasses.

The plane's door opened, the bottom half folding down and creating steps to the ground. Dumond, his expression grim, appeared in the plane's door where he paused for a moment before climbing down the steps. A pair of bodyguards followed him onto the tarmac.

The Frenchman strode over to Krakoc, acknowledged him with a faint nod and moved past him. Without realizing it, Krakoc scowled but turned and rushed to catch up with the other man. He held his tongue until they'd put some space between themselves and the still-idling airplane.

"It's good to see you," Krakoc said.

"Where's my car?" Dumond demanded.

The German pointed at one of the storage buildings. "It's in there," he said. "It's an old Mercedes. We put a new engine in it, so it is reliable."

If Dumond heard him, he gave no outward sign of it.

"Perhaps you should stay here," Krakoc said. "We can clear out one of the buildings and you can stay there. This would be a good place to hide."

Dumond snatched his glasses from his face and gave the other man a withering stare. "Hide? Who in the hell said I need to hide?"

Krakoc licked his lips. "No one," he said. "I just thought…"

"You thought I needed to hide," Dumond snapped.

Krakoc noticed that the bottoms of the other man's eyes

were rimmed with purplish crescents. The whites were marbled with red lines. The guy obviously was stressed.

"I thought you might need to regroup."

"I don't need to regroup!" the other man said, his volume rising.

A burning sensation ignited in Krakoc's gut. His fingers curled into fists, but he let them hang at his sides even as he forced a smile.

"Of course," the German said with mock grace, "I'm wrong."

They walked the rest of the way in silence to the building that housed one of the kitchens.

Krakoc rushed around Dumond, pulled open the door and gestured for him to go inside.

The building's interior was cool, the temperature controlled by an air conditioner powered by a gas generator. The smell of coffee hung in the air. Krakoc followed the other man inside and shut the door behind them. The guards had remained outside.

Krakoc gestured at one of the chairs. Dumond gave a slight shrug, moved to the table and lowered himself into the nearest seat. Closing his eyes, he pressed the tips of his right thumb and index fingers against the lids and rubbed them in small, circular motions.

The German filled two foam cups with coffee and carried them to the table, setting the first in front of Dumond before seating himself with the second cup still in his grip. He waited for the other man to speak.

After a half minute or so Dumond cleared his throat and spoke.

"The woman knew," he said. "How the hell did she know?"

Krakoc moved forward, a concerned look on his face. "Wait, what did she know?"

"She knew about the weapons."

"The ones going to North America?"

Dumond nodded.

Krakoc scowled. Feeling as though someone had punched him in the gut, he placed a hand on his stomach.

"You're sure?"

"What the hell do you think?"

"Sorry, I meant no disrespect."

Dumond pushed the coffee away. The phone on the side table rang. When Krakoc made no move to answer it, Dumond frowned, then picked up the receiver.

"Yes, hello… I'm just passing through, Cyril… What? Not right now."

"Can't you take that call later?" Krakoc demanded.

"I'll have to talk to you later, Cyril. Come to the depot in an hour. If I'm not here, Johann might have something." Dumond ended the call.

"Who was that?"

"Just a contact who needs fifty MP-5s. I don't want to deal with anyone while I'm in-country. You can deal with him.

"Okay, where were we?" the arms dealer asked.

"Did you tell our leader what the woman knows?"

"No."

"Perhaps you should tell him."

Dumond's head whipped toward Krakoc. His eyes narrowed into slits, he stared at the other man.

"Shut up."

"Of course."

Dumond looked away and lapsed into silence. He'd pulled a gold lighter and a pack of cigarettes from his pants' pocket. Clicking open the lighter, he coaxed a flame from it and lit the cigarette. He set the lighter on the table next to his pack of smokes. He kept his stare fixed on the wall.

Krakoc studied the man. He could feel a grin coming

and squeezed his lips together to suppress it. Dumond was an arrogant prick. Krakoc had for all intents and purposes held his nose while working for the French bastard. And he couldn't help but enjoy seeing the other man suffering from shell shock.

"You can stay here at the facility," Krakoc said. "Or we can fly you out of the country."

Dumond plucked the cigarette from his mouth, held it sideways and studied it for a few seconds.

"You heard what happened, right?" he asked.

"A little."

"He took out our entire team," Dumond said, eyes still fixed on the cigarette.

"He? Who's he?"

A long, pale gray ash had formed on the tip of the cigarette. Dumond flicked it onto the floor and took another drag from the smoke.

"I don't know," he said, shaking his head. "I saw the bastard on the security monitors before they cut out. He was big. He was dressed head to toe in black. He killed—hell, I don't know how many he killed."

"All by himself?"

Dumond shook his head. "He had a second man with him. They both fought like hell. I've never seen anything like it."

Krakoc scowled. "You? Please, my friend. You've been in several battles. You've spent your life around guns and soldiers. How could this man be any different?"

Dumond looked at the German. His eyes were wide, but when he spoke he sounded defensive.

"Trust me, they were different. The big man especially was different. There were bullets cutting through the air all around him, yet he kept moving forward. His guns seemed like extensions of his body. He seemed…" Dumond's voice trailed off and he stared down at his lap.

"He seemed what?"

"Never mind."

"No, I want to know."

"He seemed unstoppable."

Laughter burst from Krakoc's mouth. Dumond raised his head and glared at him.

"Don't laugh, you son of a bitch," Dumond said. "I know what I saw."

Krakoc swallowed his laughter and nodded in mock sympathy. Standing, he patted the other man on the shoulder.

"Of course, you do," he said. "I have no doubt you believe what you're saying. Who knows? Maybe he was a supernatural force! A vengeful spirit seeking retribution for all your wrongs against humanity."

"Fuck you," Dumond muttered. He fell silent and went back to staring at the floor.

Krakoc walked over to the coffeepot and poured himself a fresh cup. Turning, he leaned against the stove and looked at Dumond. How does a man break so easily? he wondered. Perhaps it was because Dumond had no real convictions. Krakoc, on the other hand, knew he had deeply held convictions, beliefs and goals that drove him out of bed every day. He knew for a fact he'd never break under pressure like this French coward.

He took a final sip of his coffee, set it on the counter and sighed gently. Truth be told, he was about to do Dumond a favor. The idiot appeared too shell-shocked to even think straight, let alone survive, especially in the world Reinhard Vogelsgang was promising to bring.

If the Frenchman knew he was helping the ideological successors to the Nazis gain a new foothold in the world... He'd fall apart.

Krakoc walked back toward the other man, approaching him from a direction putting him just out of Dumond's peripheral vision. He slid his pistol from its holster. When he got within a couple of feet of the arms dealer, he cocked the weapon's hammer. Immediately recognizing the sound, Dumond started to turn his head toward Krakoc.

The pistol cracked once, dispatching a single killshot into Dumond's skull. He toppled from the chair.

Holstering the pistol, the German turned from the corpse and began gathering his things. Mission accomplished. Now it was time to head to America.

CHAPTER EIGHT

Tunisia

The Peugeot 308 was cramped and stank of cigars and spilled wine. The engine hesitated every time Bolan punched the accelerator. The CIA liaison who'd hooked him up with the car had looked sheepish as he'd handed over the keys. The agent had said it looked like hell and ran even worse. He'd tried to soften the blow by pointing out the car's new GPS unit. He also bragged about the air conditioning, which Bolan later found out blew hot air, forcing them to drive with the windows down. Bolan had shrugged it off even though, truthfully, he would have preferred a good car to a good GPS system. A beat-up compact car would likely attract less attention than a new sedan, though.

As the car rolled through the city, Bolan took in his surroundings. He was struck by the absence of tall buildings. Most of the structures lining the streets stood no more than a single story and they weren't much to look at, either. The exteriors were faded, the paint weathered by the relentless heat and sun.

A pair of young men stood in the shadow cast by one of the buildings. They stared at the car as it rolled past them. His eyes hidden behind mirrored aviator shades, Bolan sized them up. He saw no visible weapons and neither made an effort to hide his interest in the Peugeot. Maybe they were genuinely curious about a pair of strangers or maybe they were acting as lookouts.

Bolan glanced at the rearview mirror and saw they continued to stare after the vehicle. One of the men raised his hand to his head. Was he bringing a phone to his ear?

"Are you worried about them?" Rodriguez asked.

Bolan shrugged. "Aware of them," he said. "They seemed interested in us."

"Maybe it's the fabulous eye candy next to you," Rodriguez said.

"That must be it," he replied. "Mystery solved."

Bolan guided the little car another half block and turned right. He drove another minute or so before pulling over to the side of the road.

Rodriguez exhaled deeply and released her seat belt. She reached into the backseat, grabbed a duffel bag and set it on her lap. Resting her hand on the door handle, she looked at Bolan.

"Five minutes?" she asked.

"On the dot," he said.

Nodding, she exited the vehicle, shut the door and slid her bag over her shoulder. Bolan stared after her while she walked past a couple of buildings before disappearing around the corner of the farthest one. The soldier threw the car into gear and rolled away from the curb. The man they'd questioned at Dumond's estate had said "Evergreen" and mentioned the name Monet. They'd come to Tunisia hoping to find Cannon Monet, one of Dumond's top associates. From what the Farm had dug up, Monet and an acquaintance ran one of Dumond's logistics centers for his gunrunning operation.

Bolan guided the car farther down the street before he found an empty lot to park the vehicle. Stepping from the car, he went to the trunk, opened it and pulled out a briefcase that contained his MP-5 and extra magazines.

He slammed the trunk lid closed and walked from the lot, which was little more than an empty parcel of land covered with gravel and tall weeds.

Bolan had passed Monet's office on his way to park the car. Leaving the parking lot, he turned and walked back toward the building. The plan was pretty simple. He and Rodriguez wanted to grab Monet and quiz him about his boss's whereabouts and any other information they could glean from him.

When Bolan reached the office building, he kept walking, trying to memorize as many details as he could without actually stopping and staring at the building. The place was squat and ugly. Steel bars covered the windows. A chain-link fence topped with razor wire surrounded the property.

Otherwise, it looked similar to the buildings around it. He also noted that no guards were stationed outside the building, a fact that disturbed him more than it comforted him. If one of Dumond's executives was inside the building, then where was the security team? From what the soldier had seen, there was no reason to believe Monet would leave the place unguarded.

The soldier walked past the building and, when he reached the end of the block, pulled out his phone and dialed Rodriguez's number. It rang once and she answered.

"Yes?"

"Have you seen any guards?" Bolan asked.

She paused for a second. "Negative," she said.

"Does that make any sense to you?"

"No," she said. "He's a high-value target. You'd think he'd have a small army roaming the grounds."

"Right. And there are no trucks parked outside."

"I noticed that, too. What do you make of it?"

"I'm not sure," Bolan replied. "It does seem weird, though."

"Maybe he ran."

Bolan had wondered the same thing. "It's possible," he replied. "Maybe he heard about the attack on Dumond's place in Monaco and closed up shop."

"Or Dumond contacted him and told him to shut the doors."

"It's possible," Bolan said. "There's only one way to find out, though."

"Do we stick to the plan?"

"Right," Bolan said.

Retracing his steps, he moved to the gate and found it unlocked. This only intensified his concerns. He couldn't imagine a high-level gunrunner leaving the place unlocked. A silver call-box stood on a post next to the gate. Bolan pressed the white button under the speaker. Several seconds passed while he waited for a reply.

He pushed the gate aside, stepped through it and began walking up a curved driveway leading to the front door.

If his approach triggered alarms in the building, he saw no sign of it.

When Bolan arrived at the front door, he reached over and turned the knob, which also wasn't locked. He pushed the door inward, tensing slightly, as he anticipated a sudden burst of gunfire to lance through the doorway.

Nothing happened.

Switching the briefcase to his left hand, the soldier reached under his shirt and fisted the Desert Eagle. He went through the front door. His first impression was of cool air brushing over his face and arms, cooling the sweat. His eyes and the Desert Eagle's barrel moved in tandem as he looked for threats. His eyes immediately flicked to the bodies on the floor. He counted three, all males, all lying on their stomachs, their faces pressed into red pools of their own blood. As best he could tell each man had been shot in the back of the head execution style. Shell casings lay on the floor near the bodies.

Flies already had gathered on the corpses. Bolan caught traces of the smell of decomposition floating on the air. He moved to check the corpses and immediately recognized Monet.

The soldier rose to his feet and moved through the other rooms. The only other living person in the house turned out to be Rodriguez who had come through the rear door.

"Monet?" she asked.

"Dead," Bolan replied.

He turned and exited the main building. A second single-story structure, as nondescript as the first, stood at the rear of the property. Four bay doors lined the front of the building. Bolan walked around the corner and found a single door. Turning to Rodriguez, he gestured at the door with his chin. She nodded her understanding. Turning the knob, he pushed the door inward and she went through it, her micro-Uzi at the ready.

Bolan followed her inside. A Caucasian man in a dark T-shirt, denim shorts and flip-flop sandals lay on the floor. He was on his back, his head turned toward the two Americans, dead eyes staring at them. A small hole in his forehead, streaks of blood trailing from it, seemed to stare at them, too. A gun lay on the floor a few feet from the dead man's right hand. Unlike the others, this guy apparently had made a play for his gun and been killed in the process.

Bolan noted a single shell casing on the floor several feet from the dead guy's outstretched legs. Apparently he'd been shot at fairly close range, and it obviously hadn't come as a surprise.

Running his gaze over the building's interior, the soldier felt his blood run cold. Along one wall stood a multidrawer tool chest, like those used by mechanics, and a shelving unit stuffed with bottles of oil, windshield wiper fluid and antifreeze. Several boxes still covered in plastic wrap also were piled on the shelves, and Bolan guessed they were unopened packages of vehicle parts. A few other large cardboard boxes were stacked along one wall, along with some empty pallets. A forklift was parked in another corner of the rectangular building.

"The weapons are gone," Bolan said.

"And if they're not here," Rodriguez said, "Dumond won't come here, either."

A LITTLE WHILE later they were back inside the main building, searching Monet's office. Bolan had looked for a laptop or a tablet computer, but found neither. The same went for cell phones. Bolan and Rodriguez had found none on the property.

They also found three shell casings, all in 9 mm, on the floor near the bodies. The men had been killed without a wasted shot. All that told Bolan was that the killers hadn't been considered an immediate threat and they'd been able to quickly get control of their targets. The casing in the garage had been a .40-caliber round so it was likely a different shooter. If the dead guy had known his killer, it was possible he'd allowed the shooter to get close to him, he'd heard shots from inside the house and made a play for his own pistol and caught a bullet in the forehead.

Maybe. It was one of a half dozen possible scenarios swirling around Bolan's brain as he thought about what they'd found. Exactly how it all had happened mattered little to him.

He wasn't a detective. What he, as a soldier, needed to know was whether Dumond's own people had pulled off the hit. And, if they were killing each other, what did that mean? If it was a rogue element, what did they want? Was it something Bolan could exploit? The soldier had learned a long time ago that, when the savages he hunted turned on one another, his best course of action was to sit on the sidelines while they tore each other apart. Once they thinned the herd, he could swoop in and eliminate those left behind.

It was a strategy that had worked in countless battles. However, Bolan didn't have the intelligence at hand to know what he was dealing with.

The soldier sat on a corner of Monet's desk and took out his sat phone.

Punching in a number, he waited as the call passed through the cut-out numbers before it started ringing.

Price answered. "Hello?"

"Hey."

"Striker, what did you find?"

Bolan quickly brought her up to speed on finding Monet and the others dead, as well as the lost weapons.

"We have other options," Price said. "I'll talk to Bear to see whether he can get a trace on the guy's phone or computer. One or both of them have to have a GPS unit inside them. We can get his number. It may take a little while."

"Good thinking," Bolan said, knowing Aaron Kurtzman, the cyber team leader, would stop at little to find a trace.

"That doesn't ease your mind much, does it?"

"Not really," Bolan said. "We need to find those weapons."

"Give us time to run some taps on our end," Price said. "We might be able to find something."

BOLAN WAS SITTING in Monet's kitchen, drinking a bottled water when the Farm called him back. Though she hadn't said anything, Rodriguez also seemed uncomfortable hanging out in a house filled with dead people. She averted her eyes from the room that contained the bodies and instead spent a lot of time looking out a window.

When his sat phone beeped, Bolan took the call.

"Did you get a location?" he asked.

"We did," Price replied. "We also were able to get some voice intercepts. Apparently, whoever took Monet's phone also is making phone calls on it."

"Okay."

"They have the weapons," Price said, "and they're going to transport them by ship."

"Not all the way," Bolan said.

"Doubtful," Price replied, "but that's how they're going to get them out of Africa. After that they probably have a flight lined up somewhere."

"Did they name a recipient?"

"Negative. No recipient, no final destination. It's not much."

"But it's all we have."

"Unfortunately, yes."

Bolan drank some water and set the bottle back on the counter.

"We've moved with worse intelligence," he said.

"And it turned out great," Price pointed out.

"I always walked away in one piece," he said.

"That's something. What's your next move?"

"I'm still thinking about it. What else?"

"I've been combing through some of the texts and other information. It looks like, whoever this is, he or she is associated with Dumond. And Dumond was the one who ordered Monet killed."

"Why?"

"From what I'm gathering, Monet already was on Dumond's list before you showed up. He's been skimming money for some time, or at least Dumond believed that to be the case."

"So it may as well be true."

"Exactly."

CHAPTER NINE

Seated in the Peugeot 308, while Rodriguez drove, the Executioner read through the contents of an encrypted email Price had sent regarding the weapons shipments. It likely would be the first of several as Price and the Farm's cyber team tracked down additional information.

Monet had spent months smuggling the weapons from neighboring Libya into Tunisia.

Now Dumond's people were going to use a boat named *Trident III* to move the weapons across the Mediterranean Sea to Europe. Price had already contacted Washington and asked them to flag authorities in Tunis. If they could snag the boat before it left the dock, the weapons problem would end quickly.

If that didn't happen, they'd need to locate the boat as it crossed the sea and seize it before it arrived in Europe. The soldier didn't want to storm the boat once it docked. Even if they tried to keep it under wraps, it was almost impossible to seize a ship of the *Trident III*'s size without attracting attention. Even if they succeeded, there was always the possibility a local policeman might leak the information to the media. The White House probably could concoct some kind of a cover story that would deflect attention. But the soldier would rather not attract the attention, period.

Grimaldi was flying ahead, following the most likely route to Tunis and trying to get a fix on Dumond's trucks. Bolan wasn't optimistic. The trucks had a long lead time on them. While the Farm's cyber team had combed through enough intelligence reports to ID at least a couple of trucks owned by Dumond, there was no guarantee they were the right trucks. Unfortunately, it was the best they could do under the circumstances. Bolan could have waited for more information to surface, but that would have taken time and he needed to act.

"You let me drive," Rodriguez said. "I'm impressed."

Bolan shrugged. "Renaissance man."

She smiled.

"Are you finding anything from those files?"

Bolan shrugged again. "You know the bottom line as far as what he plans to do.

"Apparently he's been shipping the weapons into Tunisia from Libya through one of his front companies, Evergreen Logistics."

"Does that mean anything to you?"

"When we were at Dumond's house in Monaco, we quizzed a man who turned out to be his head of security."

Rodriguez made a face. "Bellew?"

Bolan nodded. "We asked him where Dumond would run to. At the time, he said Evergreen and Monet's name. It made no sense, but now it does. According to the tiny bit of information out there, the company runs medical and other humanitarian supplies into Libya."

"Because Dumond's a humanitarian."

"Sure, but still businessman enough to realize he's losing money driving empty trucks back into Tunisia. So he stuffs them full of surplus weapons, probably leftovers from when Khaddafi was in power, and drives them to Africa."

"He's smart," Rodriguez said.

"To a point."

"Meaning?"

"Look at it this way. If you were smuggling weapons, what's the best way to stay underground?"

She considered the question for less than a minute. "Send weapons to small countries fighting small wars."

"Pretty much. You want to support the wars nobody pays attention to. And, since the U.S. and other countries are watching Libya, you don't want to smuggle weapons out of the country, either. Not if you want to keep a low profile, anyway. Dumond couldn't keep his hands out of there, though."

"He's arrogant as hell. He could've assumed no one would catch him."

"I'm not sure I buy that," Bolan said. "I'm sure he's arrogant and a risk-taker. Those are standard qualifications for an international arms dealer. He's probably not an idiot, though. Anyone in his business had to know they were going to attract attention moving weapons out of Libya."

"True. But if the payday's good, he's probably going to do it."

"Sure. I guess my point, though, is he had to have something really tempting that he wanted from Libya. Or his customer really, really wanted something from Libya."

"There were rumors that he was looking for portable air-defense systems," Rodriguez said. "That's how he first came to my unit's attention. We'd heard he was looking for shoulder-fired rockets, though we hadn't heard anything about Libya at the time. We assumed he was going through Afghanistan, buying up some of the old stock there."

The road split into a vee. Rodriguez tapped the brake to slow the car and veered right.

"When Khaddafi's government collapsed, a lot of those weapons went missing," Bolan said.

"Of course. And, if he got his hands on them, they'd fetch a good price. But that doesn't even touch the other elephant in the room. If he gets that stuff, how does he sneak it into the U.S.?"

"We both know it's possible," Bolan said. "Not easy, but possible."

She nodded.

"Unfortunately," she said, "that raises still another question. Who is the end user? He's about as apolitical as they come. He has to have a payday waiting for him on the other end or he isn't interested. And, once we identify the buyer, we'd have to figure out why he wants the weapons."

"Unless we can just find them and deal with them."

"By deal with them, you mean kill them."

"We already went over this," Bolan said.

"What if the customer is an American?"

"We've already been over this," the soldier said. A hard edge had crept into his voice.

"I'm raising a legitimate point," Rodriguez told him.

"It is legitimate. No argument there. If you'd like some time to think about it, I'll drop you off in Tunis and you can have a few days to think about it. I got over that moral and ethical dilemma a long time ago."

Turning her head, Rodriquez shot Bolan a withering look.

"You don't have to be an asshole."

"No, but I have to stay focused on my job, which is finding these guys."

"That's my job, too."

"Yeah, but the other piece of my job is eliminating the threat. That doesn't include arresting them, collecting evidence or securing arrest warrants. And, frankly, even if I was open to doing those things, my gut tells me we don't have time for that. This is a high-risk operation. Whoever's pulling the strings here is willing to shoulder that risk in order to secure a payback of some kind."

"A payoff we haven't identified."

"Right," Bolan said, nodding. "Dumond wants money. We can assume someone else wants the weapons because they want to do something awful with them. I want to find Dumond because of what he's done, but we also need to find him so he can lead us to the next target."

"I understand," Rodriguez said.

"And you're going to let me handle this my way?"

A few seconds passed before she pursed her lips and nodded slowly.

"Washington said you're in charge," she replied. "You're in charge."

They both fell silent. Bolan could understand her point of view, especially with her law-enforcement background. If the roles were reversed, he might balk at his methods, too.

However, Bolan wasn't a cop. He carried federal agent credentials only because it made his job easier. When all was said and done, he was a soldier, one who'd dedicated his life to hunting down and eliminating the savages who preyed on innocent people and civilized society.

CHAPTER TEN

The local CIA station chief was a guy named Mauldin.
Bolan had met him on a previous mission in another country, while operating under his Matt Cooper alias. Mauldin
was dressed in a T-shirt, Bermuda shorts and sandals.
When he saw Bolan uncoil from inside the Peugeot, he
mimed a gun with his right hand, aimed it at Bolan and
fired.

Bolan acknowledged him with a nod.

"Coop!" Mauldin yelled. "What did you think of the
wheels? Sweet, huh? Blended right in with the locals."

"It worked fine," Bolan said.

"Good, good," Mauldin said. He jerked a thumb over his
shoulder at a Black Hawk helicopter nearby. "Well, here's
my next gift to you. Don't ask me how I got it. But here it
is. That skinny bastard you run with—what's his name?"

"Jack."

"Right, Jack. He loves it. Thought he was going to dry
hump it right here on the airfield. I almost had to ask his
little buddy Leo to hold him back."

Mauldin laughed and slapped Bolan on the arm. The
guy seemed to have a lust for life and for his job. Mauldin
always seemed "on." However, the soldier occasionally
caught a hardness in the guy's eyes or an edge in his voice
that let the soldier know at least some of Mauldin's frat-
boy behavior was an act. It made him easy to underesti-
mate, and Bolan guessed the smarter people who tangled
with Mauldin dismissed him altogether—to their peril.

Bolan allowed himself a grin. Rodriguez exited the car and appeared at his side. She extended her hand to Mauldin, who took her hand and shook it.

"Special Agent Rodriguez," she said.

"Mauldin," he replied.

"Is that your first name or your last?"

"Yes."

"Yes?"

"Exactly."

"Excuse me?" Rodriguez asked, irritation creeping into her voice.

"He doesn't give his full name," Bolan said.

"Protects my identity, you know," Mauldin explained.

Rodriguez smirked. "Wow," she said. "Spooky."

"Ain't it, though? Look, Coop, good to have you and your lady friend here in my country. We love having guests and all…"

He paused.

"What?" Bolan asked.

"I gotta ask you something," Mauldin said. "It's gonna piss you off, but I have to ask the question. Okay?"

Bolan nodded.

"Look, the last time you and I met—" he looked at Rodriguez then back at Bolan "—in a country not to be named, you left one hell of a body count. You also left me with one hell of a mess to clean up. I mean, it's okay. You want to make a few omelets, you got to break a few eggs, blah, blah, blah. Am I right? But it took a little finesse on my part to keep the local officials at bay."

"Thank you."

"You don't need to thank me."

"Then there's a point?"

"Well, I'm just saying, if you're going to run around killing people or starting international incidents, a little warning would go a long way toward making ol' Mauldin's life a little easier. You feel me? Loud and clear?"

"I feel you loud and clear," Bolan said.

Mauldin's grin broadened and his shoulders relaxed. "Good," he said.

Bolan told him about the bodies they'd found at Monet's house.

"Shit, see, it's starting already. Okay, no worries. A couple of phone calls and I can make it all disappear. Give me the address."

"Fine," Bolan said. He recited the address and the CIA agent repeated it.

"Got it," Mauldin said, nodding.

"How's the rest of the list coming?" Bolan asked.

"It's all good. I'm trying to scare up a satellite or a drone, maybe get you kids some thermal imaging capabilities."

"And the additional helicopters?"

"Got a couple on contract. Also scared up a couple of agents, though they're mostly for support purposes. The one's pretty handy with a gun, the other's a linguist. Freaking genius of a girl—"

"Nice," Bolan said, interrupting the other man.

"The other ships will just be for show. It was all I could do to find helicopter pilots and hardware on such short notice. I mean, I'm good, but I'm not a miracle worker. I can get some people to search the ship, but if you want more guns, you're going to have to wait a day or two."

"Understood," Bolan replied. "We have enough people to take the *Trident III*."

Mauldin made a show of craning his neck and peering past Bolan at the empty space behind him.

"Enough people? What, you and Barbie here?"

"Barbie's about to break her foot off in your ass," Rodriguez stated.

"Ignore him," Bolan said. "He's trying to bait you."

He turned to Mauldin. "We have enough people. Just track down the additional helicopters. I want to be off the ground and after the ship as soon as possible."

CHAPTER ELEVEN

The Black Hawk helicopter flew over the Mediterranean Sea, staying close enough to the churning waves to foil radar detection. Grimaldi was piloting the craft.

Bolan was in the combat chopper's belly, checking his equipment. Turrin and Rodriguez, seated near him, did the same.

Wearing a combat blacksuit, Bolan had picked an M-4 outfitted with a cut-down Remington 870 shotgun fixed underneath the assault weapon's barrel, similar to a grenade launcher. The shotgun was loaded with three 12-gauge breeching rounds. Along with his usual sidearms, he also had packed white phosphorous, fragmentation and flash-stun grenades.

Turrin and Rodriguez had acquired MP-5 submachine guns. In addition to his .38 revolver, for this mission Turrin also was packing a Glock 22 chambered for .45 ACP rounds. Rodriguez was carrying her Glock.

Two more Black Hawk helicopters were trailing the one carrying the Stony Man warriors.

Grimaldi's voice buzzed in their headphones. "Two minutes to contact," he said.

"Roger that," Bolan replied.

The cargo ship was large, but as best they could tell it had no helipad or any place large enough to land a helicopter, let alone three. That meant Bolan and the others would have to use a fast rope to reach the cargo ship's deck, fan out and try to neutralize any crew members who fought back. Bolan originally had balked against having Rodriguez come along. The woman knew how to fight, but he wasn't sure she would be able to rappel onto the ship by rope. She told him she'd trained with the FBI's Hostage Rescue Team a couple of times during her career and could make her way to the deck with no problems.

Bolan still felt uncomfortable. It wasn't a gender issue. The Executioner had fought alongside women several times during his War Everlasting. He could tell Rodriguez was tough and resourceful. She knew how to use a gun and fight. On paper, her credentials looked impressive. But he hadn't seen her in action, which, man or woman, made her an unknown in his book. Still, with Grimaldi piloting the craft, he wasn't about to turn away the help, especially when Rodriguez was so resolute about stopping the weapons shipment.

Grimaldi's voice crackled again. "We have visual contact," he said. "We should be in position in thirty seconds."

Bolan and the others acknowledged the information and waited in silence. They'd already gone through most of the critical data before they'd left Tunisia. What information they had was thin and suspect. Without the designs for the *Trident III*, they'd been forced to use plans from the original manufacturer of the ship. The plans were more than twenty years old.

They had no way of knowing for certain whether the ship had been modified since it had been built. Considering its history under several owners of moving contraband, though, Bolan could only assume there'd been changes, such as false panels and hidden rooms, made to the boat over the years.

The other intelligence had been only slightly better— and not from lack of trying.

Dumond had registered a series of front companies, all based in Africa. The cyber experts at the Farm had accessed the computers of the controlling corporation and secured a list of employees and payroll numbers. The payroll records indicated the company had twenty employees, seventeen men and three women. Whether they were muscle, bookkeepers or maintenance workers wasn't clear from the hacked files. Bolan also had to assume the information in the files was inaccurate, given he was dealing with a criminal enterprise.

The Black Hawk swooped over the Trident's deck and hovered.

In addition to the copilot, the CIA had provided a skeleton crew that included two men, both of whom Bolan pegged as being in their early thirties. One of the men, a wiry guy who'd introduced himself as Bernie, rose and moved to the now-open doorway. The second man, who'd identified himself as Ted, remained seated, the expression on his suntanned face one of boredom. He occasionally entertained himself by doffing his black baseball cap and scratching at his shaved scalp.

Bernie, serving as jump master, tested the rope to make sure it was moored securely to the craft. He nodded his satisfaction and, when Grimaldi gave the signal, he tossed the rope through the doorway.

Bolan had slipped on a pair of gloves to protect his palms. He grabbed the rope, went to the door, set his feet on the bottom of the frame and jumped. He squinted against the rotor wash and felt it whip at his clothes as he slid down the rope.

As he hit the ground he saw Turrin step off the door frame and begin sliding to the ground. A second later he heard a voice saying something in French, the words smothered by the whipping of the chopper blades and the roar of the ocean.

Bolan already knew the message: "We are agents of the

United States' government. Throw down your weapons. Surrender your ship."

Once Rodriguez set her feet on top of the bridge, Bolan began moving.

From his vantage point, he could see dark shadows stepping onto the deck and moving toward the bridge. The copilot repeated the message again in both French and English.

They'd raised the volume so his words could be made out over the loudspeakers. Bolan was sure the people moving along the deck could hear if not understand the message blaring from the helicopter.

Bernie and Ted were the last ones down the rope. They'd come equipped for combat, complete with M-4 rifles and Beretta 92 handguns. But their primary job was to operate the ship once the team gained control of the bridge.

A ladder led from the top of the bridge to the deck below. Bolan descended the ladder quickly, moving into a crouch when his feet touched the deck.

Peering through the windows, he saw three crewmen. One, an older Caucasian with a flowing, white beard, stood at the center of the bridge and stared up at the ceiling, apparently focused on the sound of the helicopter blades. Another crew member was seated and staring at a computer monitor. Bolan assumed the man was getting a feed from radar or trying to radio other crew members for help. A third man stood on the opposite side of the bridge, peering through a window and gesturing for the others to join him at the window.

Bolan saw no immediate signs of weapons.

Moving in a crouch, he reached the door and tried to open it, but found it was locked. He backed up a couple of paces from the door, aimed the launcher and squeezed the trigger. The weapon cracked and a single round punched through the lock. The door sprang inward and Bolan fol-

lowed it inside. The crew wheeled in his direction. When
their eyes lit on the black-clad warrior, they put their hands
up and began speaking rapidly in French, the tones of their
voices ranging from fear to indignation.

Bolan crossed the room, gesturing for the men to turn
and put their hands on windows, consoles or tables. The
guy who'd been fixated on the monitor screen and the man
who'd been staring out the window immediately got Bolan's meaning and complied.

The third man, his beard and hair white and unkempt,
his cheeks ruddy, glared at Bolan and snapped something
in German.

Turrin and Rodriguez were positioned on the deck outside the bridge while the other two Americans had followed Bolan inside.

From the guy's demeanor, Bolan pegged him as the
captain or another ranking officer.

He fixed Bolan with blood-shot eyes; he reeked of alcohol. Bolan thought he saw the guy waver just slightly.

"Do you speak English?" Bolan asked.

The guy stared for a second then shook his head. "No,
no English."

Bolan scowled, unsure whether the skipper was jerking
his chain or telling the truth.

Ted brushed past Bolan. "I speak German," he said.
"Ask the questions and I can translate."

Bolan nodded. "Ask him how many people they have
on the boat."

Ted asked the question in what sounded to Bolan like
fluent German. The captain spit out something. Bolan
didn't understand most of the words, but the belligerence
was unmistakable. Before the Executioner could say anything, Ted stalked forward and began speaking rapidly,
occasionally gesturing at the big American.

The officer glanced over at Bolan for just a second before turning back to the other American. He said something and while tone remained defiant, he'd crossed his arms over his chest. The two men went back and forth like that for what seemed like forever.

Bolan felt himself growing more impatient, knowing there were gunners on the way to the bridge.

Finally the man's shoulders slumped and he began answering questions.

Ted looked at Bolan.

"Fourteen guys," he said. "Only half that many are armed. The rest are maintenance workers and the like."

"You believe him?"

The other man grinned. "I told him you were crazy, that you'd hunt down his kids, his grandchildren, if he didn't talk. He agreed you look crazy enough to do it."

"Thanks," the soldier said.

He keyed his throat mike and relayed the information to the others.

"Striker," Turrin said, "I need you out here."

Turning, Bolan strode quickly toward the door. "What's the problem?"

"That's just it," Turrin said. "There's no problem."

"What?"

"The crew is surrendering."

EXITING THE BRIDGE, Bolan saw Grimaldi and Rodriguez positioned at the rails, their weapons fixed downward at something beyond his vision. He moved to the nearest rail and saw seven men standing on the next deck, their hands on their heads.

CHAPTER TWELVE

Poised on a catwalk, Friedhelm Geiger looked down on the brick warehouse's interior. He watched as one of his men steered a forklift to the back of a large trailer and slid the forks underneath one of the wooden pallets stored inside. The driver worked the lift lever, raised the pallet off the trailer floor and backed away from the vehicle, bringing a wooden crate with him. It was the fourth such crate the man had unloaded from the truck. Two more trucks packed with similar payloads idled outside the warehouse.

The contents of most of the crates was insignificant. Each contained standard-issue assault weapons, boxes of empty magazines and cartridges, army surplus gear and other items Dumond had sold to some small African country's army. The transaction was legal, with Dumond selling the hardware through one of his front companies to a legitimate buyer. While not a favorite of Washington, the African dictator cutting the check wasn't at odds with the United States. There were no embargoes against him buying the weapons, no Treasury Department seizures of his assets, or other blemishes that might call undue attention to him. That meant that, while foreign intelligence agencies knew he was buying guns, they had no reason to scrutinize the shipment or to try to stop it.

That worked fine for Geiger.

To his right, he heard someone stomping up the metal stairs to the catwalk. He turned and saw one of his men approaching. The guy was a tall, rangy German with sandy-brown hair and a wide face. His name was Klaus Schenker. Ostensibly, Vogelsgang had assigned him to work with Geiger because Schenker had superior organizational skills. However, Geiger assumed the man's main role was to act as another set of eyes and ears on the ground for Vogelsgang. That didn't surprise Geiger. He knew two things: his boss didn't trust him and the feeling was mutual. He could live with that.

Schenker halted a couple feet away from Geiger and threw the older man a crisp salute.

"We've unloaded everything," Schenker said.

Geiger nodded. "Good," he said. "Send the trucks on their way. The longer they're delayed, the more attention we'll draw."

"I agree," the other man replied.

"And once you've done that, begin repackaging the other items."

Schenker saluted again and walked away. Geiger suppressed a laugh. Where does Vogelsgang find these people? he wondered. Apparently the industrialist had fed this guy the same line of bullshit he'd fed so many others. There was going to be a rebirth of Germany and eventually Europe. They'd succeed where Hitler had failed. They'd make Germany a country to be feared and respected, not just for its economic strength, but also its military might.

Lighting a cigarette, Geiger took a long drag then exhaled. Through a haze of smoke, he saw Schenker hurrying around the warehouse floor, barking orders at the others, gesturing for them to move the crated weapons away from the bay doors. Geiger knew the full extent of Vogelsgang's plans—at least he thought he did. While they sounded somewhat fantastic, the former spy knew that if anyone could pull it off it was Reinhard Vogelsgang. The man had money, vision, drive and, occasionally, charisma. He'd assembled a small army ready to move on short notice. More important, members of the United Front had infiltrated various parts of the government. Some were warriors; some were bureaucrats. There were true believers and people who signed up because they liked the bribes.

Regardless, Vogelsgang had established an infrastructure; one that would begin moving soon. It would shake Germany and probably the rest of the world to its core when it all came together.

First, though, something stunning needed to happen, an event of such magnitude that it would consume the world's attention, sending it reeling with panic.

That was where Geiger and the weapons came in.

He was supposed to use the weapons to create something big, a distraction that would reverberate around the globe. Unlike the other guys, he wasn't buying it. He gave Vogelsgang a 50-50 chance of making his twisted dreams a reality. And, even if he won, he'd have a hell of a battle on his hands as he grabbed for power, maybe even triggering a major war.

Geiger noticed his cigarette had burned almost to the filter. Dropping it onto the catwalk, he stomped it and began looking for another one. Why the hell not? he told himself. In a few months he'd be in the ground anyway. He had a brain tumor, the fast-growing kind that likely would leave him bedridden in a matter of months, if not weeks. The kind that killed millionaire politicians and the poor with equal viciousness.

He shook another cigarette into his palm and slid the pack into his pants' pocket.

It was his death sentence that had led him to take on the gig with Vogelsgang. Geiger had spent years running operations for German intelligence. By his own estimation, most had been successful, a few even qualified as brilliant. He'd killed with his own hands, coordinated assassinations, recruited spies, public officials and high-level corporate executives to turn against their own. However, everything he'd done had been invisible. The people he'd killed were important, but not national figures.

He'd always preferred the anonymity—until now. With death staring him in the face, he'd decided he wanted to leave something behind. Granted, people still wouldn't know he'd been involved in the events coming their way, but they'd sure as hell would know something had happened.

Schenker returned a couple of minutes later.

"They'll have everything transferred to new packaging and stowed on the plane within the hour," he said.

Geiger acknowledged the other man with a nod.

"I'm curious," Schenker said. "Dumond thought the weapons were to be shipped by boat. How did you convince Monet to bypass him and send the weapons directly here?"

A smile touched Geiger's lips.

"It wasn't hard. I told Monet that if he sent the cargo here, to the warehouse, we could cut out Dumond, and Monet would make more money. I had Dumond killed. Then, once Monet shipped the weapons, I had someone put a bullet in his head."

Schenker looked confused. "Why? He did as you asked."

Geiger shrugged. "I didn't want him to tell anyone about the diverted weapons."

"He followed your orders and you had him killed."

Another shrug. "Come on. It's all in a day's work, right? Today was bloody, but tomorrow's going to be even worse. It gives me something to look forward to."

Geiger flicked his cigarette butt over the catwalk railing. He turned and walked away from the other man, chuckling as he went.

Mediterranean Sea

SEVEN MEN. Bolan immediately wondered where the other half of the crew was.

Moving to the nearest ladder, he climbed down to the next level with Turrin following him. Bolan began motioning with the barrel of his M-4 for the seven men to line up along the nearest wall.

He looked at Turrin and said, "Start frisking them."

"Again with that?" Turrin asked.

"When you have a specialty, stick with it," the soldier said.

"That specialty being endless tolerance for bullshit," Turrin replied.

The Executioner watched as Turrin moved to the nearest sailor and began patting the guy down. Turning up a small folding knife in the guy's front pants' pocket, he turned and slid it across the deck toward Bolan.

The soldier felt his unease growing with each passing second. Part of his worry tension was easy to diagnose. They'd only located half the crew, none of whom appeared to be armed, which matched what the captain had told them. However, that also meant there was another group of armed men moving around the boat out of Bolan's sight while he, Turrin and Rodriguez dealt with this group.

The sound of feet scuffing against steel prompted Bolan to turn. He saw Rodriguez climbing down the ladder. When she reached the deck, she fisted the MP-5 and moved to Bolan's side.

"This is too easy," she said. "And you know it. I can tell by the look on your face."

Bolan nodded, but kept his eyes on the line of prisoners.

"There's supposed to be fourteen people," he said. "And we have seven. Half the crew is supposed to be armed."

"And these guys aren't armed," she said.

Bolan gestured with his chin at the box cutters, pocketknives and screwdrivers Turrin had collected from the crew. "Not unless you consider that armed," he said.

"Half these guys look like they're in their sixties," Rodriguez said. "They don't look like they're in bad shape. But they also don't look like hardened combat veterans."

"Something's wrong," Bolan said.

"What should we do?"

He reached into one of his pouches, pulled out a handful of blue zip ties and handed them to her. "Take these guys out of commission," he said. "Then we look for the others."

ERNST HOLZMAN TRIED to stretch his leg and bumped it against the side of the lifeboat. The sudden sound caused him to whisper a curse. He looked to his right and saw three other men staring daggers at him. He shrugged off their dirty looks. There was plenty of noise emanating from outside the lifeboats. The whipping of helicopter blades was constant. From belowdecks, he could hear the big engines rumbling, pushing the boat forward over the Mediterranean. No one heard the bump of a boot against the lifeboat. They just didn't.

Unfortunately he was surrounded by a bunch of wussies who were jumping at their shadows—all because some American supposedly was gunning for them. The idea that these men around him were scared of a single American both sickened and worried him. If the United Front was to achieve its goals, the last thing anyone could afford was to lose their nerve. Geiger had come up with a plan. It seemed like a simple one, but it was more than enough to make sure the American agents stopped troubling them.

The lifeboat held seven United Front fighters. Now they just had to wait for a signal to make their move.

The killing would be easy.

From Holzman's perspective, most of the crew was useless. They were nothing more than laborers who performed the most menial tasks on the ship. They'd ordered them to surrender to the Americans to create a distraction. If he and the other United Front commandoes had to mow down a few cargo handlers to get at the real targets, so be it. Maybe such moral dilemmas worried other men, but Holzman considered himself above such concerns. And it was that quality that put him and his brothers in the United Front above so many others. They realized not all men were equal. Many were weak, in body, mind, or both, and they deserved to have less. Others had weaknesses that went beyond physical or mental infirmities—their skin color, their choice of religions, whatever. Their very existence weakened society, especially when they began making noises about being "equal" to other men who so clearly were superior.

Eventually they'd kill those men, too. And their women and the children.

Holzman knew he was a patriot. He'd spent years in the German military and later the country's intelligence agencies. But over the past several years he'd become increasingly alarmed as he'd watched these foreigners come into Germany and other parts of Europe and attach themselves to it like leaches, siphoning off its prosperity and its identity. At the same time, public officials in the country were only too happy to sit back and let the bastards ravage their homeland.

It made him sick; sick to the point he knew he needed to fight back, though he was unsure how.

When Friedhelm Geiger had approached him about working for the United Front, he'd jumped at the chance.

He'd broken a lot of laws and spilled a lot of blood since then. All of the killing had been covert, a small hit here or there to eliminate someone threatening the movement. Though it'd been years since he'd run operations, he'd found, to his delight, that killing still came easily to him and he never found himself saddled with remorse over the murders. Now he was going to have another chance to kill a man, several men and a woman, in fact. He just had to wait a little longer.

CHAPTER THIRTEEN

Once Bolan gave the all clear, the helicopters lowered to the deck and hovered, off-loading a dozen people. A handful carried sidearms while others were analysts borrowed from the CIA's various offices in Africa. They spread out over the ship's deck and began accessing the various cargo bays.

Bolan watched the activity below. He felt uneasy. He'd expected more resistance in taking the ship and had encountered none. If the ship contained weapons, especially weapons for some kind of strike, why not guard them? It was possible Bolan's strike on Dumond's mansion in Monaco had pushed them into hiding. That always was the risk in making that kind of hit. Once you fired the first shot, everyone knew you were coming for them.

The soldier's sat phone vibrated and he brought it to his ear.

"Go," he said.

"Striker? It's Barb."

"Hey."

"We have a fix on Dumond."

"Okay, good. Where is he?"

"He was at his weapons depot in the Tunisian desert."

"Was?"

"He's dead."

"You're sure?"

"We have photo. I'm sending it to your phone. Give it a look. I'll wait."

Bolan opened the text message and looked at the photo. The picture was slightly blurred and tilted a little, as though someone had shot it quickly and hadn't bothered to hold the camera or phone straight. Bolan recognized Dumond's face right away from other pictures he'd seen. The slope of the guy's forehead was interrupted by a small red hole, from which a red line of blood trailed over his forehead before pooling on the floor.

Bolan closed the message and raised the phone to his ear.

"It's him," he said.

"How did we get this?"

"You can thank Mauldin. One of his sources knows Dumond and has purchased guns from the Tunisian arm of the organization. He was looking to hook up a client with some MP-5s. When he called the depot, he was surprised to hear Dumond answer. Since Dumond's a gunrunner, Mauldin was always willing to buy information about him, especially about any deals he might be cutting. The source was told to show up at the depot in an hour. According to Mauldin, his source found the door unlocked. He went inside and found our friend bleeding out."

"Did he have any theories on who might've killed Dumond or why? And why wasn't there anyone on site to stop him from getting into the facility?"

"I'll take the last question first. The facility was empty. He walked right in."

"What the hell?"

"Exactly," Price replied. "You'd think an arms dealer would have better security at his facility than that.

"Red flag number one. Then Mauldin's source told him something else interesting." Bolan heard Price shuffling some papers on the other end of the phone and stayed quiet. He guessed she was going through notes. "As for the who-dunit question, Mauldin's guy said that, when he called

Dumond, he heard a voice in the background. The arms dealer said that if he wasn't there later, 'Johann' would take care of him. From previous dealings with Dumond, he knew he was referring to Johann Krakoc."

"What's the book on Krakoc?"

"It's hard to nail down much," Price replied. "I called in a few markers at NSA. Apparently he was German intelligence for a while. He did some low-level legwork, but got bored because he believed he was destined for bigger things."

"Legend in his own mind?"

"Yes and no," Price said. "According to my contact, Krakoc underwent some pretty rigorous training to become a field operative. He grew up flying airplanes and he was naturally athletic. He excelled when it came to firearms, hand-to-hand combat, that sort of thing. They even sent him to the U.S. for some counterterrorism training."

"All he needed was an Aston Martin and a martini."

"Funny. On the technical side he was very good. Unfortunately he decided to use his powers for evil."

"Meaning?"

"The guy's a bigot. He doesn't just have beliefs out of the mainstream, he likes to act on them. He started targeting immigrants in the country."

"Targeting?"

"Not like that. No, he'd confront someone and start a fight. After he put a couple guys in the hospital and got busted, his superiors got nervous. He was an intelligence agent, but his day job was as a bureaucrat with Germany's foreign ministry. Once he was arrested, he threatened to dump his guts to anyone willing to listen."

"Damn."

"After that, it got a little hazy. He fled the country. The charges vanished. The next time he pops up on the radar, he's a mercenary, working in Africa and South America.

From what I gather, he flew under the radar while he was a soldier-for-hire. There's almost no record that I can find of him."

"That doesn't mean he behaved himself."

"Not in the least. Maybe he got smarter. He worked in some failed states, like Somalia, so I'm betting he took advantage of the general lawlessness. But here's the scary part. Apparently, Krakoc has traveled to and from the United States recently. Under aliases, of course, but he's been coming to the U.S."

"Why?"

"No clue. We're working on it, though."

"Find out what you can," Bolan said. "We've got to search this ship."

CHAPTER FOURTEEN

Holzman saw the big guy and the woman move between the crates.

He and the others had slipped from the lifeboats minutes ago and had begun fanning out over the cargo ship. He moved over the deck, hugging whatever shadows he could find. Turning to the pair of gunners at his six, he signaled for one to circle the crates to try to head off their targets. The hardman nodded his understanding. While he melted into the darkness, Holzman signaled for the other man to stay put in case their targets tried to retreat.

Holzman activated his throat mike.

"Now," he said.

The lights went off, plunging the ship into darkness. Holzman slipped his night-vision goggles down over his eyes and fell in behind the two Americans. He was ready to hunt.

WHEN DARKNESS SWALLOWED everything, Bolan froze and touched Rodriguez on the arm so she'd do the same. While he waited for his eyes to adjust to the darkness, he tried hard to use his other senses to detect threats. He strained his ears, but heard no tell-tale signs of people such as the scrape of boots on the deck's surface or the rattle of equipment that wasn't properly secured.

Turrin's voice buzzed in his earpiece. "Lights out," he said.

"You, too?"

"Yeah," Turrin said. "The only place where I see lights is the bridge. I'm assuming they have a backup generator."

"Radio Jack," Bolan whispered, "tell him to give us some light down here."

"Roger that."

The soldier began moving again with the silence and grace of a jungle cat. A full moon hanging in the black sky provided some light and the soldier's eyes had adjusted to the darkness so that he could move around with some confidence.

Gunshots shattered the silence, prompting Bolan and Rodriguez to halt again. The shots had come from belowdecks. His stomach clenched and he bit off a curse. There were a few CIA fighters on the deck below, but most of the people were analysts, linguists and other help Mauldin had pulled together at the last minute. They weren't going to be any help in a firefight.

He activated the throat mike again.

"Green Team," he said, "situation report."

"Green Team commander here," said Trish Michaels, the team leader. "Someone turned out the lights. We're taking fire. No time to talk."

"Roger," Bolan said. "Red Team, situation report."

"Red Team okay," said Lou Elliott, the team leader. "We have more shooters. Want us to peel a couple off and send them Green Team's way?"

"Roger that. One or two. No more. Keep the rest of your team together. If you can find a place you can control, do it until we get the lights back on. If they turned out the lights, there's a good chance they have night-vision goggles. If that's the case, they can hunt and pick us off almost at will."

"Thanks," Elliott replied, his tone anything but grateful.

The soldier heard a light scraping noise at his six. He wheeled and saw a shadowy figure several yards away from them. The movement by Bolan apparently panicked the guy who'd overestimated his stealth capabilities. The guy's weapon flamed and bullets chewed into the crates next to Bolan. The soldier was swinging around the M-4's muzzle to return fire when Rodriguez squeezed off a couple of shots from the MP-5. The burst tore into the man's abdomen. He let out a cry of pain and folded at the waist, closing like a jackknife.

Bolan's combat senses cued him to more danger. He spun and caught sight of another inky form, his body silhouetted by the moonlight, creeping toward them. Triggering the M-4, Bolan swung the weapon in a wide arc, the rounds lancing into the man's center mass.

Their attacker collapsed in a dead heap. Bolan crept up on the dark figure. Kneeling next to the man, he stripped the NVGs from the guy's head and brought them up to his own face for a closer look. A stray round had struck the goggles' lens, shattering it and rendering the equipment useless. Bolan set them aside. From the corner of his eye, he saw Rodriguez approaching. She now wore goggles and Bolan assumed she'd stripped them from the other hardman.

"You want these?" she asked, tapping them with a finger.

Bolan shook his head. The goggles were good, but a luxury for him. He knew he had more nighttime combat training and experience than the FBI agent, more than enough to get him through until they found a pair for him.

Getting to his feet, he continued on, winding his way through the maze of crates until he reached the first cargo hold. Derrick posts jutted from the deck and were silhouetted in the moonlight. Before he emerged from cover, the Executioner swept his gaze over the posts, studying them for signs that someone was using them for cover. While he walked around the cargo hold, Rodriguez went to the next one and checked for enemy gunners.

When they reunited, he asked whether she'd found anything. She whispered no.

Next was the forecastle, the front deck of the boat. Bolan signaled for her to approach it from the starboard side, while he came at it from the port side. She acknowledged him with a nod and they began their approach.

The soldier proceeded cautiously as he neared the forecastle. It rose several feet from Bolan's perch. The closer they got to it, the harder it was to see on the platform. That meant if someone was there, the person could rain down death with impunity on Bolan and Rodriguez.

Dying didn't bother Bolan. He'd made peace with that long ago. He traveled with the Reaper's cold breath on the back of his neck. He'd die soon enough. What did worry him, though, was that he wouldn't finish the mission. Bolan tried not to think too much about it as he moved ahead.

One of the Black Hawks had moved overhead. Its arrival was a mixed blessing. A spotlight on the belly of the craft kicked on, the white beam cutting through the inky blackness and providing Bolan some light. He glanced to his right and saw Rodriguez was slipping her night-vision goggles from her eyes. The helicopter also gave Bolan an eye—and some large-caliber machine guns—in the sky. At the same time, the whine from the helicopter's engines drowned out other noises and made it hard for Bolan to hear.

A steel ladder led to the top of the forecastle. Bolan reached it first. He set his left foot on the bottom rung and his hand from the same side reached for the rung a few inches above eye level. He let the M-4 fall loose on its strap and slid the Beretta from his shoulder holster.

Before he could begin climbing, the rattle of automatic

weapons fire crackled behind him. He whirled toward it. Yellow-orange lines streamed out of the darkness, angling up at the chopper. The bullets hit the Black Hawk's skin, sparked and whined off the steel.

"Shit," Grimaldi's voice said in Bolan's ear, "the dude's chewing up my paint job."

The whine of the engines intensified as the pilot began turning the helicopter on its axis to face the shooter.

"Careful, Jack," Bolan said into his throat mike. "We have our people in the cargo hatches."

In the meantime, Bolan switched the Beretta to his left hand and, double-tapping the trigger, unleashed a series of tribursts in the direction of where he'd seen the muzzle-flashes just before they'd winked out. Another volley of shots lashed out from the darkness, this time at Bolan. They originated from a different point than the first rounds.

Shooters on the move, Bolan thought.

Rodriguez also had spun and was unloading her MP-5 at what had been their rear flank.

Even without its spotlight, the chopper's other lights were at least creating enough of a glow to allow Bolan to see a little better.

More shots flashed out from Bolan's right. The Executioner assumed this was a separate attacker. He fired the M-4 with his right hand, the weapon grinding out a sustained burst in that direction. Flames flashed from his opponent's weapon as the shots angled up at the sky and winked out almost immediately. Probably caused by a last trigger squeeze of a dying man, Bolan thought. If it wasn't for the noise from the helicopters, he might've heard a strangled cry or the clatter of a falling weapon. As it was, he'd just have to wait to see where the next shots came from.

Instinct told Bolan to turn. Wheeling, he caught the

edge of a foot striking against his jaw. Even though it was a glancing blow, it caused him to stumble. His jaw went numb immediately. As he stumbled back, he saw a man hanging from the ladder, pulling his foot back in for another strike. The guy launched himself from the ladder. By the time his feet struck the deck, the guy had fisted a pistol and was bringing it up to squeeze off a shot at Bolan.

The soldier locked the Beretta's muzzle on the guy first. Tapping the trigger, he introduced the hardman to a face full of 9 mm Parabellum rounds that drilled through the man's mouth and nose.

Rodriguez had dropped into a crouch and was concentrating her fire at ten o'clock. Return fire whistled out of the darkness, slamming into the deck several feet in front of her.

In the same instant Grimaldi triggered the Black Hawk's front machine guns, feeding a quick blast in the shooter's direction. The bullets pierced the man's skin like the stingers of a swarm of angry bees, ripping through flesh and making part of his torso disappear in a red mist.

"I think he's down," Grimaldi said.

Bolan turned and started back up the ladder while Rodriguez continued to cover his six. As his fingers curled around the top rung, two more dark shapes appeared at the edge of the forecastle. Even in the limited light, Bolan could see they were carrying rifles of some kind. The soldier whipped the Beretta around and it chugged out three rounds, all of which punched into the first figure's center mass. His body went limp and pitched forward, falling past Bolan. Rodriguez in the meantime had seen the second thug and turned her weapon in his direction.

To Bolan's surprise, the guy dropped his rifle and threw up his hands. Bolan scrambled the rest of the way up the ladder. Climbing onto the raised deck, he kept the Beretta trained on the guy as he crossed the distance between them. When he got close enough, he kicked the dropped rifle away.

"Down," Bolan yelled.

He gestured at the deck with the Beretta in case the man didn't speak English.

Nodding, the man lowered himself first to his knees and then went facedown on the deck. Bolan knelt, rested his knee on the guy's spine and sank his weight into the guy's back. With his free hand, he snagged the man's sidearm, a Detonics .45-caliber pistol, and tossed it over the railing. He found a combat knife sheathed on the guy's other hip and tossed it over the side, too.

Rodriguez had joined him on the deck. She kept her MP-5 trained on the prisoner, allowing Bolan to reload his Beretta before he holstered it. He pulled a couple zip ties from one of his pouches and used them to bind the man's hands.

Climbing off the guy, Bolan grabbed one of the prisoner's biceps and rolled him over onto his back. He grabbed a flashlight from his gear, flicked it on and shone it in the man's face. He had gray hair cut into a flattop, but his face looked fairly young, at least in the poor lighting.

Bolan activated his throat mike. "Green and Blue team leaders, sitrep."

"We found two of these bastards skulking around down here," the Green Team leader replied. "Put bullets in both of them, took their NVGs and sent a couple of people looking for a way to turn on the lights. They should have something shortly."

"We haven't lost anybody else," the Blue Team leader chimed in. "We've been staying put."

"Good," Bolan said. "Stay sharp. There are more fighters than the captain told us about."

"Shadow Master to Striker, come in, Striker." It was Turrin.

Bolan grinned. "Shadow Master, seriously?"

"It played well with focus groups," Turrin replied.

"I take it you're still alive," Bolan said.

"Roger that. Just hanging with my new BFFs."

"We've got a prisoner," Bolan said. "I want to have a heart-to-heart with him. I'll probably bring him your way."

"More the merrier," Turrin said. "You think he knows anything?"

"Other than that his ass is in a sling? Hard to tell."

The Black Hawks continued to hover over the deck. While Grimaldi had lost his spotlight, the other two still had theirs, and they continued to sweep lights over the deck. Grabbing the guy by his biceps, Bolan hauled the prisoner to his feet. He stripped the man's NVGs from his head, tossed them aside and walked the guy to the port railing.

Rodriguez had a flashlight fixed to her MP-5. She flicked a switch and bathed the guy's face in light. The guy's jaw was set and eyebrows arched angrily. However, Bolan also noticed perspiration filming the man's face and defeat in the guy's eyes as he forced him to move.

"Where are we going?" the man demanded.

"You speak English," Bolan said. "That answers my first question."

"It's the only answer you'll get from me."

Bolan nodded once. "Sure," he said.

He took a step back from the railing and withdrew the Beretta, pointing the muzzle at the man's midsection.

"What are you going to do?" the man asked.

"We're going to have a Q and A session."

"Q and A?"

"Questions and answers. I'm going to ask you questions and beat the answers out of you."

The other man stiffened but tried to keep his expression flat. "I'm not afraid of you."

"You should be," Bolan replied.

Before he could utter another word, he felt Rodriguez's elbow in his side.

Muttering, "Screw this," she pushed past him and stepped within a foot or so of the prisoner. Shining a light on his face, she gave the guy what in another situation would be a disarming smile.

"Hi," she said.

The guy spit on her and it landed on her left breast. Her smile never wavering, she lashed out with her right leg and drove her shin into the guy's crotch. He expelled the air in his lungs and sank to his knees. Reaching down, she grabbed a handful of his hair, brought him back to his feet and shoved him into the railing hard enough that he almost flipped over it. She grabbed his belt to keep him from going over the side of the ship.

"Let's try it again," she said. "Hi."

He made a croaking noise and she smiled warmly. "Close enough," she said.

She stood by for several seconds while he continued to gasp. When he finally was able to suck in a breath, she aimed the H&K at his balls. Before she could speak, the ship's lights began to flick back on. Bolan watched as, with her empty hand, she reached up and pulled off the night-vision goggles and tossed them onto the deck.

"Look," she said. "If you think the knee-in-the-groin thing hurt, imagine what a couple of bullets will do to your junk. Can you imagine? I'm imagining it, and I kind of like what I'm thinking."

"You're crazy."

"Tell the crazy lady your name."

"Holzman," he said. "Ernst Holzman."

"Nice accent, Ernst," she said. "Where are you from?"

He hesitated. She fired a single shot between his legs

about a foot below his crotch. It passed between the rails and disappeared in the darkness.

"Germany," he said.

"What are you doing here?"

He looked up at her and sneered. "Trying to kill you."

"Why?"

He looked past her at Bolan. "Because of him," he said. He turned his eyes on her. "Because of you. We knew you were going after the weapons and we wanted to stop you."

She smiled. "Good try," she said. "Looks like we stopped them anyway."

A barking laughter burst from the man's mouth.

"You haven't stopped anything," he said.

She scowled. "What the hell are you talking about?" she asked. "We have the ship. We have the weapons."

"You have nothing, you idiot," he said. "Don't you understand? There are no weapons on this ship. There never were any weapons here. It's just a decoy."

"Bullshit."

He shook his head. By now the pain in his groin seemed to have subsided. He stood a little straighter, and some strength had returned to his voice.

"Really," he said. "There are no weapons here. We knew you'd find out about the ship so other arrangements were made."

"What other arrangements?"

"I don't know. They never told me details. We were just supposed to ride along on the ship, be here when you arrived."

"So you could ambush us," Bolan said.

The man looked at Bolan and nodded. "Yes."

"But where are the weapons?" Rodriguez demanded.

The man shook his head again. "I. Don't. Know. They never told me that."

"If you're covering for Dumond," she said, "give it up. You know he's dead, right?"

Holzman laughed again. "Dumond? He's barely a footnote in all of this."

Bolan stepped forward. "What the hell does that mean?"

"Dumond procured weapons for us, but that's all he did. He was just a supplier."

"Supplier for whom?" Bolan asked.

The man paused and stiffened a bit. Bolan expected him to become defiant again, but Holzman seemed to catch himself.

"It's way bigger than you can imagine," he said.

Bolan and Rodriguez escorted Holzman to the galley. Bolan dragged out a chair and shoved the guy into it.

"You said it's bigger than we can imagine," Bolan said. "What the hell does that mean?"

Licking his lips, Holzman looked at the soldier, then Rodriguez and back at Bolan.

"I want protection," he said.

"Protection?" Bolan asked.

"Yes, I will share what I know," the man said. "But it can't come back on me. If they knew I was talking about this, they'd kill me."

"Who are 'they'?" Rodriguez asked.

"His name is Geiger. He's a German, too. We worked in intelligence together for many years." He paused. "I'd like some coffee."

"I'd like you to keep talking," Bolan said. "So you worked in intelligence and—what?—decided to go rogue?"

Holzman's neck turned scarlet, and it quickly rose up to his cheeks. "Rogue? As in betray our country? Rogues run our country. We're trying to get the damned thing back from them."

"Meaning what exactly?" Bolan asked.

"We want to return the country to when it was strong," the man said, "to when the world was scared of us. Today, we're nothing. We're strong economically, but we have no currency of our own. We've joined the European Union and no longer are a sovereign state. We have Arabs and Africans coming to our country, polluting our gene pool and our culture. This can't continue."

Bolan sucked in a deep breath and exhaled. He hadn't heard this exact speech before, though he'd heard variations on the theme.

Rodriguez picked up the thread. "It can't continue? How were you going to stop it?"

"We have a group—damn it, I shouldn't be telling you this."

Bolan aimed the Beretta at Holzman's forehead. "Do yourself a favor," he said. "Tell us what you know."

"We have a group," the man began again. "We call ourselves the United Front."

Bolan shook his head. "Never heard of it."

The other man smirked at Bolan. "Of course you haven't heard of it. We've done everything possible to keep it under wraps. I don't know everything. I don't know who was bankrolling us. But it's somebody with a good deal of money to spend for our cause."

"And your cause is what?" Rodriguez asked. "Racial purity? Religious purity?"

"No, no," he replied. "It's so much more than that. We are patriots. We know Germany can be a great nation again. It can lead Europe and probably the world. We nearly led the world in the 1940s—"

"That's one interpretation," Bolan said.

"And we can do it again. Or at the very least we can become a superpower."

Bolan saw a glint of madness in the guy's eyes. As best the soldier could tell, the guy believed what he was saying.

"So you're part of a skinhead group?" Rodriguez asked. "You went from working as an intelligence agent to joining up with a bunch of skinheads and you call it patriotism. How exactly do you make that work in your mind?"

Holzman's face reddened even more. "Skinheads? We're not some neo-Nazi street gang, you idiot. You have no idea what you're going up against, absolutely none. Our people will succeed where Hitler failed. He had good ideas. But the UF's ideas are so far superior to his. We know what we're doing. We know how to win. We're going to do what he wouldn't do.

"We're going after America first."

THE DOOR TO the bridge flew open and Holzman stumbled through it with Bolan close on his heels. Bolan grabbed the German by the neck, guided him to a seat and shoved him into it.

Turning, the soldier pinned the captain under his gaze and the guy's eyes widened.

"Get out," Bolan said.

"I can't leave the bridge," he said. "I'm the captain. What if something happens?"

"You'll go down with the ship," Bolan said. "Now get the hell out of here. And take your entourage with you."

The man rose from his chair, gestured at the door and told the others to go. When the captain exited the bridge, he closed the door behind him. A glance through the windows told Bolan the guy was loitering outside, smoking a cigarette.

"What's going to happen to America?" the soldier asked.

"I don't know," Holzman said.

"Bullshit," Bolan replied.

"No, really, I don't know."

"You said out there, the United Front is coming for America first."

Holzman shook his head vigorously in agreement. "I did say that," he replied. "But that's all I know. That's what the weapons are for."

"The weapons we can't find."

"Yes." Holzman's lips turned up in a thin smile. "We made sure of that. You won't find them in time."

"Someone knows," Rodriguez said.

Holzman shrugged. "Of course, Geiger knows. But good luck finding him. It's not going to happen."

"Because?" Rodriguez asked.

"Because he was a spy, one of Germany's best from what I understand."

"Why'd he go rogue?" Bolan asked.

"I don't know what originally drove him out of the intelligence world. But I know he's perfect for us."

"Why?" Bolan asked.

Holzman paused and Bolan could tell he was trying to figure out how much to say. The soldier decided to help him with the decision. He aimed the Beretta just a few inches below the man's groin and fired a round. The German gasped and tried to jump up from the chair. Turrin, who was standing behind him, put a hand on the guy's shoulder and pushed him back down.

"Please," Turrin said, "these nice folks are talking to you."

"He has terminal cancer," Holzman said.

"Okay," Bolan said. "So?"

"I don't know exactly, but word is he's gone a little crazy. He knows he's going to die anyway so..."

"So why not take crazy risks?"

"Yes. He wants to do this job because it's a big deal. It's something he wants to accomplish."

"Like his bucket list?" Rodriguez asked, her voice incredulous.

The guy gave her a blank stare.

"Never mind," she said.

Bolan looked at her and then at Turrin. "Keep asking this guy questions. Whatever he knows about Geiger and Johann Krakoc, we need to know, too. That includes aliases, contacts in America, all of it. Feed the information to Barb and the others as you get it. Let's see what we can figure out. We don't have much time."

CHAPTER FIFTEEN

Arizona

The tunnel, hewn from hard earth, was cramped and hot. Dust choked the air, forcing Geiger and his entourage to wear filtered masks over their mouths and noses. As he walked the tunnel, he tried to ignore the urge for a cigarette that nibbled at the back of his mind and focus on his surroundings.

He guessed the passage was about eight feet high and five feet across, its interior supported by wooden beams. Lights fixed to the beams illuminated the space. Geiger's hand rested on the grip of his Browning Hi-Power. A slight flutter in his stomach registered with him. Was it nerves or anticipation? He couldn't tell for sure, though he guessed it was the latter.

It had been a year or so since he'd engaged in full-scale combat. He still could recall the excitement, the pleasure of having every sense maxed out as he killed while trying to stay alive, and the sense of omnipotence rushing through him when he decided whether someone lived or died. Killing for him was like heroin shooting for an addict; he needed the hit, needed to scratch the itch, or he became stir crazy in his own skin. Fortunately for him, he'd found an outlet as a contract killer, taking on work from foreign governments and organized crime, or from wealthy women and men such as Vogelsgang. It still was murder and he still broke the law repeatedly. But at least this way he got to indulge in something he'd do anyway and make damn good money doing it. Now that cancer was eating away at him, having a little pleasure every now and again was even more important to him.

But what he was going to do tomorrow…?

It was going to be huge.

When Vogelsgang had first approached him about the mission, Geiger had thought the guy was crazy and maybe certifiable. However, he had pulled all this stuff together— the United Front, the network of mercenaries, the weapons, all of it. He'd even been able to bring in some American white supremacists to help serve as extra fighters for the United Front and been willing to pay for the weapons, gear and training. For all his faults, Vogelsgang wasn't trying to do this on the cheap.

Geiger heard the murmur of voices on the door above followed by the rattle of chains being stripped away. When the double doors began to part, sand and dirt fell down in the hole. Shafts of light broke through along with a rush of fresh air.

Geiger squinted against the flood of light into the underground chamber. As his eyes adjusted to the light, he saw several silhouetted figures looking down at him.

"You Geiger?" one man asked.

"Yes," he replied.

That apparently was enough for the men above. Someone dropped a rope ladder into the hole. Geiger grabbed hold of one of the rungs, tested the ladder with a quick pull, and then climbed from the hole. On the surface, he found himself surrounded by six men that he assumed were Americans. He wasn't sure what he'd expected, but it wasn't this. It would've been easy to mistake the six men for professional military or maybe police officers. All were neatly groomed and trim. None of them had weapons in plain sight. However, at least half of them wore button-down shirts over T-shirts, and Geiger saw bulges in their armpits beneath the shirts; two of the men had belt packs strapped around their waists, while the last guy either was unarmed or was carrying a pistol in an ankle holster under the cuff of his jeans.

One man was unusually tall, standing at least six feet six inches. His shaved head gleamed under the Arizona sun. His long, thin face, covered by a black goatee made him look like the devil himself. His arms were covered in tattoos. If Geiger wasn't already standing on death's door-step, the guy might actually have frightened him.

The man thrust out his right hand.

"I'm Bud Cornett," the guy said.

Geiger ignored the man's gesture and nodded at the hole.

"Weapons are down there," he said. "I want a couple of your guys to climb in there and carry them out."

Cornett put his hands on his hips. He studied Geiger and then each of Geiger's men.

"Your people look capable of carrying their luggage," he said.

"They are. I didn't say I 'needed' your men to carry the weapons, I said I want them to do it. And here I'm guess-ing ten seconds have passed since I said what I wanted and it hasn't happened yet. Why is that?"

Cornett's eyes narrowed and Geiger saw a gleam of hatred in them. The German was going to cause the other guy to lose face in front of his own people, which was what Geiger wanted.

Finally, Cornett turned toward his men. "Mark, you and Jason go down there and help Mr. Geiger with his stuff."

The men climbed down the hole, one after the other. Nodding his approval, Geiger walked over to the tunnel entrance, stood at the rim of the opening and stared down into the hole.

"Very good," Geiger said.

His hand drifted under his shirt and he freed the Browning from its holster, cocked the hammer back and fired into the tunnel entrance at Cornett's men. The first bullet punched through the guy named Mark, severing his spine and leaving him bleeding on the ground. Geiger maneuvered the pistol to the left and snapped off two more shots, each round opening a red hole in Jason's chest. The German then swung the pistol barrel back at the first guy, the one crumpled on the ground with a severed spine, and put another shot in his head.

When he wheeled, Geiger saw his men had their weapons trained on Cornett and the other Americans, all of whom were holding up their hands. Cornett's expression was a mixture of rage and surprise.

"What the hell was that?" he asked. "Are you crazy?"

Shrugging, Geiger walked back over to Cornett and stood just a few feet from him.

"Maybe," he said. "But that wasn't the lesson here."

"Lesson? What the devil are you talking about?"

"Lesson," Geiger said, "please pay attention. Do you understand what the lesson is, Mr. Cornett? Do you? You're silent, so I assume not. Here it is. I do whatever I want with your people. If I want to kill them, I will kill them, understand? I will kill them and you will thank me for giving them such an honorable, worthwhile death. Understand?"

Cornett's lips were pressed together in a bloodless line and his hands were balled into fists. After several seconds he nodded his understanding.

"That's good," Geiger said. "Now, send two more men into that hole and have them get our weapons."

CHAPTER SIXTEEN

Phoenix, Arizona

During the flight back to the United States, Bolan forced himself to get some sleep. Over the years he'd developed the ability to sleep almost anywhere and at any time while he was on a mission. When the plane touched down at the Phoenix Sky Harbor International Airport, the soldier felt rested and alert.

An FBI agent named John Smith met them inside the airport. Smith was medium height, the crown of his head exposed by male-pattern baldness. His face, head and hands were tanned from the Arizona sun. He wore a black suit, black wingtip shoes, a black tie and black sunglasses. He broke up the monotony with a crisp white dress shirt.

"Shouldn't you be chasing aliens?" Grimaldi asked.

"Excuse me?" Smith asked.

"Never mind."

Smith led them to a pair of black Crown Victoria sedans that were parked in a lane in front of the airport's main entrance. Both cars were idling. When he stepped through the concourse's sliding-glass doors, a blast of heat hit Bolan square in the face, and he quickly felt perspiration form on his back and chest. He guessed it would dry almost as quickly.

Grimaldi had stayed with the plane. He and another FBI agent were going to unload the team's weapons and transport them to the hotel later. Once he'd finished that, Bolan had ordered the pilot to get some rest since he was the only one who hadn't slept during the flight. For his part, Bolan planned to shower, change clothes and clean his weapons.

Once he got all that behind him, he planned to kick in a few doors. While he'd been flying back to the U.S., the Farm's cyber team had been able to link Geiger to Jim Edwards, a Phoenix attorney. Once they'd made the initial link, the cyber wizards at the Farm had nailed down that Edwards had made four trips to Berlin and two to Monaco in the past sixteen months. He had also helped to incorporate an export-import business allegedly based in Munich and begun navigating it through the government approval process.

In his spare time he'd begun snatching up real estate in Phoenix for a limited-liability company he'd set up.

Yeah, Edwards had been busy spending other people's money. Bolan wanted to know more about who was supplying the money and why. The soldier found a pair of khakis, a white dress shirt, a lightweight sport coat and a pair of brown loafers in his room, all of it supplied by the Farm. It wasn't exactly a power suit, but at least Bolan could walk through the door of an attorney's office without raising any alarms.

The soldier hated to wear a jacket when the temperature outside was flirting with 100 degrees, but he had little choice. He wanted to carry both the Beretta and the Desert Eagle, and he needed a way to carry them. Bolan called down to the front desk and asked whether his rental car had arrived yet. It had, so he asked the clerk to have a valet bring the vehicle around front.

The Executioner rode the elevator to the lobby. He met the valet who handed over the car keys while Bolan slid the guy a tip.

The late-model Ford was comfortable enough, with plenty of legroom for Bolan. He considered slipping off the jacket, but changed his mind. He was carrying the Beretta in a shoulder rig and figured keeping it out of sight was best, just in case he had an accident or an unexpected encounter with a police officer. He cranked up the air conditioner to full blast and, like a dog with its head hanging out a car window, enjoyed the feel of the air blowing in his face.

The drive to Edwards's office took about twenty minutes through the midday traffic. The attorney had his office on the seventeenth floor of a downtown skyscraper. Bolan debated whether to park his car in a ground-level lot, where he could get in and out with relative ease, or in the multifloor garage underneath the office tower. Since neither option held much appeal, Bolan picked the lesser of two evils and parked in a street-level lot a half block from the building. If things got dangerous, escaping the office building and getting to his vehicle would take some hustle. But guiding through the twists and turns of a cramped underground garage at high speeds was hard enough, add people shooting at you and blocking the ramps, and escape could become next to impossible.

The soldier locked the car, left the lot, found a break in traffic and jogged across the street to Edwards's office building. The walls and floors of the lobby were covered in marble. Palm trees curved out from a large planter in the middle of the room and seemed to stare down at people like long-necked dinosaurs.

Bolan made his way to one of the elevators and pressed the button for the seventeenth floor. By the time he reached his destination, the elevator had stopped twice along the way, dropping off a trio of pretty young women on the eleventh floor and picking up a clean-cut young guy a couple floors later.

When the elevator car reached his floor, the young man stepped aside so Bolan could exit. The doors slid closed behind the soldier and the elevator continued on. Edwards was in suite 1708. Following the signs, Bolan turned right and headed for the attorney's office.

PAUL DIXON JABBED the Open Door button on the elevator and watched the big guy walk away. He did that for a couple of seconds before allowing the door to close. Without a doubt, the guy matched the physical description he'd received from Europe. The fact that he was stopping at the seventeenth floor made it even more likely he was the man Geiger had told him about.

The elevator stopped at the next floor. Dixon stepped out and made his way to the stairs. Geiger had told him to wait in the lobby and watch for the man. Though they didn't have a photo, they'd pieced together a physical description and a composite drawing of the American. Dixon, who was operating under an alias, had spent the past several hours in the lobby or outside the building, keeping watch for his target. This was the third guy he'd followed, but this time he was pretty sure he had the right one.

Slipping into the stairwell, he passed two women on the steps, gave them a friendly nod and continued to the next floor. When he reached the landing, he slid a hand under his suit jacket and withdrew a Glock 19. From a jacket pocket, he slipped out a sound suppressor and threaded it into the muzzle of the pistol. Slipping off his jacket, he wrapped it around the pistol, pushed through the stairwell door and headed for Edwards's office.

BOLAN ROLLED INTO the attorney's office, slamming the door behind him. A pretty woman, her hair cut in a pixie style, green eyes highlighted by dark-framed glasses, inhaled sharply and looked up at Bolan. A guy with a big head, his wide belly poorly concealed beneath an expensive suit, was seated in the waiting area. He looked up from his magazine and gave Bolan a dirty look before turning his attention back to an article.

Eyes obscured by a pair of mirrored shades, Bolan sauntered up to the desk. The young woman set down her papers, folded her hands on the desk and smiled at Bolan. Her name plate said Julie Lance.

"Hello," she said.

"Hello," Bolan said. "I'm looking for Mr. Edwards."

"Do you have an appointment?" She swiveled slightly to her left. With one hand, she tapped the space bar on her computer keyboard and with the other she gripped the mouse.

"Do I have an appointment? Sort of," Bolan said.

Her smile faded slightly. She turned back to Bolan and cocked her head slightly, the move telegraphing her confusion.

"Sorry, you sort of have an appointment?"

"I'm going to meet with him," Bolan said. "It's just not on his calendar."

"If you were going to meet with him, it'd be on his calendar."

"If it was on his calendar, it'd say, 'This afternoon, get ass kicked around ears.'"

She paled a little and had to lick her lips before she spoke again.

"I'm sorry?"

She now had turned toward Bolan and had her eyes locked on him warily, the way someone would watch a swaying cobra.

A chair squeaked behind Bolan. He turned to see that the guy in the fancy suit had jumped out of his chair and was at the door, his hand wrapped around the knob. He gave Bolan a frightened glance over his shoulder, opened the door and exited the office.

Bolan jerked his head at the door.

"You'd better follow Mr. Big Head," Bolan said. "I want to have a private con-fab with your boss."

"Sir, who are you?"

Bolan reached inside his jacket, pulled his DOJ identification card from an inside pocket and tossed it on the desk. She slid it toward her with her right hand, flipped it open and looked at his credentials.

"Matt Cooper," Bolan said. "I'm with the Department of Justice. Your boss, Mr. Edwards, has been a bad boy and I need to talk with him."

"He's in trouble?"

Bolan nodded.

"What kind?"

"The kind you don't want to know about, Ms. Lance," Bolan said. "Seriously, do yourself a favor and get the hell out of here. You don't want any part of this. Best thing you can do is grab your purse, leave for lunch and never come back."

"I…"

"You need to get going. Is there anyone else here?"

She shook her head. "No," she said, "our paralegals are out to lunch."

"You have their numbers?"

"Yes."

"Call them and tell them the same thing I told you," Bolan said. "Tell them to take the day off." He jerked a thumb over his shoulder at the door. "Now get out of here before I change my mind."

She was gone in less than a minute. Bolan locked the front door behind her and headed for the offices, taking out the Beretta as he moved.

Moving down a hallway, Bolan heard a scratchy male voice that he assumed belonged to Edwards. He'd seen the guy's picture, but hadn't heard his voice before. The guy sounded as though he gargled with acid and gasoline.

"Look," he said, "I did my part. I set up the companies, I filed all the documents. I even paid to get the information you wanted. I've done everything you've asked. Why drag me deeper into this crap?"

The guy fell silent and Bolan assumed he was listening to someone on the telephone.

"With all due respect, Johann, that is complete bullshit. I followed his orders to a tee and now you guys are asking me for more? When is it ever going to be enough? C'mon, man, a guy can only do so much of this stuff before it catches up with him, you know what I'm saying." Another pause. "Turn you guys over to the Feds? Hey, I call bullshit on that one. I never said anything about turning you over to the Feds.... Out? No, I don't want out. I just think I've done enough for now.... No, no, don't be like that, Johann. Look, don't go down that road. Johann? Johann?" Bolan heard a phone being slammed into its cradle. "God damn!"

Bolan went through the door and found Edwards seated behind his desk. A small mirror topped with three lines of a white powder the soldier assumed was cocaine and a razor blade rested on the desktop in front of Edwards. Bolan locked the muzzle of his pistol on the attorney's chest. The attorney's head jerked up and his eyes flicked from Bolan to the Beretta's snout and back to Bolan.

"Who the hell are you?"

"Hello, Counselor," Bolan said.

"I asked you a question."

"You don't get to ask questions. You answer them."

"The hell I do. I know my rights."

Edwards reached for his telephone. The Beretta coughed out a single Parabellum round that drilled into the top of Edwards's desk. The attorney flinched and jerked back in his chair.

"You're crazy. You can't come in here and start shooting at me. I'm not armed. I'm a lawyer. I know my damn rights."

"Yeah," Bolan said. "So you said. Someone else might actually care about that. Me? I don't. I want answers and I don't care how I get them."

Edwards swallowed hard.

"You were speaking with Johann," Bolan said. "Johann Krakoc?"

"I don't have to answer that," Edwards replied. "There is such a thing as attorney-client privilege in this wonderful country of ours."

Bolan fired two more rounds into the desktop.

"The next one goes between your eyes," Bolan said. "Now, either change your attitude or I'll kill you. I don't care. It all pays the same to me."

Edwards licked his lips. He stared at Bolan for several moments. He seemed to be trying to gauge whether the guy really would kill him and finally came up with an answer.

"Ask your questions."

"Where is Krakoc?" Bolan asked.

Edwards shrugged. "You mean at the moment? I don't know. Supposedly he's on his way here."

"To Arizona?"

"That's 'here,' right?"

"Why is he coming here?"

"I don't know. Don't look at me like that. I have no idea why he's coming. I don't ask those kinds of questions. It's better off not knowing."

"Plausible deniability has benefits."

"Something like that. You never know when some Beretta-wielding prick's going to bust into your office and squeeze you for information. At least this way I can say I don't know and really mean it."

"Because your word is your bond."

"Screw you."

"When will Krakoc get here?"

"He said another twelve hours maximum."

"He's flying into Sky Harbor?"

"I have no idea. Knowing that kind of thing is little above my pay grade. I do know that he's not coming alone. I've heard he'll be bringing a team of guys with him."

"All by plane?"

"I have no idea," Edwards said.

"He'll be traveling under an alias?"

"He always travels under an alias."

"Give."

"You think he shares that level of detail with me? Look, I'm just his lawyer. I don't want to know that kind of information. It does me no good to get caught up in that kind of thing. I just keep my head down and process their paperwork."

"You're just an innocent guy getting swept along in all this, is that right?"

"I didn't say that."

"Then what are you saying?" Bolan asked.

"Exactly what it sounded like. I don't want to know any more than is necessary. It's not smart for a guy like me to get in the middle of this shit."

"Yet here you are. How did you get here?"

Scowling, Edwards closed his eyes and pressed the heels of his palms against the eyelids.

"You really want to go there? All right, we can do that. I started doing work for Krakoc and another German—a guy named Geiger. You familiar with him?"

Bolan remained silent.

"Oh, that's right. I answer all the questions around here. Fine, I started handling some projects for these two Germans. Most of it was bullshit. Incorporate a business here, set up a real-estate trust over there…whatever they needed.

What I didn't know was that some of the entities I'd set up were involved in criminal activities, such as money laundering."

"You had no idea?"

"Did I suspect something was messed up? Hell, I suspected something was wrong. But I had no idea about their criminal activities. I thought they were buying property here to launder money or to dodge taxes somewhere else. Then I found out there were other issues."

"Issues?"

"Issues. Geiger and his people own an old gym. The place was a dump on the inside, but it's built like a fortress. One day, some kids are climbing on the fire escape. The kids are idiots. They shouldn't be there. Anyway, one of the little bastards falls down the stairs and breaks his leg. Immediately, I thought, 'Shit. This isn't good.' Sure enough the parents hire a lawyer."

He nodded at a pack of cigarettes lying on the desk. "May I?"

Bolan nodded.

Shaking a cigarette from the pack, Edwards lit it, took a long drag and after a couple of seconds exhaled a stream of smoke. He seemed to relax a little.

"Anyway, the next thing you know, they've filed a lawsuit against the holding company. It doesn't matter that the kids were trespassing. They sue us. Us! I get served with an armload of documents. I tried getting hold of Geiger and Krakoc. I sent them emails. I called them. Since I hadn't been in touch with them for a while, I wondered if there was anybody at the building. I went there. The place was closed. I almost left. Then I thought, 'What the hell? I should make sure everything's okay.'"

Edwards's eyes were fixed on a point just behind Bolan as though the events were playing out in front of him on a movie screen only he could see.

"What happened?" Bolan asked.

"This is going to destroy me," Edwards said before he took another puff.

"I think we're past that point," the Executioner said.

Edwards licked his lips, then nodded slowly.

"I suppose so. I have a key and I know the alarm codes, in case they get triggered accidentally. I go in there thinking the place hasn't been touched since—I don't know—probably since the Germans bought it. I was wrong. Someone had been stockpiling stuff in there. From the looks of it, they'd been sneaking stuff in there for months."

"'Stuff'? What kind of stuff?"

"In one corner there was a bunch of gym equipment—weights, benches. They had those freaky martial arts practice dummies. You know. The ones that look like a guy's torso?"

"That doesn't seem out of place."

"No, but elsewhere in the building, I found three Hummers. The black ones with armor. There are black uniforms hanging on the wall. Like the clothes SWAT teams wear. Someone had been stockpiling other stuff—pistols, ammo, holsters, grenades. They had all kinds of stuff. Next time I spoke with Krakoc, I asked him about it. He flipped out and started threatening me. I told him I'd keep it quiet.

"Hey, don't look at me like that. I had no choice. The guy said he was going to kill me. And he would've, too. Besides, by then I was up to my neck with these guys. I'd done so much of their legal work, knowing it was dirty, that I would've lost my license."

"I assume they held your nose over that one, too," Bolan said.

"Yes, they did."

"When was the last time you heard from Krakoc and Geiger other than just now?"

"A week ago," Edwards said. "They told me they would

be coming to Phoenix, and they asked me to make sure they had some things at the gym."

"Like what?"

"Just food. But lots of it. I just told you Krakoc was bringing a team"

Bolan stepped up to the desk and Edwards shrank back a little. A legal pad lay in the corner of the desk. Bolan shoved it over to the man.

"Draw me a layout of that place. Don't leave out anything."

Edwards picked up the pad and a pen. "What's going to happen to me?"

"Depends on how much I like your drawing."

WHEN DIXON REACHED the attorney's office he found it was locked, the waiting room dark. Scowling, he placed the pistol on the floor, took out a set of lock picks from his pocket and began working on the lock. After a little time, the lock released and the door handle yielded to him pushing against it.

Picking up his weapon, he crept into the office. No one was sitting behind the receptionist's desk and a ringing phone went unanswered. He could hear voices coming from down the hall. He headed toward them.

By the time he reached Edwards's door, Dixon could hear the voices easily. Edwards's voice sounded strained, as if his throat was a little too tight to talk. The other guy sounded cold and assured. Dixon had heard about the carnage in Monaco, and he had a good idea what he was going up against. Face to face, the American probably would put up a hell of a fight. He might even take Dixon down in a face-to-face fight.

Dixon knew better than to try that.

He moved around the door jamb, the Glock coughing out bullets.

BOLAN WATCHED AS Edwards tried to sketch a diagram of the old gym. The guy's forehead was filmed with perspiration, his breathing heavy. He tried to draw a line, but it came out crooked. "Damn!" he muttered. He tore off the paper, crumpled it, tossed it aside and started again while Bolan looked on, impatience churning in his gut.

The soldier's eyes drifted up. Just beyond Edwards stood a cabinet with glass doors. On the inside shelves were framed copies of Edwards's various degrees, his training certificates as well as framed pictures of him, usually clad in a tuxedo, mugging with various politicians. Motion in the glass caught Bolan's eye. He whirled and saw a man—the guy who'd ridden the elevator with him—standing in the doorway. The soldier yelled Edwards's name. The attorney looked up just in time to catch a bullet in the forehead.

Bolan dropped into a crouch and squeezed off two rounds from the Beretta. One of the bullets zipped just past the other guy's head while the other cored his left eye.

As the shooter's body began to crumple, Bolan moved through the office and down the hallway, the Beretta held in front of him and seeking new targets.

He found nothing.

Bolan bit off a curse and returned to Edwards's office. The guy's face was pressed on the desktop. Blood was leaking from the wound and spreading over the desk. Bolan looked at the legal pad. If the guy had made any notes worth keeping, they were covered with his blood and illegible. The soldier found the balled-up paper, pulled it open and looked. The drawing told him nothing, but at least he now had an address to work with. It wasn't much, but he could have the cyber team get more details on the property.

The last thing he needed was to have someone find him standing over Edwards. Since he'd identified himself to the secretary, and the other guy in the office probably had heard it, Matt Cooper's name was going to come up. Bolan was going to need to let Price know so she could have Washington run interference for him.

First, though, he needed to get out of there.

CHAPTER SEVENTEEN

Bolan walked past the front door of the abandoned gym. From the corner of his eye, he took in the double doors. The paint had begun peeling back years ago and the exposed metal had rusted. A length of chain was wound tightly around the handles and held in place by a padlock the size of the soldier's fist. The chain and lock glinted in the sunlight.

"The chain looks new," Rodriguez said.

Bolan, who'd been thinking the same thing, nodded.

"We won't go in that way," he said.

"We could cut it off."

"And draw lots of attention."

She cast a quick look around at the steady stream of cars and passersby and nodded in agreement. They reached the corner of the building, turned and continued walking along its perimeter.

The building ate up about half the block. Boards covered the first-story windows. From what Bolan could tell, they'd been nailed on years ago, the planks now weather-beaten or covered by graffiti. If they could find a window out of public view, they could rip away the boards and make their way inside, but Bolan preferred to find a door. Aaron "the Bear" Kurtzman had laid out the basic story over the phone.

The two-story building had once housed a boxing gym. When the gym's owner had died, the place had fallen into foreclosure and disrepair. A hot-shot Phoenix developer and self-proclaimed knight in shining armor had purchased it with a grand plan to transform the eyesore into loft condos. The recession had put a knife in the heart of that idea. The building had sat empty for a few more years until a company called New Dawn snatched it up for a bargain price.

Once Kurtzman unwound all the other shell companies behind New Dawn, he'd found the trail led straight to a German named Reinhard Vogelsgang, who also happened to own a large interest in the shipping company that had been moving weapons from Dumond and shipping them to the U.S.

When Bolan and Rodriguez moved around the rear of the building, they found a single door, as well as a truck bay.

Bolan tried to memorize as many details as he could while continuing to circle the structure. Before they went in, he wanted to know the location of all the exits, possible escape routes and the size of the opposition forces.

He and Rodriguez wore street clothes. He had on jeans, a T-shirt and tennis shoes. A button-up shirt covered the Beretta and the Desert Eagle, and he was wearing a baseball cap and sunglasses.

The lady Fed also wore a T-shirt and jeans, all of which accentuated her curves to a point Bolan found pleasantly distracting. Since leaving Europe she'd altered her appearance by cutting her hair and dying it blond. Her hand was out of sight in her shoulder bag, and Bolan guessed she was gripping the micro-Uzi stowed in the bag.

They returned to the rental car, which was parked a couple of blocks away. Bolan opened the trunk, unzipped the large duffel bag stowed there and made a final inventory of the weapons. He'd brought along the sound-suppressed MP-5, as well as an assortment of knives, garrotes and grenades.

Grabbing the MP-5 but leaving most of the ordnance inside, he slung the duffel over his shoulder. They returned to the gymnasium, this time approaching from a different angle, and returned to the rear door.

Bolan keyed his throat mike.

"Striker to Ace," he said.

"Go," Grimaldi replied.

"Ready to work your magic?" Bolan asked.

"Always," the pilot replied. "Give us sixty seconds."

"Roger."

Grimaldi and Turrin were positioned at a nearby phone relay box where, with long-distance coaching from Kurtzman, they would be able to disable the building's alarm. In less than a minute, Grimaldi called back.

"Alarms down," he said.

"Roger," the soldier said, already moving for the back door, Rodriguez a couple of steps behind.

The Executioner reached inside the bag, withdrew a crowbar and pried the lock from the door. Tossing the crowbar aside, he took out the MP-5, flung open the door and moved inside as quickly as possible, ending up inside a sprawling room with a high ceiling that probably once served as the gymnasium.

Shouts to his left snagged Bolan's attention. He wheeled and spotted a couple of men running for the door, each grabbing for hardware of some kind.

Bolan triggered the MP-5 and swept the weapon in a short arc. The rounds chewed into the oncoming thugs, both of whom wilted under the fire. The soldier was on his feet and scanning the place for more targets. The large room, however, was empty of people and vehicles.

"We're too late," Rodriguez said, her voice hushed.

Bolan nodded once, but headed across the room. There was a set of stairs on the far side and, from what Bolan understood, the second floor was another wide-open space, probably an old basketball court. He first walked to the dead men, knelt next to the nearest one and found a two-way radio clipped to the guy's belt. The soldier took it, turned the volume down and pulled the earpiece cord from the jack.

Suddenly he could hear an excited voice coming through the speaker.

Bolan knew enough German to recognize when he was hearing the language, but not enough to grasp what the man was saying. He shot Rodriguez a questioning look, but she only shrugged. If the speaker was in the building, Bolan hoped the guy also knew English. Otherwise it was going to be a short, unproductive interrogation.

The soldier dropped the radio onto the corpse's bloodied chest, rose to his feet, jerked his head at the stairs and began marching toward them. Rodriguez walked parallel to him, but put several yards between them so a shooter wouldn't be able to put them both down easily.

Bolan moved up the steps first, the MP-5 raised in front of him. Obviously they'd missed their major target. Other than a single vehicle parked inside the building and a small cluster of guards, the place appeared to be empty. That raised a couple of questions. Where were Geiger and his men, and how had they known Bolan was coming? If they'd known, that meant someone was leaking information, which would make Bolan's mission harder and more dangerous. He'd deal with that if he needed to. First things first.

When he was just a few steps from the top, he felt his combat senses flare, warning him of an impending danger. He gestured for Rodriguez to stop behind him. An instant later a guy stepped into view at the top of the stairs, a submachine gun held at hip level. The guy fired off a fast burst from his weapon, the bullets drilling just past Bolan's scalp before clanging off something metallic at his six. The

MP-5 coughed out a punishing burst that pounded into the shooter's chest, the onslaught whipsawing his body like a leaf caught in gale-force winds. When Bolan released the trigger, the guy crumpled to the ground.

The soldier plowed ahead until he reached the top of the stairs. He stepped over the corpse, burst through a door to his right and found himself momentarily disoriented. The bottom floor was dilapidated—the air hot and tinged with mold, the floor soiled with brick dust and scuffed by shoes. The upper floor, however, was well lit by recessed fluorescent lights in the ceiling, the walls bright white. The smell of fresh paint wafted in the air.

Moving to the nearest wall, he glided along it. His footsteps were nearly silent, muffled by carpet and the white-noise of an air conditioner's humming. After a few seconds a voice sounded in one of the rooms ahead, speaking in German. Immediately, Bolan recognized it as belonging to the man he'd heard on the dead hardman's radio. This time it sounded louder and tauter, not only because of the speaker's emotional state, but because he was on the move.

The sound of footsteps thudding against the floor reached Bolan, and an instant later he saw the hint of a shadow poking through a door just ahead and to his right. The Executioner drifted up on the door, flattened himself against the wall and waited.

Rodriguez mimicked his moves.

A lanky man with a thick head of gray hair and a matching beard came through the door.

He apparently was agitated enough that he didn't see Bolan out of his peripheral vision.

When his eyes settled on Rodriguez, who had the barrel of her Uzi trained on him, the guy jerked to a halt. Only then did the presence of Bolan, who also was aiming a weapon at him, register. He put up his hands and sputtered something German.

Bolan grabbed the guy by the upper arm, spun him a quarter of a turn and shoved him against the wall. The guy had a Walther stowed in the small of his back. The soldier slid the weapon from its holster and handed it to Rodriguez. A pat-down of the German turned up a second Walther hidden in an ankle holster, a large folding knife, a wallet and a cell phone. Bolan cinched the guy's hands with plastic restraints and led him back into the room he'd just exited. He shoved the guy onto a couch while Rodriguez broke away long enough to clear the other rooms.

The German glared at Bolan.

"You are the police?" he said. He shot a questioning look at the door. "Where are the others?"

"Your guys? Dead."

The man nodded once. "I see," he said. "And now will you arrest me? Or will you kill me?"

"I don't arrest people," Bolan said. "As for whether you live…" He let his voice trail off and gave a little shrug.

"You are not the police," the man said. He gestured with his chin at Rodriguez, who was coming through the door. "What about her?"

"No," Bolan said. "In other words, don't expect us to read you your rights and let you have an attorney."

He shot a glance at Rodriguez who had her lips pressed together in a thin line. She nodded in agreement and Bolan turned back to the man.

The soldier flipped open the man's wallet and studied it. Inside, he found a California driver's license issued to an Arnold Schuster of Palm Springs. He skimmed through a half-inch-thick stack of credit cards, all under the same name, before slipping them back into the wallet and handing it to Rodriguez.

"I'm going to go out on a limb and say this isn't your name," Bolan said. "Am I right?"

The guy stared at the floor.

"Where are the others?" Bolan asked.

"I have no idea what you're talking about," the German said.

Bolan nodded slowly. He tossed the driver's license into the other man's lap.

"Here's the thing, Arnold," Bolan said. "You're an armed foreigner, traveling this country under what I assume is a fake name, stalking around an old building that most of Phoenix assumes is empty. Two of your buddies are downstairs going stiff." Bolan paused and looked around for effect. "Unless my eyesight has gone to hell, the other guys you're working with are gone. That means you're alone. Off the grid."

The man kept his eyes locked on Bolan's, but he no longer was glaring at the big American. He licked his lips and fidgeted in his seat. Bolan took a step forward and crossed his arms over his chest.

"And the thing about people who fall off the grid? When they die, nobody notices it. Same goes for when you whisk them off to a cell somewhere. They just sort of fall into a hole, never to be seen again."

"You're full of shit. You won't kill me. I'm unarmed."

Bolan shrugged. "Keep telling yourself that," the soldier said. "But think about this—what's to stop me? No one knows you're here. They don't know you exist. We shut down the surveillance cameras before we ever stepped foot inside this place. Keep telling yourself these stories if it makes you feel better. But I already know how this will turn out for you if you don't talk."

The guy stared at Bolan, apparently searching for some sign of weakness, an indication he was bluffing. He flicked his gaze to Rodriguez, whose face was inscrutable.

The German heaved a heavy sigh and his shoulders slumped. "The people I work for, they can reach me," he said.

"You mean Geiger?"

The guy flashed him a thin smile.

"Yes, Geiger. Of course, Geiger. But not just him."

"Meaning what?" Rodriguez asked.

"You didn't think Geiger organized all this, do you? You didn't think he paid for all of it, right?"

"He didn't?"

He shook his head. "He doesn't have the resources for something like this. He doesn't have the ability to pull it all together. Hell, he is not the man pulling the strings on the United Front. I would've thought that was obvious."

"He bought the weapons," Bolan said.

"Sure, he bought them and he'll use them. But he isn't the one with the money. For him, this is no different than acting as a mercenary in Africa. He has no passion for what he is doing."

"Which is what exactly?" Rodriguez asked.

"Changing the world. At least, that's the goal. Returning Europe to its former glory. Geiger's a tool, a deadly tool. But he's no visionary, no leader. He won't remake the world."

"So who's pulling the strings?" Rodriguez asked.

"Reinhard Vogelsgang."

"The German industrialist?" Rodriguez replied. "He's the guy behind all of this?"

"He's the main one behind all of this, the United Front," the guy corrected her. "He's definitely supplying the money. But there are others, too."

The woman shook her head. "I can't believe that," she said. "You're telling me they have major backing from a guy who appears regularly in the financial press?"

She gave Bolan a questioning look. He shrugged and pinned the other man under his gaze. It made sense. The guy was in this up to his eyeballs.

"My friend thinks you're full of shit," he said. "I'm inclined to agree."

"It's the truth!" the other man protested.

"Vogelsgang owns this building," Bolan stated.

The man nodded.

"He even paid for the upgrades."

"Because?"

"We needed a staging area."

"For?"

"You know who's in Arizona today, right?"

Bolan did know, because Brognola also was slated to be there. But the soldier kept his expression flat.

"No," he said, "enlighten me."

"Your president is meeting with the German chancellor today, here in Arizona. They're supposed to discuss economics and trade, as well as some intelligence sharing."

"There's been nothing about that in the news," Bolan said.

The guy flashed a thin smile. "We have our sources. And we plan to be there."

"Be there why?" Bolan asked.

"To kill everyone we can, of course."

The guy looked past Bolan's shoulder. The soldier turned his head slightly, wary of sudden moves, and followed the guy's gaze and saw he was staring at a wall clock.

"It's going to start soon," he said.

KRAKOC PAUSED AT the entrance to the gym. The red light on the alarm's keypad was dark. When he'd punched in the pass code, no beeps had accompanied the keystrokes. The alarm system was unresponsive. He set his hand on the doorknob, ready to turn it, but he stopped himself. Instead he removed his cell phone from a pocket and tried to call a couple of the men who were supposed to be here waiting for him. No response. What had happened to the others?

Slipping his cell phone back into the pocket of his jeans,

he pulled his 9 mm Walther pistol from beneath his wind-breaker and cocked back the hammer. The gun, along with several magazines of ammo, had been waiting at a dead drop located a mile or so from the airport. During previous visits to America, he hadn't carried a weapon. But this time, with the raid looming, he had wanted to carry a gun. He wasn't part of the strike force. His job was to oversee the logistics of the mission. But, if things went wrong—say someone figured out the purpose of this abandoned gym—he'd be up to his neck in police. If that happened, he planned to shoot his way out. He'd already decided he'd rather go out on a slab than betray the cause.

Pushing the door open, Krakoc entered the building. He found himself in a sprawling room. He eased the door closed behind him, raised the Walther and turned left. He stopped cold and took a sharp breath. Across the room bodies were sprawled on the floor, blood splattered on the wall.

When he took a couple of steps forward, his foot struck something that generated a metallic clink. A shell casing. More shell casings littered the floor.

A quick scan of the room told him no one else was there, dead or alive. He hurried across the room, entered the stairwell and headed to the second floor. Should he call Geiger to tell him they had been compromised? Maybe. First, though, he needed to find the intruder and eliminate him. He assumed it wasn't the local police. If it had been, there would have been a couple dozen cops going over the grounds, patrol cars, ambulances and other emergency vehicles parked outside.

He also guessed it wasn't the CIA, since they operated overseas. Maybe it was someone from another federal agency. How had they found this place, though? The answer came to him a second later: Jim Edwards, the attorney. That seemed to be the most logical answer. Edwards would be dealt with later. First he needed to deal with the situation at hand.

When he reached the top of the stairs, Krakoc paused for a second at the door leading to the second level. He heard voices murmuring on the other side, though he couldn't make out what they were saying.

With his free hand, he pushed down on the release bar and moved through the door. A big man with black hair was exiting a room down the corridor, a machine pistol clutched in his hand. Was this the man who had been tracking the weapons overseas? There was no way for Krakoc to know for sure. All he knew was that there were bodies on the floor below and this man was armed. Anything beyond that didn't matter. What mattered now was preserving the mission.

Krakoc raised his pistol.

BOLAN FELT A presence. He looked up the corridor and spotted a man leveling a gun. The Executioner swung the MP-5 toward the threat and unleashed a burst. The bullets sliced through the air to the guy's left. Though they missed flesh, the rounds slammed into the stairwell door and forced the hardman to move farther into the open.

The new arrival fired off two more shots. The rounds chopped into the floor just in front of Bolan's feet.

The MP-5 flared to life again. This time the volley drilled into the man, tapping crimson geysers from his torso. The guy collapsed to the ground. Bolan closed the distance between himself and the fallen man. The soldier kicked the guy's pistol away and studied his face. Up close he recognized Johann Krakoc from photos Price had provided. While he had no doubt that the man deserved to die, Bolan wished he'd had the chance to interrogate him. The soldier mentally shrugged it off, knowing that he and the others had to act quickly to avoid unspeakable carnage in the desert.

Rodriguez joined him.

"We need to move," Bolan said.

CHAPTER EIGHTEEN

The abandoned filling station and diner had sat empty for nearly a decade. Sheets of plywood—discolored and warped by the relentless desert sun—covered the windows of the buildings. Heat had blistered and curled the paint on the exterior walls. The previous owners had removed the gas pumps. Crews had unearthed and removed the underground petroleum and diesel fuel tanks years ago. Discarded plastic soda bottles, shards of brown or green glass, the remnants of shattered beer bottles and discarded fast-food bags littered the grounds.

Inside the diner, Friedhelm Geiger leaned against the lunch counter, chewed a toothpick and swept his eyes over the building's interior. Anything of any value had been stripped out, either by the owners or by teenagers or drifters. The floor was charred in several spots, apparently where trespassers had built fires to ward off the desert's overnight chill.

Both his men and Cornett's thugs milled around the old building's interior, smoking cigarettes, chugging water and grumbling as they waited for the raid. The sound of footsteps to his right caused Geiger to turn. He saw Cornett walking toward him, his thin lips turned down in a scowl. The American was dressed in blue jeans, a black T-shirt and dark blue sneakers, his gun belt looped over one shoulder. Cornett halted about a foot from the German.

"You hear anything?" he asked.

Geiger shook his head.

"Not a damn thing," Geiger replied. "Why, you got someplace to be?"

Cornett's face reddened and, for a moment, Geiger thought the guy would throw a punch.

"Just asking a question," Cornett said. "I got a right to do that, don't I?"

Geiger shrugged, already bored with the conversation.

"We'll hear something when we hear it," he replied.

"But you have someone inside?"

"I do."

"And he can get us access?" Cornett asked.

"Total access."

"How?"

Geiger plucked the toothpick from his mouth, tossed it on the floor and leveled his gaze at the other guy.

"You ask too many questions."

Cornett stiffened.

"I'm sending my people in there," he said. He jerked his chin at his men. "That gives me the right to know. Hell, you killed two of my people yesterday in cold blood. Give me answers or I walk the hell out of here and take my people with me."

The corner of Geiger's mouth twitched, and he could feel rage boiling up inside him. He checked himself, though. He could take out Cornett, but it would unnerve the American's men, maybe cause some of them to leave. If they were angry enough, they might—what was the old American expression?—drop a dime on him.

He couldn't afford that so close to the operation. It would be best to just give the guy what he wanted and leave it at that.

"We have a couple of guys on the interior security team working for us," he said.

"Secret Service?"

"Hell no. It's Wolfe's personal security team. The second in command is a former Phoenix cop. He kept putting his dick where it didn't belong and running up big gambling debts. An organized crime boss was threatening to kill him."

"He sold out his team?"

Geiger shrugged. "We promised him money, said we'd make it look like he tried to stop us, but got conked in the head. He walks away and maybe looks like a hero."

Cornett smirked.

"You actually sold him that line of bull?"

Geiger was impressed. The American was smarter than he looked.

"Desperate people are willing to believe anything," he said. "We told him we'd fix his problems. We will. Just not in the way he expects."

"You're a stone-cold bastard," Cornett said.

Geiger smiled.

"You have no idea."

CHAPTER NINETEEN

Seated in the back of the limousine, Hal Brognola stared out the window at the desert landscape next to the highway. The tinted windows had given the seemingly endless lengths of hard-baked earth, interrupted by occasional clusters of scrub brush, a bluish cast. A glance at his phone had told him the temperature had exceeded 100 degrees, prompting one of his security guards—a tough former FBI agent named Maggie Bennett—to eyeball his dark blue suit and shake her head with mock pity.

"You'd better hope the car doesn't overheat," Bennett had said. "I'd hate to see you walk in the desert dressed like that."

"No, you'd better hope it doesn't overheat," Brognola had growled good-naturedly. "If it does, you'll be carrying me on your back. I'm the big shot, remember?"

She'd grinned. "How could I forget?"

Brognola and Bennett went back a ways. She was one of the Farm's blacksuits, the armed commandos charged with keeping the ultrasecret facility safe.

When he'd first joined the Justice Department, Brognola had met Bennett's father, who had been in the twilight of his career at that point. The two had hit it off and had stayed in touch, even after the elder Bennett retired.

When Brognola had learned that Maggie worked for the Bureau and had an exceptional record, he'd arranged to have her rotated into the Farm's security force. And, while the world at large knew almost nothing about Brognola or his job, he'd ended up in near-lethal danger enough times that the President believed the man merited a security contingent from time to time, especially when Brognola was involved in high-level talks. This was one of those times.

Bennett was seated in the front passenger's seat. Brognola couldn't see her from where he sat, but he guessed she was taking in the surroundings, scrutinizing them for any signs of trouble.

Another blacksuit was driving the limo while a second vehicle containing three more guards trailed several car lengths behind them. Brognola had thought the second car and extra guards was overkill, but the Farm's security chief had insisted. If something happened to Brognola's limo, the security people didn't want him sitting in the middle of the desert waiting for a tow truck, especially since he usually carried classified documents with him and untold amounts of secret information in his head. The last thing they needed was for him—and the classified data—to be sitting on the side of the road where it'd be easy pickings. It had been that argument, with some nudging from the President, that finally had led Brognola to relent on the additional security.

"How much longer do we have?" Brognola asked.

Bennett threw him an over-the-shoulder glance. "Ten minutes," she said.

Brognola nodded. He turned his attention back to the documents resting in his lap.

The big Fed shuffled through the papers for several more minutes, only looking up when he felt the limo start to slow. Bennett turned in her seat and made eye contact with him.

"We're here," she said.

Nodding, he shoved the documents back into the folder as the vehicle drove into a slow right-hand turn, accelerated briefly, rolling several yards before coming to a complete halt. Brognola peered through the side window and saw two men clad in camouflage and ballistic vests. Each carried an M-4 rifle and a sidearm, though Brognola saw no official military insignia on their uniforms. One of the men remained at his post while the other marched around the rear of the big car and stood there, his stony gaze locked on the vehicle.

Guard number three approached the driver's window and gestured for the window to come down, while his other hand rested on his sidearm. The limo driver rolled down the window and passed his ID and some other documents to the guard. Even as those two men conversed, Brognola noticed a fourth guard appear, seemingly from nowhere, walking a German shepherd dog, which he directed to begin sniffing the car. It was several more minutes before the guards finished checking out the vehicle and waved Brognola and his entourage through the gate.

The limo rolled through a curved driveway and came to a stop outside the main residence, a sprawling Southwestern-style home, with its stucco exterior and a roof covered in curved red tiles.

Brognola stepped from the vehicle's interior and felt a wave of heat smack him in the face.

He scowled and against his better judgment, threw a sideways glance at the sun's yellow glare, before quickly looking away. When he stepped from the vehicle, he had his suit jacket draped over his arm. However, he slid it on to hide the Smith & Wesson Model 4006 riding in shoulder leather. The pistol had a stainless-steel frame and slide with a four-inch barrel. Favored by several law-enforcement agencies, it included a slide-mounted de-cocking and safety as well as an 11-round staggered-column magazine.

"How hot is it supposed to get?" he asked Bennett.

"About 110 degrees," she replied. "Maybe more."

"Welcome to hell," he muttered.

Lou Minotti checked his watch and scowled. Just a few minutes before the fireworks started and his life changed forever.

His mouth felt dry, his tongue thick. He drummed his fingertips on his knee and stared at the wall in front of him without really seeing it. He knew what he was about to do, knew why he was going to do it, knew he was going to regret it probably for the rest of his miserable life. He also knew he had no intention of stopping himself.

He was going to commit treason, maybe end up an accessory to murder. All to settle some gambling debts and to make some compromising pictures disappear. Minotti's right hand began to tremble. He squeezed it into a fist in hope of stilling the tremors.

"Hey, Lou, you okay?"

Minotti turned toward the voice and saw a young man standing there, some fresh-faced kid named Bailey. His hair trimmed close to his scalp, his suit pressed neat, shoes shined as if he still was in the Army. From what Minotti knew, the kid had served three tours in Afghanistan. He had a wife and kid in Phoenix that, if Minotti was honest with himself, Bailey would never see again. Minotti knew that should fill him with guilt. It didn't. All he cared about was settling some gambling debts with the Mafia Don running the casino.

He'd sell out a dozen Baileys to make that happen.

"I said, are you okay?" Bailey repeated.

Minotti gave him a thumbs-up. "Good as gold, kid," he said. "Think I'm just dehydrated. Drank too much last night. Hauled my butt out of bed and ran three miles this morning, in this heat. I just need some aspirin and a bottle of water. You got things here?"

Bailey pressed his lips together, cast a look over Minotti's shoulder at the door and then back at the former cop.

"Davis said there's supposed to be two of us here at all times," he said.

Jesus, what a boy scout. Mike Davis was the head of security, a former Marine drill sergeant and a tough SOB. Most of the security guards followed his orders to the letter.

"I just need a couple of minutes," Minotti said. "What could happen?"

"Considering who our guests are," Bailey replied, "a hell of a lot could happen."

"The place is crawling with Secret Service, okay? We're just window dressing. Trust me, kid, with all the guns roaming around the estate nothing's going to happen. Nothing. You're acting like an old woman."

Bailey heaved a sigh. "I guess you're right," he said. "But if Davis sees that you're gone..."

"He won't. He's too busy kissing ass at the main event. Besides, if I don't get some water, I'll be worth shit anyway."

Bailey sighed and gestured for the older man to go.

"I'll cover for you. But make it fast. I don't want any trouble."

Minotti winked. "Calm down, kid. Who's more reliable than me?"

Bailey muttered a reply that only vaguely registered with Minotti. He was already focused on his next goal. Just in case Bailey was paying close attention, he made his way to the kitchen, where he grabbed a bottle of water and talked with the cook, an attractive Latina. He always spoke with her, and he didn't want to do anything to trigger suspicion. After a couple of minutes of banter, he excused himself and exited the kitchen.

He'd been on the security detail here for four years, more than enough time to learn every nook and cranny of the sprawling mansion, including the spots not covered by surveillance cameras. One of those spots was the Jacuzzi room, where the owner occasionally entertained women other than his wife and had been emphatic about not having cameras in place to catch his straying on video.

Minotti slipped inside the room and pulled a cell phone from his jacket pocket. The phone wasn't the one issued to him by the security company, but instead had been provided to him by his co-conspirators. With his thumb, he dialed a number and waited as the call rang through.

On the second ring, a man's voice answered.

"Yes?"

"I'm alone."

"Go ahead."

Minotti quickly recited the security codes the caller requested. Davis was a fanatic when it came to security, and he made sure critical security passwords changed daily and were only circulated among a small cadre of the security team.

The man on the other end of the phone made Minotti repeat the numbers.

When he finished, Minotti asked, "Are we good? We're good, right?"

"No."

The creases in Minotti's forehead deepened with confusion.

"Hey," he protested, "I did as you asked."

"You did. Now I want more."

MINOTTI POCKETED HIS phone two minutes later. Cursing under his breath, he dug his cigarettes from his pocket, lit one and puffed on it. He hadn't agreed to this. Sure, he'd been willing to hand over some security codes, guard dossiers and other intel. But this...

He couldn't do it. But what choice did he have?

He'd already taken it this far, had already sold out his

country. Even if he tried to turn things around and warn someone of the mayhem about to erupt here, what good would it do?

There was a group of heavily armed men ringing the place, ready to burst in. By the time he spread the word, convinced the others of his story and explained his last-minute change of heart, Geiger and his men would have descended on the estate. They'd put a bullet in his head. Or, if he survived, the Feds would reward his last-minute tip with a trip to federal prison where Geiger could easily arrange to have someone slit his throat for a few cartons of cigarettes.

Whatever he did, he was screwed—as usual.

His phone began to vibrate again. It was time. Minotti scraped the cigarette against the wall until the lit end died. He pocketed the rest of the smoke, pushed himself from the wall and started for the door.

By now, the boy scout probably was getting nervous and was mentally rehearsing the ass-chewing he planned to dish out. Enjoy your last few minutes, Minotti thought with a rueful smile. It's about to get damned bloody around here.

A couple of minutes later Minotti climbed the stairs to the second floor and made his way to a short hallway. Three doors led off the corridor to his right and two to his left.

He marched toward the last door on his right. Along the way, he glanced into another room on the same side, a former bedroom that now served as an office for the security team, and found it empty. He considered that a stroke of luck, since it would allow him to reach his ulti-mate target more quickly.

Pausing outside the door, he slid a .40-caliber Glock from his shoulder holster. From an inside jacket pocket he took out a sound suppressor and threaded it into the pistol.

When he'd been handed the suppressor by Geiger's people, he'd been told it was only for an emergency, if someone discovered his treachery and he quietly needed to kill the person. That he'd believed such a bald-faced lie only underscored how badly he'd wanted to believe.

Sliding his card through a reader that hung next to the door, he punched a seven-digit security code into the keypad. When the lock clicked open, he pushed the door open.

A pair of uniformed security guards was seated inside the room at a control panel, staring at a wall of monitors. One guy whirled in his armchair, a questioning look on his face. His face relaxed when he realized it was Minotti and his mouth opened to say something. Before he could utter a sound, though, Minotti raised the Glock and squeezed the trigger. The slug drilled between the man's open lips before it burst through the back of his skull, killing him.

By then Minotti was working on autopilot, swinging the pistol toward the second guard.

The guy's hand dropped to his handgun and he brought his other hand up defensively, palm facing Minotti.

The ex-cop squeezed the Glock's trigger again. The weapon coughed and a red hole opened in the guard's outstretched palm, marking the bullet's path before it slammed into the guy's forehead.

Minotti had killed before. Officially he'd shot two drug dealers while working narcotics for the Phoenix police. Six months before that, he'd popped one of his fellow narcs in the back of the head after the guy found out Minotti had been taking bribes from a Mexican drug lord. Minotti hadn't lost sleep over it; it'd been the fastest way to get what he'd wanted. Just like now.

He crossed the room and moved to the control console. It took him less than a minute to punch in the right codes and turn off the exterior alarms, the surveillance cameras and to override the auxiliary alarms.

Unfortunately, within sixty seconds of the alarm shutting down, a backup system fired text messages to Davis and a couple other supervisors, all of whom would react quickly.

All hell was about to break loose. Minotti had less than a minute to grab some distance before he got swept up in the chaos.

Exiting the monitor room, he returned to the first floor and moved to the nearest exit. He still had the Glock out, but the pistol was pressed against the top of his thigh. An emergency tone began to buzz on his two-way radio and he pressed a button to acknowledge the alarm, even as he stepped outside.

Squinting against the sunlight, he grabbed his sunglasses from the breast pocket of his shirt and slipped them on even as he broke into a dead run away from the mansion. Since he knew where to look, he could see several figures crouched outside one of the security fences; he assumed they were cutting through it.

Minotti watched as a pair of black GMC Acadias barreled toward the intruders. He didn't recognize the vehicles, and guessed they belonged to the Secret Service. A hissing sound caught his attention, and he turned toward it in time to see a pair of objects arcing over the fence before they began carving twin trails toward the vehicles.

The rockets punched into the speeding SUVs. Dual thunderclaps pealed, and boiling masses of orange-yellow flames swelled inside the vehicles, gutting them and sending them veering off course.

He jogged for the fence, but kept his pistol down. All the figures were dressed in black, including ski masks. A couple of them swung their weapons at Minotti. He threw up his hands.

"I'm with you," he shouted. "It's Minotti!"

The two men hesitated for what seemed like forever before one of them nodded and gestured for him to join them. Hoping no one would see him, Minotti walked over to the two intruders. When he got closer, he saw one of them was tall and rangy while the other was of average height.

"You did well," the tall man said. His thin lips turned up in a smile. "We got in here with no problem."

Minotti felt a wave of nausea wash over him. From the moment he'd clocked in for his shift today, he'd known exactly what he was doing, committing treason. But hearing someone else say it caused his stomach to roll. It was one thing to rough up a drug dealer and steal his money. This was something else entirely.

"Okay," Minotti said. "I'm looking for Hans. You guys seen him?"

"I'm Hans," the tall man said.

"Okay," Minotti said, "you know the drill then. You guys are supposed to hit me in the head or something, make it look like you overpowered me. That way they won't suspect anything."

Hans flashed another cold smile.

"Sure," he said. "Of course, we need to step it up a notch. Give me your gun."

Minotti shot the other man a confused look.

"My gun? Why?"

Hans held out his hand, palm up. "Please. We don't have time to discuss this. Give me your gun."

"That wasn't part of the deal."

"Trust me. It will make it more believable."

Minotti scowled. Finally he placed his service pistol into Hans's outstretched palm.

"Good, good." Hans studied the pistol for a second before stretching his arm back and thrusting it several yards away.

"Hey!" Minotti said.

"Now, you run."

"What? I'm not running, damn it."

Hans aimed the MP-5 at the ex-cop. "Trust me, you should run."

Minotti hesitated for a second, searching the other man's eyes for some sign that he was kidding. After a few seconds passed Hans pointed his MP-5 skyward and fired a burst.

"I said run!" he yelled.

The sound of a gunshot snapped Minotti from his trance. He spun and began running away. A searing heat stabbed into his shoulder, causing him to cry out and stumble before crashing to the ground.

He heard Hans laughing just before he blacked out.

GEIGER WATCHED HANS shoot the turncoat security guard as the guy ran away.

The gullibility of desperate people never ceased to amaze Geiger. Why else would the guard have thought a group of foreign invaders, because that's essentially what they were, would actually deliver on a promise? Once they completed this day's operation, Geiger didn't care what else happened to the morons and turncoats who were helping him. Hell, he really didn't care what happened to Vogelsgang. All Geiger knew was the industrialist had promised him a big payday for his efforts. The money was to be rolled into four black accounts in the Cayman Islands.

Geiger knew that realistically he'd soon have little use for the money. The things he once would have bought—fast cars, expensive penthouses and the like—soon wouldn't matter. He'd end up pumping the money into more practical things, like morphine, a hospital bed and twenty-four-hour medical care. At least he could go out comfortably, though. He didn't give a shit about dying with dignity. He considered that a myth. By the time he slipped into the big sleep, he'd look like a damned refugee, so he had no illusions about his final moments.

At least he could buy enough drugs to stay comfortable. And, if he really got tired of it, he could have a nurse help him into a wheelchair and push him onto the beach where he could watch the frothy surf roll in and out one last time—before he put a bullet in his brain.

First, though, Geiger needed to win the day.

A security helicopter rose above the house. It hovered there for a few seconds before the pilot turned the aircraft in the direction of Geiger and his people.

He keyed his throat mike. "Am I the only one worried about this?"

"On it," one of his men replied.

A second later he heard the whoosh of a shoulder-fired rocket being activated. The rocket pierced the helicopter's exterior and a second later a rumble passed through the inside of the craft. The doors bowed outward, blew off the hinges, as did the windshield. Orange-yellow flames rolled out through every opening as the craft suddenly began to turn in the air before dropping from the sky and crashing to the ground.

Two more Acadias barreled out from behind the house and bore down on Geiger and his entourage.

"Deal with it," he said into his mike.

Another volley of shoulder-fired missiles speared through the air and struck the vehicles. The double blasts rent the vehicles' metal frames and threw the SUVs into the air while engulfing the insides with flames. The metal carcasses slammed to the ground. A flaming figure burst from one of them in a final deadly sprint. Geiger brought his MP-5 to hip level and showered the human matchstick with a torrent of bullets. In his case, it wasn't an act of mercy; it just amused him.

He and his men fanned out into a long, ragged line. He

reloaded the MP-5 and when one of the guards stepped out from the cover of a shed, Geiger gunned the man down. It was funny. For some people, a look at their own mortality made them appreciate life more. In his case, he just enjoyed dealing out death all the more, like a black angel taking as many people with him as possible.

When they neared the house, a couple of guards were standing near the pool, unloading their guns at the intruders. Geiger's mercenaries responded by hosing them with sustained bursts from their submachine guns.

Before they reached the house, Geiger ordered several of his gunners to stay outside, in case reinforcements arrived as he suspected they would. When he reached the house, he heard a scream and a young woman in a business suit burst from behind a shed. Geiger guessed the woman had tried hiding, but was overcome with fear and tried to flee.

"Freeze!" he yelled.

The woman stopped running and threw up her hands.

"Turn," Geiger ordered.

She turned in his direction. Tears streamed down her face and her chest was heaving. Geiger flicked the selector switch to single shot and fired two bullets into her gut. She screamed and folded to the ground. He walked by her, hesitating long enough to see her arms clutched around her middle, her face a mask of pain, before he opened the sliding-glass doors and stepped inside the house. The other gunners followed him inside.

It was all he could do not to lick his lips. He was just getting started.

CHAPTER TWENTY

Bolan tried Brognola's number again. It rang a few times before kicking him to voice mail. He ended the call. The soldier already had left his old friend a message a few minutes ago and saw no need to do so again. He slipped the cell phone into the pocket of his jeans.

"Nothing?" a female voice asked.

Bolan turned and found Rodriguez standing behind him. He shook his head and her look of concerned deepened.

Before he could say anything, though, he heard the squeak of metal rubbing on metal and turned toward the sound. He spotted Grimaldi pushing open a glass door and stepping inside the small building. He was alone. Turrin had returned to Washington.

The pilot gave Bolan a hopeful look, but it evaporated almost immediately when he saw the soldier's grim expression. The large square building they stood in usually served as an office and waiting area for the small airport they'd come to. Most occupants of the air park made their living selling helicopter flights to tourists. However, with a couple of phone calls, Bolan and a handful of FBI agents had been able to commandeer the place, ground most of the helicopters and turn the building into a makeshift command center.

The federal agents had lied to the pilots and others occupying the airport. They'd said Rodriguez was a key witness in an organized-crime case and they were trying to smuggle her out of Phoenix, which they obviously couldn't do at Sky Harbor Airport. If the story had triggered anyone's bullshit meter, Bolan thought, that person had decided to keep mum about it and give the authorities a wide berth.

Considering the mood he was in, that suited Bolan just fine.

Moving fast, Grimaldi marched up to Bolan and Rodriguez.

"I got us a helicopter," the Stony Man pilot said.

"Good," Bolan replied.

The pilot shrugged.

"Maybe good," he said. "It'll get us there, but that's about it. It has no weapons at all. All we'll have is what we're carrying."

"Which is considerable," Bolan pointed out.

"True," Grimaldi replied.

Bolan nodded at a man standing a few yards away.

"That's the local special agent in charge," Bolan said. "If we need more weapons, he said he could get them for us."

"I'm sure he's happy to sit on the sidelines," Grimaldi said, "while we march into town and handle this."

"If by happy you mean 'wants to put two bullets in my brain,' then, yes, he's happy."

As they'd driven to the small airport, Bolan had contacted Stony Man Farm and asked for aerial photos and floor plans of the large ranch as well as information about the facility's security setup. Accessing an encrypted email account, he pulled down the documents and began looking through them, his soldier's mind formulating and dismissing options as he scanned the information. Grimaldi, who'd spent years fighting alongside Bolan, fell silent, smoked a cigarette and stared out at the choppers parked on the tarmac. Bolan's sudden withdrawal into silence barely registered with him.

Rodriguez, on the other hand, appeared uncomfortable.

She crossed her arms over her chest, chewed at her lower lip and stared expectantly at Bolan.

She checked several times as two minutes ticked by. "Should I go get myself some coffee?" she said.

Bolan lifted his eyes from the tablet computer's screen and looked at Rodriguez. Her brows were arched, but the eyes themselves appeared wider than usual and her mouth was turned down in a scowl. If she was scared or nervous, the soldier couldn't blame her.

The stakes suddenly had spiked, and he guessed she was feeling it.

"We're leaving," he said.

"You have a plan?"

"Fly in, kill the bad guys. Save the good guys."

"The genius lies in the simplicity," Grimaldi said.

BROGNOLA CAUGHT A glance of Jim Preston, the head of the Secret Service's protective detail, just seconds before everything went to hell.

Pressing his index finger to his earpiece, the guy's lips tightened into a slash; he nodded a couple of times as he listened. His eyes immediately flicked to the President and he took a step toward the Man.

Brognola felt the small hairs on his nape rise, and his gut knotted. Something was wrong. The big Fed wanted to jump up from the chair, step in and take charge of the situation, but he stopped himself. If things were about to turn bad, the best thing he could do would be to get out of the Secret Service's way. He guessed agents had scouted the property days before the visit, formulating contingency plans in case things went south.

They had a handle on it. The last thing they needed was a middle-aged bureaucrat jumping into the fray.

Brognola felt a hand press gently on his left shoulder. Turning his head, he looked up to see Bennett standing behind him, letting him know his own security detail was close by. He acknowledged her with a quick nod before turning his attention back to the protection detail. The agents already were crossing the room, swiftly and silently, and converging on the President. The chancellor's head of security noted the men bearing down in his direction, and shot them a confused look.

Before he could blurt out a question, though, the agents swooped in on the Man.

The agents walked to either side of the President. Brognola watched as each placed a hand on the Man's shoulders. The security chief leaned down and began speaking into the politician's ear. He listened for a few beats, nodded once, rose to his feet, smoothed his suit jacket and gestured to the Germans.

"Madame Chancellor," he said, "we may have a situation…"

Her lips parted to speak, but before she could utter a word, thunder pealed outside the house and an instant later the big Fed heard the screech of metal twisting, followed by something thudding against the house, shaking loose plaster dust from the ceiling. As the noise died down, Brognola heard a series of small pops he pegged as gunshots.

Brognola's heart rate kicked into overdrive and blood thundered in his ears as adrenaline began coursing through his body. They were under attack.

The politicians flinched and the Secret Service agents began to react, two of them grabbing the President and leading him to the door while others formed a tight ring around him.

One Secret Service agent broke from the others and moved to the chancellor and her entourage. Her own security detail was beginning to encircle her. The agent gestured at the door.

"Madame Chancellor," he said, "we have a place for you, but it won't hold everyone. Let's go!"

The woman hesitated for a moment, but her own guards began ushering her from the room.

By now the big Fed was on his feet, the two blacksuits next to him.

Bennett grabbed his biceps. "We should get you to safety," she said.

Brognola swept his gaze over the other occupants of the room. Most were bureaucrats, men and women who spent their days trying to keep the wheels of government turning. They weren't warriors. Several were covered in plaster dust, talking and gesturing rapidly.

If someone had breached the house, Brognola thought, these people were going to die.

Bennett squeezed his biceps again. "Sir—Hal—I said…"

Brognola turned to her and her partner.

"I heard you," he said. "Take care of them. Get them to safety if there is such a thing."

"I can't…"

"She's right, sir," the second blacksuit said. "Our priority is to make sure you're safe."

Brognola shot the guy a hard look.

"I decide your priorities, son, and I've decided that your priority is to get these innocents out of the way."

Brognola wheeled and began to head for the door.

"Sir," Bennett shouted after him, "what are you going to do?"

Brognola didn't bother to answer. At that point he wasn't sure what he could do.

CHAPTER TWENTY-ONE

The estate backed up to a jagged mountain range.

In the pilot's seat, Grimaldi flew the chopper parallel to the line of mountains, using them for cover as they approached the property. Otherwise the aircraft would stand out against the clear blue sky.

Bolan was seated in the back, where he could perform a final equipment check. In addition to his usual sidearms, the Beretta and the Desert Eagle, he'd also packed a Steyr AUG 3 submachine gun. Chambered for 5.56 mm rounds, the bullpup-style weapon was outfitted with a scope, flash suppressor and flashlight. Bolan also had donned military webbing over his civilian clothes and was carrying an assortment of flash-bang and fragmentation grenades.

Rodriguez was seated nearby, her attention focused on feeding a magazine into an MP-5 supplied to her by the FBI. Three other agents, all of them also armed with MP-5s as well as their service handguns, also had hitched a ride. Two of the three agents had served on SWAT teams before becoming federal agents. The third had served three combat tours in Iraq, most of it hunting al Qaeda terrorists. Like Rodriguez, the three men were battle tested. Bolan didn't question their courage, skill or patriotism.

However, an unsettled feeling in his gut told him he still wasn't comfortable with the situation.

If Vogelsgang's people had planned this raid well—and Bolan had no reason to think otherwise—it was possible they'd stationed lookouts in the mountains or along the roads. They could already know that help was on the way or they could've set traps for rescue teams. Bolan saw a million things that could go wrong with this operation, but it didn't matter. They had to go in anyway.

The helicopter touched down and Bolan was the first one out. He dropped into a crouch and watched for any threats.

The carnage was striking. The soldier counted two helicopters, their twisted and charred remains lying at ten and three o'clock. Fire ate away at the frames and pumped thick black columns of smoke into the sky. A quick sweep of the terrain revealed five dead guards, all of them uniformed. Two corpses floated facedown in the swimming pool; the water around them clouded crimson by blood. The bodies of two other men, both dressed in black, were sprawled on the ground. Bolan assumed they were part of Geiger's crew.

He also saw the bodies of least a half dozen men and women, all of them dressed in khaki pants and dark green polo shirts, strewed around the property. All of them wore black leather equipment belts with a holster, a pouch for additional magazines and a pair of handcuffs. The defenders had suffered multiple gunshot wounds to the torso, arms and legs. It hadn't been a fight; it'd been a slaughter.

Bolan's combat instincts flared, urging him to look to his left. He whipped his head in that direction and spotted two men sprinting into view from behind a stucco building near the swimming pool. Like the corpses Bolan had noticed earlier, these men were dressed head to toe in black. One of the men cut loose with his weapon, firing at Bolan.

The rounds lanced into the ground just a few feet in front of him, the bullets kicking up small plumes of dirt.

The Executioner swung the Steyr toward the nearer man. He tapped the SMG's trigger and a spray of flames and 5.56 mm rounds burst from the muzzle. The swarm of bullets flew low, ripping into the man's legs and lower abdomen, sending the guy flailing to earth. Seeing his comrade fall, the second guy wheeled a quarter turn and sprinted away from the downed man.

However the barrel of his SMG spit jagged muzzle-flashes in an apparent bid to cover his escape.

Maneuvering the Austrian-made weapon, Bolan loosed another blast. This one drilled his target's torso and arms, transforming the hardman's sprint into a jerky death dance before his corpse pitched forward.

By now the others had disembarked from the helicopter. Bolan turned toward them and said, "We're finished here. Let's go."

The Stony Man warrior wanted to check on Brognola, but he knew he needed to focus on securing the President first. That would be Brognola's priority and Bolan knew it should be his, too. Without another word, Rodriguez, Grimaldi and a couple other agents began fanning out over the property. In the meantime, Bolan kept moving with one of the other FBI agents, a guy named Charles Olson.

Bolan had barely taken another dozen paces before a shooter rose from behind a large concrete planter. The guy's quick movements caught the Executioner's attention even before the guy could squeeze off several rounds with his pistol. Bolan threw himself to the ground and rolled away as the shots passed harmlessly through the space where Bolan had just stood.

Olson reacted like a pro, tapping out a punishing burst from his MP-5. The swarm of 9 mm killers was aimed too low, however, and slammed into the wall of the planter, kicking up small fragments of concrete.

The slugs never went near the shooter, but the onslaught drove him under cover.

That reprieve bought Bolan the time he needed to rise from the ground and start circling the planter. Olson con-

tinued to put on the pressure, firing waves of bullets. Just
as Bolan rounded the planter, the agent's MP-5 clicked
empty and he began scrambling for another magazine. The
hardman who'd been riding out the automatic weapons fire
from Olson stood again, ready to deliver a killing strike.
Before he could squeeze the trigger, though, Bolan hosed
him with the Steyr's special brand of hellfire.

Even as the guy's shredded form crumpled, Bolan heard
gunshots and an anguished cry from his six and he whirled.
He saw Olson taking fire, eyes bulging and mouth agape.
Bullets began to burst from his throat, filling the air with
a red mist of blood, bone fragments and bits of flesh. As
the agent's ragged form collapsed to the ground, his killer
came into view.

The guy had his arm extended and a large black pistol
clutched in his hand. He maneuvered the barrel toward
Bolan. From over the guy's shoulder, the Executioner also
saw two more armed men, both of whom he assumed were
Geiger's people, approaching in the distance.

The Executioner stroked the Steyr's trigger and it delivered a fiery gut punch to the thug who'd just killed the
FBI agent. The shooter sank to his knees, his midsection
ravaged by bullets, just as the Steyr clicked empty.

Bolan released the weapon and, by the time its weight
pulled the strap taut, he'd set a hand on the Desert Eagle.
Sliding it from its holster, he thumbed back the hammer on
the big handgun and darted to his right. One of the hardmen had frozen in place, knees slightly bent and SMG held
snug against his torso. The second had decided to charge
at Bolan, leaning on the trigger of his submachine gun and
sweeping it in short arcs. The second guy's initial marks-
manship was sloppy and the rounds zipped over the soldier's head. Bolan had no doubt the guy was going to get
better, or at least luckier, fast.

Spinning on his heel, Bolan snapped off several shots

from the big Israeli handgun while also darting for the concrete planter. As he closed in on it, he bent at the knees, uncoiled his legs and launched himself into the air, his body knifing over the planter.

While he landed on his feet, the soles of his shoes touched down in some of the blood pooled on the concrete and caused one foot to slide out from underneath him and leave him lying on his side. The slip saved his life as the two shooters began to unload in his direction and bullets whizzed overhead.

Maneuvering himself into a crouch, Bolan plucked one of the fragmentation grenades from his web gear. He pulled the pin, but held on to the weapon, waiting for the shooting to die down. When the rain of autofire eased, Bolan reached over the planter and threw the grenade. A second later he heard someone yell just before the grenade blew. The Executioner dropped back behind the planter, letting it absorb the fragments of razor wire and the concussive force of the blast.

As the explosion died down, Bolan was up on his feet, the Desert Eagle again in his hand. He saw two men lying on the ground near where the explosion had occurred. The wire fragments had done their job.

The soldier turned and started for the house. He made sure the Desert Eagle had a fresh magazine, holstered it and reloaded the Steyr.

Rounding the pool, Bolan looked at the bodies floating facedown in the glittering water. A third body lay a few yards from the pool. Bolan hadn't seen it before. It was a young woman, her petite form balled up between a pair of outdoor loungers. The jacket of her high-dollar business suit was bloodied. Her eyes were closed and her lips parted. Bolan saw that her hands were still clutched at her middle and her knees drawn up. Even in death she was trying to protect her battered body. Bolan saw no signs that the woman was armed. He guessed she was a staffer for the President or the chancellor. She hadn't posed a threat, but had died just the same, for being in the wrong place at the wrong time.

Bolan hadn't had any illusions when he'd come here. But now, looking down at an innocent, unarmed person, her body ravaged by gunfire, Bolan knew what he was dealing with. They were fanatics willing to mow down anyone who stood in their way.

Good to know.

The soldier reached the sliding-glass doors. He paused outside, chancing a glance through the glass, but saw nothing amiss. Pushing aside the door, he moved into the house's cool interior. From the outside, he heard bursts of machine-gun fire and he felt his body tense. The fighting was a distance from him, but that meant Grimaldi, Rodriguez and the others had run into trouble.

He considered checking in with Grimaldi for a situation report, but stopped himself. He needed to focus on securing the President. The soldier made it through a few more rooms before he came across a body. A man in a black suit lay on his back, arms and legs splayed. A bullet had snapped the nosepiece of his mirrored sunglasses before burrowing into the bridge of his nose. A micro-Uzi lay just inches from the man's dead hand.

He guessed the dead man was a Secret Service agent. His stomach clenched as he entered the house, knowing he'd see more fallen heroes inside.

BROGNOLA EXITED THE meeting room and traveled down the corridor, its walls covered by large and probably expensive paintings. From somewhere in the house, he could hear the popping of gunshots, the noise causing his heart to race. He began to question his decision to leave the blacksuits behind while he ran toward the gunfire. He'd been in plenty of tough situations. He'd killed. He could fight, but he wasn't a soldier or a former member of an elite SWAT team, not like the warriors he commanded at Stony Man Farm.

He was a middle-aged bureaucrat, one who hadn't been on the pistol range in weeks, and he was diving headlong into what sounded like a hell of a fight. Maybe the adrenaline had gotten the best of him.

His phone vibrated in his pocket. Muttering a curse, he pulled it from his pocket, glanced at the screen and saw he'd received a text from Service Exporters LLC. Without stopping, he opened the text and glanced at it. Service Exporters was a cutout organization that Stony Man sometimes used when sending messages.

He read the message.

"Striker on way."

The news brought him some relief. Having Bolan arrive could make all the difference—if the Executioner got here soon enough.

The hallway emptied into a large dining room. He'd passed through the room earlier, along with the rest of the group. Tables topped with dishes, coffee urns and stainless-steel chafers filled with food stood against one wall. Folding tables and chairs were arrayed around the room. Large rectangular windows looked out on the jagged mountain ranges that butted up to the property.

Through the windows he saw the mangled remains of a downed helicopter, the steel skeleton engulfed in flame, lying on the ground less than a hundred yards from the house. A look to the right showed him the propeller blade had snapped free and stabbed into the exterior wall of the mansion. Another thing struck him—what he didn't see. Not a single person was fighting the fire. The wreckage just burned, the flames pumping long columns of oily black smoke into the air. If there were any emergency crews operating, they were fighting the army of killers laying siege to the estate.

The chatter of automatic weapons grabbed his attention from the downed aircraft. He whipped his head toward the noise and saw two guards—a man and a woman— crouched behind a forest-green SUV while a hail of bullets from an unseen gunner pulverized the car's windshield and windows. Both still had there guns in their hands, but he wondered if they'd spent all their bullets.

Brognola swore under his breath.

Those people weren't his responsibility, damn it. In the big picture, they weren't even a priority, considering the major players he had to help protect.

Who was he kidding?

At the other end of the room he saw a door. As the big Fed crossed the room to it, he could see a pair of gunners advancing on the guards. He popped open the door and stepped outside into the blistering heat. He squinted against the brilliant sun and, for a moment, wished he'd brought his sunglasses. They were still in the conference room in his briefcase.

Once Brognola had moved to the outside, he lost his clear view of the advancing hardmen. To get a look at them, he knew he needed to step away from the house and put himself in the open, an act that likely would put him on the bull's-eye.

He moved away from the house until he could see the gunners. Raising the pistol, he bracketed the first man in his sights and squeezed the trigger. The .40-caliber slug punched into the guy's cheek, jerking his head to one side as though he'd been hit by a prize fighter, before it burst out the side of his head in a spray of blood and brain matter.

Even as the first shooter whirled in a quarter turn, the second man jerked his gaze in Brognola's direction and raised a machine pistol at the big Fed.

Brognola had an advantage. The two shooters had been so focused on the guards, they hadn't anticipated someone coming at them from another direction. It was a rank amateur mistake, one Brognola exploited.

The pistol in his hands cracked twice more. The bullets drilled into the hardman's chest, opening rosy geysers of blood. A death reflex caused the guy's submachine gun to fire once more before he collapsed.

Brognola moved to the dead thugs and gathered up their weapons. Moving to the other side of the SUV, he shouted, "Department of Justice. Don't shoot." He found the two guards still crouched behind the vehicle, both eyeing him warily.

"You ran out of ammo, right?" he asked.

"We carry two magazines apiece," the woman said. "We're not exactly equipped for a major firefight."

Brognola dropped the stolen guns in the sand at their feet.

"Past tense," he said.

"Thank you," the female guard said.

Brognola nodded and turned away.

CHAPTER TWENTY-TWO

Brognola circled the outside of the house, trying to size up the situation he faced. He'd counted a dozen dead guards, three dead Secret Service agents, two downed helicopters and several burning SUVs sprinkled throughout the property. The corpses of more than a half dozen bad guys also were visible on the grounds.

That so many good people had died already bothered Brognola, but he knew he couldn't dwell on it. The attackers had superior weapons and obviously had been planning this for some time. Arming the estate guards with pistols and semiautomatic rifles had been a bad decision on someone's part, one that probably would get hashed and rehashed through endless Congressional hearings and other venues.

When he reached a corner of the house, the big Fed flattened himself against the wall and peered around the corner. One of the invaders was standing at the front door, his rifle at the ready, acting as a sentry. Moving slowly, Brognola rounded the corner and aimed the Smith & Wesson at the hardman.

"Psst," Brognola said.

The guy turned toward the noise, bringing up his rifle. The Smith cracked once in Brognola's grip, sending a slug hurtling into the guy's heart.

Even as the noise of the gunshot subsided, Brognola heard the metallic click of a hammer being cocked at his six. Without thinking, he threw himself to the ground, landing on his stomach. By the time he'd rolled onto his back, a gun barked and a bullet sizzled through the air above him. A towering man dressed all in black, a smoking gun clutched in his hand, was swinging the pistol at Brognola, preparing to fire off another shot.

The Smith & Wesson cracked again and a red spray exploded from the man's throat. His baseball-mitt-size hand flew to his neck and clutched it. His knees went rubbery and he stumbled back a step. Brognola doubletapped the trigger of his pistol and cored two more shots into the man's torso.

Brognola headed for the front door. He stepped over the first guy he'd shot, paused and turned back to him. Bending next to him, he took the guy's M-4 rifle, slung it over his shoulder and pocketed an extra magazine. He heard gunshots inside the house and swore under his breath. Time to get back inside.

A GUNSHOT CRACKED at Bolan's six. He wheeled toward the sound, his Steyr coming up.

A hardman was collapsing to the ground. Over the guy's shoulder, he saw Brognola. Smoke was curling up from the muzzle of the pistol in the big Fed's hand. Bolan acknowledged his old friend with a nod.

Letting the pistol drop, Brognola walked over to the Executioner and they shook hands.

Bolan started to ask for an update. He was cut short by the sound of gunfire from upstairs.

Without a word, he turned and rushed toward the battle.

BOLAN RACED UPSTAIRS. With screams and automatic gunfire cutting the air, he didn't bother to hide the thud of his booted feet striking the steps. He doubted anyone would hear him. And he'd consider it a victory if his noisy approach drew his adversaries away from innocent people and to him.

They'd quickly learn that finding him was one thing, killing him another.

By the time he'd covered two-thirds of the steps, a pair of hardmen stepped into view.

Without breaking stride, Bolan squeezed the Steyr's trigger and hosed the two men in a vengeful rain of bullets before either fired a shot.

He gestured for Brognola to hang back.

The soldier reached the top of the stairs a second later. Another thug was waiting for him. The guy leveled his assault rifle toward Bolan and fired a deadly salvo. The Executioner dived forward. As he struck the floor, the Steyr spit flames and bullets. The rounds struck the wall behind the guard, stitching a short ragged line. Though the shots missed their target, they rattled him enough that his next shots hammered into the floor.

Bolan delivered a kill burst. Slugs tore through his adversary's chest and stomach, his body staggering back until he slammed into a wall, his shredded body sliding to the ground only when Bolan let off the trigger.

The soldier changed out the Steyr's magazine. A glance over his shoulder told him Brognola was behind him. The big Fed held an M-4 Bolan assumed he'd liberated from one of the fallen.

Experience told Bolan a warrior faced some of the greatest danger when passing through a small space, such as a doorway. Any shooters left inside knew what was about to happen and they likely had their guns trained on the door. The first one through the door would get cut down in a blistering hail of bullets.

The soldier headed to the nearest corpse.

Even as he moved, he heard another burst of autofire ring out, followed by more screams.

"Shut up," someone yelled. "Everybody shut the hell

up!" Another burst from a single weapon was audible and people began to quiet down.

Bending, Bolan grabbed the guy by the back of his neck and jerked him to his feet. He turned to Brognola and gestured for him to come over. When the big Fed reached him, Bolan shoved the corpse forward.

"Seriously?" Brognola muttered.

Bolan nodded once and Brognola's scowl deepened. Holstering his pistol, he grabbed the corpse by the back of the neck and his belt, and wrestled the guy toward the door. The dead guy wasn't heavy; Bolan put his weight at 130 to 140 pounds without the weapons, spare ammo and other gear. Still, his body was limp, which meant it required Brognola to use both hands to control the guy.

The Executioner was right behind his old friend.

The big Fed moved to the door and, with a hard shove, launched the corpse through the door.

The rattle of gunfire started up immediately. A heartbeat later Bolan went through the door and darted to the right. A quick count told him there were three guards inside the room. One was still staring at the corpse, while the other two were on the move, bringing their guns to bear again on the doorway.

The guy fixated on the corpse was standing next to a woman. Bolan recognized her as Bennett, one of the blacksuits from the Farm.

The other two men were maneuvering their weapons toward Bolan. They cut loose with twin streams of autofire in the soldier's direction. The rounds sliced through the air several inches over his head before striking the walls at his back. By the time the Steyr had churned through the rest of its magazine, the hardmen lay sprawled on the ground.

TEN MEN.

Gone in minutes.

How the hell does that happen? The property's owner employed some tough security. Geiger had seen the dossiers. There were former Navy SEALs and SWAT team commanders, men who'd taken bullets and knife blades, men who'd killed. It was possible that someone was acting on his own. While the President's security team had impressive credentials, they were mostly clustered around the big man himself. They weren't skulking around, taking his people out one or two at a time.

Was there someone else? The American had been running pretty hard behind them, ever since he'd surfaced in Monaco. But could he be here already? Geiger forced the thoughts from his mind. He had no way of knowing for sure. What he did know was that every man died. Every damned one. If the bastard had come here, fine.

He'd die just like the others. In the meantime, Geiger needed to focus.

As he neared the top of the stairs, he motioned for the others to stop. He knelt, resting one knee on the stairs, and slithered forward, stopping just before the top of his head would poke over the top of the landing. Slowly, using his knee and one hand, he pushed himself forward until just his head poked into view. He saw four guards, lined two and two on either side of the hallway.

The ones in front waited in a kneeling position, the barrels of their H&K assault weapons pointed in his direction. The two stationed further back were standing, their weapons also at the ready.

Turning to look at his people, Geiger used gestures to tell them about the guards, told them how to respond.

One of his people pulled a flash-bang grenade from his gear. He yanked the pin with his teeth and tossed the bomb upward. It cleared the stairs and dropped to the landing.

Geiger heard the scuffle of boot soles. A loud crack

from the device swallowed up the sound and an intense white light flared.

Geiger rose and ascended the stairs. The guards closest to the stairs were moving their heads around, but didn't seem to see anything. One had a hand clapped over one of his ears while continuing to hold his weapon. The two men who'd been standing were moving around, obviously disoriented.

A grim smile on his lips, Geiger squeezed the assault rifle's trigger and began spraying his targets with an unforgiving stream of autofire. The guards staggered under the angry swarm of bullets. One of Geiger's men had moved by his side and also began filling the corridor with autofire.

Geiger didn't stop shooting until his magazine ran empty. By then all the guards were dead, their bodies sprawled throughout the cramped area, their blood splattered on the walls. He moved to the nearest door to the left, slid through it and checked the room. He found it empty other than furniture and left. It took him and the other hardmen less than two minutes to clear most of the other rooms.

He moved to a final door located to his right. He stood next to it, not wanting his feet to cast a shadow along the bottom edge, and listened. The guards obviously had been protecting something. Since the panic room was located on the next floor above, Geiger guessed that was their first priority. However, he knew that room would hold a limited number of people, all of whom would be the most important. The more expendable people would be on the other side of this door, he guessed. However, he also knew some would be armed. Better to deal with them now than to have them create trouble later.

By now, he'd reloaded his rifle. Geiger set a hand on the knob, started to turn it. He swore he could taste the blood. Before he could touch the doorknob, the sound of whispering at his back prompted him to turn.

He wheeled in time to see one of the estate's guards, his shirt drenched in blood, standing at the top of the stairs. A grin played on his lips. It was Bailey, his second mole. Although he was covered in blood, the American was un-injured. Geiger assumed the blood all had come from the dead and wounded. Judging by the reddish-brown stains stretching up from Bailey's fingertips to the middle of his forearms, like ragged gloves, the guy had been extremely busy dealing out death.

Geiger looked at him. "The President, is he in there?"

Bailey shook his head no.

"There are armed guards, though," Bailey said. "If they start to get adventurous…"

"It would be a mess for us. Look, I've got a way to handle this."

CHAPTER TWENTY-THREE

Bennett happened to glance at the door at the right moment and saw the doorknob begin to turn. She felt an icy rivulet of water race down her spine. Left packed in a room with panicked civilians, some of them Type A personalities with more bluster than brains, she and the other blacksuit were trying to keep control over the situation.

The meeting room's overpriced furniture included a few large tables topped with thick slabs of hardwood. Bennett and the others had turned them on their sides, creating at least some cover for those assembled inside the room. They'd been able to fit the unarmed people behind the barriers, but that had left her and the other blacksuit exposed.

A couple from the chancellor's security entourage also had drifted back downstairs and were ready to pitch in, too. One of the guys was of medium height, but burly. Even in the current crisis, the guy kept his back ramrod-straight and his expression flat. The other guy was short—several inches under six feet tall—and thin. But Bennett sensed no weakness in the guy.

The bigger German held a machine pistol in his big hands.

The smaller man had produced a Walther pistol from beneath his jacket.

Bennett was glad for the help and guessed her partner was, too. Occasionally her thoughts had traveled back to Brognola, which triggered pangs of worry and guilt. Should they have followed his orders? Technically, she had no choice. Doing otherwise amounted to insubordination. But she could have argued harder for him to stay where they could watch him.

Would he have listened? Probably not, but at least she would've made the effort. As it was, she'd let the one man whose safety she was responsible for disappear. If something had happened to him, she knew it'd cost her her career. She cared little about that. She was more worried about making sure he was safe, about protecting an old family friend and fulfilling her duty.

So, yeah, she hadn't done any of that, which left her with only one palatable option—to continue to follow his orders.

She looked to the other blacksuit. She found him staring back at her. When their eyes met, he jerked his head toward the door, as though posing a question. She answered him with a curt nod. They both were armed with H&K MP-5s, which Stony Man's armorer had selected for them because they could be concealed beneath a jacket or in a briefcase.

He moved to the nearest wall and aimed his machine pistol at the door.

For her part, Bennett knelt behind a tall cabinet that had been laid on its side. She locked the pistol's muzzle on the door and curled her finger over the trigger. Fear contracted the muscles of her chest and made breathing difficult. Sweat rolled down her temple, over the curve of her cheekbone before ultimately dropping off her jaw and onto her shirt collar.

The knob turned. Silently, slowly, the door swung open. On some level that nagged at her. Commandoes would kick in the door, not open it with such care, the way her ex-husband did when he'd try to sneak into the house in the dead of night, reeking of alcohol and a strange woman's perfume.

As the door opened fully, a familiar figure followed it, hand gripping the knob. Judging by the slight tilt to one side of his body, he was using it as much for a crutch as anything else.

It was one of the guards. She'd met him briefly when they'd first arrived. At that point he'd looked crisp, strong and confident. What was his name? Bailey. Now, as he released the doorknob and tried to raise his hands, he swayed unsteadily on his feet. The front of his shirt, the skin of his exposed forearms, were smeared with blood.

"Help." He stumbled forward, dropped to his knees and wrapped his arms around his midsection.

Without lowering the pistol, the big German threw Bennett a questioning look.

Something about this felt wrong to Bennett, but what? She jerked her chin in the injured man's direction. The big European guy nodded and began to cross the room.

From her vantage point, Bennett could see the big man flicking his gaze at the fallen guard, then out the door, then back at the guard. When he reached the guard, he lowered his weapon. At the same time, the second German was moving toward the door so he could shut it.

Then it all fell apart.

BAILEY'S HAND WHIPPED up from his waist, filled with a gun. Before the man next to him could react, he squeezed off a shot. The slug punched into the man's heart and he seized up, his face a mask of surprise and terror. A second shot drove the man down.

At the same moment shots drilled through the door and caught the second German, punching through his torso. The little man stumbled back from the door a couple steps before collapsing.

Bennett had no time to think. She raised her pistol again at the traitorous estate guard, just as he swung his own weapon toward her. She stroked the trigger twice, the sound of the shots melding into a single crack. The rounds drilled into the man's torso, and he fell to the floor in a boneless heap.

Bennett hauled herself from the floor just as four men, all heavily armed and dressed in black, moved through the door. It was as though everything around her had faded away. The fearful cries of the civilians only barely registered with her. She was aware of her partner closing in, his own gun aimed at the new threat.

But first and foremost, she saw the small band of killers arrayed in front of her.

Her pistol cracked again. The bullet caught one of the hardmen in his shoulder. The hollowpoint slug blew out his back, taking with it a spray of blood and gore. The injured man dropped his weapon, fell to the floor and writhed in pain. At some level she knew he wasn't dead, but he'd bleed out quickly.

Even as she was moving her pistol, acquiring another target, her partner took down another of the hardmen with a burst from his SMG.

Two more shots from her weapon knocked down another of the thugs. At the same time three more burst into the room. She bracketed one of them in her sights and applied pressure to the trigger.

A burning sensation erupted suddenly and seared her midsection. She gasped. A scream bubbled up from within, but got caught in her throat. Her body fell forward and she threw a hand down to stop herself.

Her partner was by her side, then had stepped in front of her. She could hear the chugging of a machine pistol, could see the hot brass cascading to the floor. It sounded far away, as though it was happening at the other end of a tunnel.

Sit up! her mind screamed. *Fight, damn you!*

Her body wouldn't respond. Instead her arms gave in and she fell to the floor. She'd been shot before. A bullet had grazed her arm years ago during an FBI raid. It'd hurt, but nothing like this. She wanted to raise her pistol, but her arms refused to move. Black spots swam in her vision and things began to fade. She heard more gunshots, a subdued popping, heard something thud against the floor near her head. From the corner of her eye, she saw a booted foot on the floor next to her head.

Then everything went black.

CHAPTER TWENTY-FOUR

Grimaldi hoofed it away from the drop zone, his long legs propelling him at a fast clip.

Though struggling a bit to keep up, Rodriguez was at his side. In the distance the pilot could hear the crackle of gunshots. They'd fall silently almost as quickly as they began, only to start up again a few seconds later.

"Sounds like they're fighting a small war over there," Rodriguez said.

Grimaldi nodded.

"And your friend ran toward it," she added.

"Kind of his specialty."

"What about you?"

He grinned.

"I'm a lover, not a fighter," he replied. "Do you have a handle on what we're doing here?"

"It's not exactly rocket science."

"Of course not. It's my plan."

"We make sure Marine One is clear in case we have to evacuate the President."

"Right."

"And if they killed the pilot? You can fly that thing, right?"

"Of course. I'm not just another pretty face."

"Thank God. I hate a man who's all show and no go."

The helipad stood on the other side of the house, at the northwest corner of the property. A road connected the helipad to the house. Grimaldi guessed they'd shoved the Man into the back of the limo and drove him directly to the house for the meeting. Even in the middle of nowhere as they were, the Secret Service wouldn't want to have the guy standing in the open for too long, even if they only had to move him a few hundred yards.

A line of buildings stood between Grimaldi and the helipad. One was long with a curved roof, obviously a hangar. A second appeared to be a long garage with multiple doors. He guessed it was for security and other service vehicles. The others all had the same southwestern look as the main house.

They sprinted across the open space that lay between them and the cluster of buildings. Once they reached the garage, they slipped into a narrow space between it and another neighboring building. Grimaldi took the lead as they moved through the cramped passage.

When he reached the edge of the garage, he paused and studied the area in front of him. From his vantage point, he saw that three men, all dressed in tan-colored guard uniforms, lay on the ground, their limbs turned at hard angles, their clothes and bodies bloodied and tattered from bullets. About fifty yards from the helicopter, one of the security Jeeps lay on its side, the windshield spider-webbed by gunshots.

Five men—all of whom were armed—stood outside the helicopter. Two had binoculars pressed to their eyes. They swept them over the area outside the fence. Two other men seemed to pace nervously while the fifth was more concerned about his cigarette than his surroundings.

Grimaldi brought his M-4 to his shoulder, flicked it to single-shot mode and locked the crosshairs on one of the guys who were pacing. The way he saw it, the men holding the binoculars and the guy playing with his cigarette could wait.

He stroked the trigger. The M-4 cracked once and the

slug drilled into his target's eye. Before the guy could hit
the ground, the second thug who'd been moving paused
and whirled toward the first and gaped for less than a second as his mind processed what was happening. He raised
his rifle and whipped his head toward the line of buildings,
looking for the shooter. By then Grimaldi had the guy in
his sights. He fired off another round. This one drilled into
the man's chest and spun him a quarter turn.

The other thugs were springing into action now. The
smoking man let the cigarette fall from his lips and began
scrambling for a weapon. The other hardmen with the binoculars, almost in unison, released their devices and let
them fall taut on the straps.

They also began clawing for hardware while moving
in separate directions.

All three had been able to pinpoint Grimaldi.

The Stony Man warrior flicked the selector switch to
automatic and squeezed off a quick burst. The rounds
passed over the heads of the thugs, but at least kept the
pressure on them.

Grimaldi saw Rodriguez dart past him and dive forward, landing flat on her belly. She raised the MP-5 and
began tapping out short blasts. One of the bursts caught
Mr. Cigarette just as he'd cleared leather with his pistol. Another of the thugs had dropped to one knee and
was emptying his machine pistol at Rodriguez. Before
Grimaldi could do anything to help, she hosed her opponent with another hail of bullets.

Grimaldi showered the fifth guy with another storm
of 5.56 mm slugs. The rounds bit through the man's torso
and jerked him violently before his death.

As Grimaldi emerged from cover, Rodriguez pushed
herself up from the ground.

Apparently drawn by the sound of gunfire, three more
guards streamed out from one of the hangars. Fire spit from

the muzzles of their weapons and, while most of the rounds passed overhead, a couple singed the air next to Grimaldi's cheek. The M-4 blazing, he fired as he marched forward. Rodriguez was doing the same. The gunners withered under the savage assault.

As they neared the helicopter, the Stony Man pilot saw several nicks on the craft's outer skin, though he considered them of little consequence. From what he knew, the special craft had an armored hide and could withstand much worse than a peppering of small-arms fire.

He heard the telltale growl of the engines coming to life. He swore under his breath and surged forward. There was no way the pilot could get the helicopter's engines warmed and ready for takeoff in a matter of seconds. But if they sealed the craft before he could get on board, they could wait him out.

In the distance he also thought he heard another sound, though faint. Sirens wailed from the main road. He wasn't surprised. The White House had told them up front they had a short amount of time to bring things under control before Washington ordered the FBI and the police to move in.

A man appeared in the side door of the helicopter. He aimed the muzzle of an AR-15 through the door and drew a bead on Rodriguez. She squeezed the trigger on her MP-5.

The bullets pounded against the helicopter's skin. Bullets lashed out from the muzzle of her opponent's weapon and pounded into her. A cry of shock and pain burst from her lips. At the same time Grimaldi triggered the M-4. The spray from the weapon caught the guy in the chest. He released his hold on his gun, folded in on himself and pitched forward through the door.

A second man appeared in the doorway. Though Grimaldi wanted to stop and check on Rodriguez, he forced the idea from his mind. He worried that the guy would just slam the door closed and seal it, effectively taking it out of commission. Maybe they'd just seal themselves inside. Maybe they'd take off with the helicopter. If the latter happened, it would cost them an important vehicle for evacuating the President. Plus, Grimaldi guessed the craft was stocked with sensitive communications and other equipment, as well, and possibly access to other sensitive information.

He couldn't let it happen.

When the Stony Man pilot came within a few yards of the door, he bent his legs, coiling his muscles, and sprang forward into a sideways jump. His body hurtled through the doorway.

Landing on the floor of the helicopter, on his side, he slid forward a few feet until his back collided with the base of one of the seats.

The man who'd been sliding the door closed let it go and spun toward Grimaldi. The hardman clawed for the pistol riding on his hip, a last-ditch effort to save his own life. The M-4 cracked once, sending a 5.56 mm round lancing into the man's head. His body backpedaled a step and bumped up against the chopper's fuselage.

The Stony Man warrior wheeled toward the cockpit in time to see a man in a blue flight suit step away from the pilot's seat. He had an Uzi in his hand and was raising it to draw a bead on Grimaldi. With quick movements, Grimaldi swung the M-4 around and double-tapped the trigger. The first round missed its target, slicing through the air between the man's biceps and his ribs. However, the second round pierced the man shoulder. A cry of pain exploded from his lips, and the Uzi rattled off a short burst, the rounds ricocheting around the cabin of the helicopter. The M-4 chattered again and this time the bullets opened up the man's midsection, tapping a spray of blood and gore, and sent him stumbling back into the cockpit.

"Clean-up in aisle seven," Grimaldi muttered.

CHAPTER TWENTY-FIVE

Grimacing, Rodriguez turned her eyes on the bullet hole in her shoulder. Blood was leaking from the wound, turning the shirt fabric around it dark. She reached into one of the pockets on her cargo pants and pulled out a field dressing. Slinging the MP-5 over her good shoulder and letting it hang under her arm like a purse, she clamped part of the wound kit's plastic wrapper between her teeth and tore it open. When she pressed it against the wound, pain seared the area and caused her to inhale sharply.

She put a little more pressure on the compress and turned toward the helicopter. When the side door opened, she tensed for a moment until Grimaldi appeared in the doorway, a grin fixed on his face. She greeted him with a nod.

He pointed at her and mouthed the words, "You okay?"

When she nodded, he gave her a mock salute and disappeared back inside the craft.

Between dehydration and blood loss, Rodriguez was beginning to feel light-headed. She turned and stumbled away from the aircraft and headed for the nearest hangar. She hoped to lean against it for a couple of minutes to rest. She'd also try to raise Cooper on her communications link to let him know they'd taken the chopper back.

Before she'd covered too much ground, she looked to her right at the long stretch of scrub brush leading up to the fence. A white flash of light winked at her from within the scrub brush and, instinctively, she halted and grabbed for the MP-5's pistol grip.

The light winked at her again. She looked harder and thought she could see a lump. The harder she stared at it, the more it began to look like a person, not a sniper trying to aim at her from a prone position, but a body curled up.

She was probably going to regret this. Turning, she pressed the button that activated her throat mike.

"Ace?"

"Yeah."

"I think I spotted someone lying in the scrub brush to the west of here. I'm going to check it out."

"You should come back here to rest," he replied. "You're injured."

"I need to check it out."

"Wait, I'll come out and help."

"Negative," she said. "Time for go."

She crossed the hot sand with a halting gait. From somewhere outside the grounds, the wail of sirens was growing louder. She guessed the FBI and other law enforcement would probably start scrambling helicopters to the scene any minute, if they hadn't already. But as she got closer to the shrubs, she saw it definitely was a man. He was lying on his side, legs drawn protectively into his stomach, at an angle where his face was pointed in Rodriguez's direction, though she saw no signs of him being conscious. The mirrored lens of his sunglasses gleamed under the bright sunlight. He was wearing a security officer's uniform.

When she reached him, she knelt and could see he was breathing, though just barely.

She touched his shoulder and he jerked.

"It's okay," she said. "I'm here to help. I'm an FBI agent. You're going to be okay."

She realized she didn't know his name. She leaned over him and looked for a badge with his name on it. She found one, small and rectangular, pinned over his left breast. She read and rested her good hand on his shoulder reassuringly.

"Mr. Minotti," she said. "I'm Agent Jennifer Rodriguez. FBI. It's going to be okay."

BROGNOLA BRUSHED PAST the Executioner and went to Bennett's side. An older man, paunchy and balding, and a younger woman, a well-dressed blonde, had emerged from cover and also were kneeling next to the injured blacksuit. The woman was gingerly pulling up the bottom seam of Bennett's shirt so she could get a better look at the wound. As Bolan approached, he produced a field dressing from one of the pockets on his pants and handed it the blonde, who began to tear open the packaging.

The big Fed looked up at him.

"This isn't where you're needed," he said.

Bolan nodded his understanding, returned to his full height and started for the door, reloading the Steyr as he moved.

BEFORE EXITING THE room, Bolan saw a blood-covered guard lying in a heap on the floor. Things were moving fast and Bolan wasn't certain about what'd happened.

From what he'd gathered so far, from the murmurings of those around him, from the position of the guard's corpse relative to Bennett's injured body, an ugly picture was forming in Bolan's mind. Stopping at the body, he leaned down and stripped the guy of his keys and his security card.

Returning to the second floor's main corridor, he again found himself surrounded by carnage, though it only vaguely registered with him. It wasn't that he was immune to the violence and bloodshed, especially when friends and comrades were wounded. Instead, Bolan over the years had honed his ability to focus on the mission at hand, especially when lives were at stake, by filtering out anything that didn't further the mission. He wasn't a robot or a cold-blooded killer. He wasn't immune to anger, shock or remorse, though he rarely wallowed in them.

Earlier, when the Farm had sent a dossier on the ranch, Price had made it a point to flag Bolan about the panic room.

Crossing the hall, he slipped into a room furnished with a desk, a hutch and a circular conference table, all made of wood and stained reddish-brown. The hutch had been shoved to one side, revealing a steel vault door.

Moving to the door, Bolan studied the keypad and a card reader. Pulling the card from his left pocket, he brought it to the lock, inserted it into the reader and prepared to slide it through.

Bolan paused, not even for a full heartbeat.

He let the card slip from his fingers and spun, his hand a blur as he raised the Steyr.

The shooter squeezed off a couple of shots from his pistol. Both rounds sliced through the air, passing through the space between Bolan's arm and his ribs. The rounds struck the vault door, sparked against the steel before whizzing away.

In the same instant he recognized Friedhelm Geiger, the Steyr rattled. The storm of bullets pounded into Geiger's chest, piercing flesh and breaking ribs. The pistol fell from his hands and he stumbled backward before his legs went rubbery and he dropped to the ground.

Moving around the desk, Bolan kicked Geiger's pistol away. The bullets had savaged Geiger's body so much that Bolan had no doubt the man was dead. The soldier began to move back toward the panic room, but checked himself. Figuring the Secret Service agents probably were on edge, the Executioner decided it was best to have them see

Brognola or a member of the White House's entourage on the other side of the door.

Light footfalls caught Bolan's attention and he whirled, leveling the Steyr.

"Whoa! It's just me," Brognola said. The big Fed clutched his pistol in both hands, but had lowered the muzzle so that it was pointed at the floor. "I heard the shots and figured I should check it out. In case the other guy won." The big Fed shrugged. "I had faith in you, but shit happens."

"It does. How's our lady friend?"

"She's okay," Brognola said, hurrying forward. "But she's probably looking at some serious hospital time."

"Glad she's going to be okay."

"The police are going to lock down this place tight. Secret Service reinforcements won't be far behind. It might be a good time for you to disappear. You have your DOJ credentials in case you get stopped?"

"Yeah. The soldier jerked his head toward the panic room. "Maybe you should greet our friends in there, make sure everyone is okay."

"Right. I'll do that after you leave."

With a curt nod Bolan slung the Steyr and headed out.

"Hey, Striker," Brognola called after him. "This could have been a catastrophe."

"We won the battle," the Executioner replied. "But this isn't over. Not yet."

CHAPTER TWENTY-SIX

Germany

Reinhard Vogelsgang tried to listen, but found it difficult.

His board just had entered the second hour of its meeting. The chief financial officer had unfurled a series of bar graphs tracking sales and earnings for the company's Asian operations. He'd spent the past fifteen minutes speaking about projected cost spikes in cold-rolled steel.

Vogelsgang was pretending to care. It was his company, after all. But his mind was a world away, in Arizona. He wanted to know the outcome of Geiger's mission. It was the only thing that really mattered.

From the corner of his eye, he saw someone staring at him. He turned and locked eyes with Fritz Kruger, a white-haired man with the reddish complexion and bulbous nose of a drunk. A well-heeled lush, but a lush, nonetheless.

Vogelsgang held the other man's stare and flashed a cold, thin smile. Kruger was an executive with a German car manufacturer and had held a seat on the board for twenty years or so. Vogelsgang took pleasure in the old man's thinly veiled disapproval.

Kruger, who'd been a child in post-World War Two Germany, had adopted the same view as so many Germans. Hitler had been wrong; a murderous tyrant who'd brought shame upon his country, one it never could live down. On more than one occasion, Kruger had said it was wrong that Hitler had killed so many Jews.

Whenever Vogelsgang saw Kruger, he saw the reason Germany wasn't a superpower, wasn't *the* superpower. Instead it had been carved up after the war like a damn Christmas turkey, with the Allies and the Soviets each grabbing a share, turning it into a proxy battlefield for ideological enemies during the cold war.

Germany's reunification had helped the country, of course. It still wasn't enough for Vogelsgang, though. It had ended up just another damned European country.

And he blamed people like Kruger. They'd rather Germany bowed and scraped when it should be soaring.

Hitler had made a deadly mistake. He'd been too soft, too merciful. He'd built a ferocious war machine, one that had chewed through Europe. It should've been unstoppable. Instead the stupid guy had lost it all.

Years ago, after too many beers, Vogelsgang had made the mistake of describing his beliefs over dinner with Kruger. The other man's reaction had been swift and intense.

"Hitler was a monster," Kruger had said.

"He started out as a genius," Vogelsgang had replied.

"A genius who murdered millions."

"It's not murder when the killer is superior."

The color had drained from the other man's face, and he'd leaned back from Vogelsgang.

"You think the Nazis were superior?"

Even with several beers in his belly, Vogelsgang had known better than to say that while living in Germany.

"Only a smart man could've accomplished what Hitler did," he'd said. "That's all I'm saying."

"But you said he was 'superior,'" Kruger had said.

He had given the old man a pitying smile. "I think you misheard me. I'd never say such a thing."

"I heard you just fine."

Vogelsgang had clapped his hands once and forced a

laugh. "Ah, my friend, you are stubborn. But it obviously has served you well. Shall we move beyond this?"

"I heard what I heard."

"Yes, you are right," the industrialist had conceded. He'd forced a smile and kept his tone light, patronizing, as though speaking to a child. "I love Hitler. In fact, I am not a businessman. I am a Nazi. There, do these words satisfy you?"

"I never said…"

"Shall we move past this?" the younger man had asked. He'd jerked his chin at the other man's nearly empty beer glass. "I'd like to think it's simply the alcohol talking. But if you press the issue, I might begin to take offense."

The other man had nodded his agreement and they'd turned the discussion to quarterly profits.

Vogelsgang had kept Kruger on his board, mainly so he could keep tabs on the sanctimonious prick.

One day, Vogelsgang assured himself, you won't have to hide from the Krugers of the world. They will cower before you.

One of the glass doors swung open and one of Vogelsgang's assistants, Mathias Schmidt, entered the room. The former military intelligence officer strode directly to his boss, ignoring the other executives gathered around the table. In spite of his stylish suit, the younger man moved like a soldier, his gait quick and efficient. He stopped next to Vogelsgang and bent to his ear.

They'd already agreed on the code. Schmidt was to say, "The repairs were successful," before excusing himself. As Schmidt approached, Vogelsgang could feel his excitement growing. He looked at his assistant, whose face betrayed nothing.

"There's an issue, sir," Schmidt said.

Vogelsgang looked at the man for several seconds as the words sank in.

"Sir," Schmidt began, "there has…"

"Been an issue. Yes, yes, I heard you."

The executive stood from his chair. Several pairs of eyes looked at him expectantly. He flashed a smile.

"Nothing to worry about," he said. "Please continue with the meeting. I'll return in a few minutes."

Schmidt was already at the door, holding it open for Vogelsgang. The two men put several yards between themselves and the conference room before Vogelsgang growled, "What the hell happened?"

"The plan failed," Schmidt replied.

"What does that mean? The target's still alive?"

"Yes."

"How did that happen?"

"We're still piecing it together," the man said.

"Have we heard from Geiger? Or Cornett? Anyone?"

Schmidt shook his head again.

Vogelsgang felt his stomach clench. His hands curled into fists and he had to squelch an impulse to take a swing at the man. "Find out if Geiger is dead. If he's been arrested, we need to get to him. He can't talk. The same goes for anybody else who might've gotten picked up out of this. Understand?"

"Yes, sir."

"We can't let them talk. If they end up in jail, we're going to have to deal with it somehow."

"Understood, sir."

Vogelsgang moved past the man and headed for his study. Once inside, he fixed himself a Scotch whiskey on the rocks, dropped into his chair and stared at the television.

Thirty minutes later someone knocked on the door and he called, "Enter."

The door opened and Schmidt stepped inside.

"We may have something."

Vogelsgang nodded once, but stayed quiet.

The other man gestured at Vogelsgang's computer. "If I may?"

Vogelsgang nodded again.

Schmidt walked around his desk. Vogelsgang wheeled to one side, giving the man some space to access the computer. His assistant opened a web browser and navigated to CNN's web site. The raid obviously was the top story on the web site.

Vogelsgang scowled, feeling impatience welling up inside.

"There's an armed raid and someone saves the President's life. Of course it's the top story."

Schmidt ignored him. Instead he opened a photo gallery and began clicking through pictures until he found the one he'd been looking for.

Three people, two state police officers and a civilian were standing next to a patrol car. Vogelsgang could tell one of the troopers and the civilian were females. With a couple of keystrokes, Schmidt enlarged the photo until the civilian filled much of the frame. The woman had her long black hair pulled back in a ponytail. Her skin was light brown. She wore a black T-shirt and her right shoulder was in a sling. The face looked familiar. Within seconds, he recognized her.

"It's the woman from Monaco," Vogelsgang said, nodding his approval. "This is good. Can you find her?"

"Of course."

"Then do it."

"There is one more thing."

"What is it?"

"We know who hired the American private investigator, Gruber, who was killed in Monaco. It was your board member, Fritz Kruger."

"How do you know that?" Vogelsgang snapped.

"Apparently he funneled money through one of his shell corporations and it made its way to the investigator's widow. It was a rather complex setup. He obviously didn't want to be associated with all of this."

"Obviously."

For a moment the industrialist thought of his former associates. The ones he'd killed because he'd assumed they'd betrayed him. Then he let the thought fade. He'd kill fifty more just like them, hell, five thousand more, to get what he wanted. They barely mattered at all in the greater scheme of things.

Schmidt stepped forward. "Would you like me to deal with him?"

"No. Bring him to me."

VOGELSGANG SAT ON the edge of his desk. His smartphone rested in his hand. He was studying stock market quotes displayed on the screen. A knock at the door caught his attention. He looked up and said, "Come in."

The door swung open and Schmidt stepped inside. Fritz Kruger hobbled in behind him.

"My old friend," Vogelsgang said. "Come in and sit down." He gestured to the array of chairs set in front of his desk.

Kruger shuffled across the room until he reached one of the chairs. His eyes squeezed shut with pain as he lowered himself into the seat.

"Don't get old," Kruger said. "It's like waking up in hell every day."

Vogelsgang gave him a sympathetic smile. "It must be difficult. Would you care for a drink?"

"No, thank you. It's much too early."

"I admire your discipline."

"You're full of shit. Why did you want to see me?"

"I have a problem," Vogelsgang said as he pushed away

from his desk and walked to the fireplace. "You see, I found out someone I am close to has been spying on me."

"What?"

"I know," Vogelsgang said. "It's unnerving Someone has been spying on me, and I can't have that. I thought you might help." He picked up a poker, testing its weight by slapping it against his palm, and walked back to the chair.

Kruger cleared his throat. "I am sorry to hear of that. But I'm not sure what I could do to help."

Strolling around the chair, Vogelsgang pinned the old man with his gaze. "I considered hiring a private investigator just to figure out what was going on here. I thought you might know one."

The old man laughed. "A private investigator? My boy, I haven't hired one of those in twenty years, not since my second divorce. I can hardly see where I can help you."

"You can't help?"

No, I cannot."

Vogelsgang nodded slowly. "How unfortunate," he said, raising the poker above his head like a club. "I guess I'll have to solve the problem another way."

The heavy iron rod fell. The old man threw his hand up defensively. The impact pulverized several bones in his hand, causing him to scream before the metal collided with his skull. Blood flew everywhere as Vogelsgang continued clubbing Kruger, even after he was dead.

Finally the industrialist tossed aside the poker, his arm worn out, his breath coming in ragged gasps. He stared at the battered corpse for several seconds, allowing himself a smile before he went to get a towel.

It was just the first taste of revenge he planned to have.

CHAPTER TWENTY-SEVEN

Minotti sucked in a breath of air and his eyes flickered open. The onslaught of white lights caused him to screw his eyes shut almost immediately. Groaning, he opened them again, this time more slowly, letting his eyes adjust to the overhead lights. From somewhere behind him, he heard a soft steady beeping and recognized it as a heart monitor. He'd had a heart attack three years ago and always swore he'd never forget the sound of the monitor. Apparently he'd been right.

As awareness returned, he also recognized the dull ache of an IV poking into his arm. He started to recall what had happened, being shot, then passing out in the desert, figuring—hell, hoping—he was going to die.

His limbs felt heavy, his mouth parched. He guessed it was painkillers of some kind. He tried to raise himself up from the bed, but his body wouldn't respond.

A television was moored to a wall opposite his bed. On the rare occasion when he was conscious, all he could do was lie there and stare at it. A pretty brunette was draping her body over a red exercise ball. The sound was off, but he didn't care. He was too focused on her lithe figure, the curve of her buttocks, the rippling muscles in her thighs and calves. Well, if you can't move, you may as well have something to look at, he thought. The tempo of his heart monitor sped up. He grinned. At least something was working on him.

It was a few seconds more before he became aware of

the presence next to him. Twisting his head to the right, he saw a woman dressed in hospital scrubs standing next to his bed. Her blond hair was pulled back in a tight ponytail. She smiled sweetly enough at him that he didn't notice the coldness in her eyes.

"You shouldn't be watching this," she said. "You have a heart condition."

He opened his mouth to speak. It took a couple of tries before his parched mouth worked again.

"Is that why I'm here?"

She nodded.

"Apparently you were shot, then had a mild heart attack," she said.

"Shit," he said.

"This is your second?"

He nodded.

"You're also dehydrated."

"I need a beer," he said.

"You're tough, Lou."

He shrugged as best he could manage.

She patted him on the arm. "Don't be modest," she said. "What you went through out there?" She jerked her head over her shoulder. "It would've killed most guys."

He tried to force his best aw-shucks grin at her. She reached down and squeezed his biceps, letting her fingertips dig in just a little. He winced and tried to jerk his arm from her grip, but she kept her hold on him.

Her other hand dipped into the pocket of her scrub shirt. She pulled a syringe from it, held it up so he could see it and gave him another smile. This time he noticed the hardness in her eyes. A shudder passed through him.

Holding the syringe high, she tapped it with her index finger.

"This is adrenaline," she said. "It's enough to make a dead guy's heart start beating."

Again, she displayed the sweet smile. "Can you imagine what it'd do to a beating heart? Especially one that's survived a heart attack or two?"

Blood thundered in Minotti's ears.

"Lady, what the hell—?"

She patted his arm again.

"I don't mean to scare you," she said, her tone soothing. "I just wanted your attention."

"Well, you got it."

"I just have a couple of questions. Then everything will be okay."

"Fine, spit it out."

"A woman found you, right? She was the one who waited by you for the paramedics?"

"Yeah," he said.

"Did she give you a name?"

"Name?"

"A name. You know, like your name is Lou. Understand?"

He licked his lips and tried to remember. He'd been weak from blood loss. Her words had seemed to reach him from a great distance even though she'd been right next to him.

"I didn't get her name."

The faux nurse pouted a little.

"Really, Lou? A stud like you and you didn't get her name?" She raked a hand through her hair. "I'm blond, but I'm not dumb, sweetie."

Twirling her hair around an index finger, she used her other hand to maneuver the needle toward his arm.

His body pushed up against the restraints for a second or two before he dropped back into the bed.

"Hold it," he said. "Give me a second." She nodded and waited. "Rodriguez."

"She have first name?"

"I don't know. Swear to God. I don't know. She said her name was Rodriguez. Said she was an FBI agent."

"Anything else?"

He shut his eyes and struggled to remember. God, he didn't want to die. Not like this.

When he opened them again, tears blurred his vision.

"Jennifer! Yeah, she said her name was Jennifer. She said she lived in Phoenix. When I got better, she said we could hang out."

"How nice. Hold on to that happy thought."

The syringe sank into his chest. He gasped in surprise and pain. The woman rested her other palm on his chest, leaning forward to put some weight on him and hold him in place.

The roar in his ears grew louder. A vise-like pressure squeezed his chest, accompanied by sharp pains that stole his breath. As the pain worsened, it seemed to consume him, erasing the woman, the hospital room and, finally, his thoughts. Then his heart exploded and blackness overtook him.

As MINOTTI SUFFERED through the last seconds of his life, Dagmar Gabriele pocketed the used syringe and slipped from Minotti's hospital room.

The cop's heart monitor had kicked into overdrive as the adrenaline worked its way through his system. As much as she wanted to stay and watch, Gabriele knew she needed to leave before the monitor brought a herd of doctors and nurses to the ex-cop's room.

She heard the scuffing of rubber-soled shoes against the linoleum and excited voices behind her. A door was open to her right. She slipped through it and found herself in a room identical to the one where she'd killed Minotti. However, this room's one bed was made and the television screen sat dark. A minute passed before she calmly exited the room and continued down a corridor, keeping her pace artificially slow so she attracted no attention. Ducking into a stairwell, she descended two flights to the ground floor and exited into the emergency room waiting area. Thirty seconds later she passed through the automatic doors of the ambulance entrance and began winding her way down the driveway leading to the ER's entrance.

She wasn't worried about being followed. There would be no reason for the staff to consider Minotti's death suspicious, at least not immediately. A middle-aged man with a history of heart problems had just died of heart failure right after surviving a harrowing experience.

If someone became suspicious and pushed for an autopsy, they might discover he'd been killed. Once that happened, they'd scour the surveillance footage and see whether anyone had come or gone from his room in the minutes before he died.

Gabriele wasn't worried. Her employer had a team of computer hackers at his disposal.

He'd told her they probably could break into the hospital's system and erase the footage. Failing that, though, she'd taken additional precautions. A blond wig covered her short black hair. Strategically placed padding made her look heavier than she really was. As she kept moving, she peeled off the latex gloves that had kept her from leaving prints in the room.

None of that made her bulletproof, of course. However, her imminent departure from the country would add another layer of protection.

By the time Gabriele reached her red compact car, sweat had begun collecting under the special padding beneath her scrubs and dotted her forehead along her hairline. Climbing into the front seat, she began thinking about her next mission: returning home to mix up a gin and tonic on the rocks. She stoked the engine to life, kicked up the air conditioner, guided the car away from the curb and began humming along with the radio. Lou Minotti already was becoming a distant memory for her.

Two minutes later her phone began to ring. Turning down the radio, she answered the call in speaker mode.

"Yes?"

"It's me," Vogelsgang said.

"I took care of your issue if that's why you're calling."

"Good," he said. "Was it any trouble?"

She recalled Minotti's body jerking, his back arching and his cries of pain as his heart surged into overdrive before it finally burst.

A smile tugged at the corners of her mouth. "No trouble at all," she said.

"Did you learn anything?"

"He gave me a name—Jennifer Rodriguez."

"Good."

"So you'll have another problem for me to handle?"

"Yes."

"Same price?"

The line went silent for a couple of seconds.

"Yes."

"How soon?"

"It depends. Depending on how your information plays out, it could be today."

She swore in German.

"It can't be helped," he said. "It's all related."

"Understood," she said.

"You'll need other people."

"I doubt it."

"Trust me," he said. "You'll need help. These are difficult problems to deal with."

"Send me the information. I'll handle it whatever it takes."

BEFORE GABRIELE RETURNED to her apartment she stopped at a city park and ducked into a restroom. She stripped away the wig and the hospital scrubs, squeezed the clothes into her backpack, changed into shorts and a sleeveless T-shirt and returned to her car.

She was in her apartment, showered and halfway through her second gin and tonic when another of her phones rang. This one was an encrypted satellite phone that Vogelsgang had provided for her so they could speak more freely.

"Your information checks out," he said.

"Of course it does," she said. "You should've seen him. There was no way he was going to lie to me."

"I want you to grab Jennifer Rodriguez," Vogelsgang said, "and anyone who is with her. I'll decide what to do with them later."

CHAPTER TWENTY-EIGHT

The Ford rolled into the driveway of Rodriguez's house.

Grimaldi, who was driving the rental, threw the car into park and let it idle. The headlights cast a whitish glow on the front of the house. The beams passed through the living room windows and cut through the blackness, allowing Rodriguez to make out the vague outlines of her furniture. She sighed without meaning to.

"You okay?" Grimaldi asked. "How's your arm?" Rodriguez had spent the rest of the day being checked out medically. Her arm had been bandaged.

"Sure," she said. "I've just been gone a while. I'm hoping the toilet flushes and the lights work. That's all."

"You could stay at my hotel. If the water or power has been shut off, you can't deal with it tonight. Come back tomorrow."

"You mean stay in your room?"

"If you can behave yourself," he replied.

A flash of anger caused her to whip her head toward him. When she saw the playful grin on his face, she cooled down immediately.

"We'd get separate rooms," he said. "Uncle Sam will pick up the tab. I'm too tired to handle a pajama party."

"Somehow, I doubt that."

"Somehow, I think you're right," Grimaldi told her.

She started to move her right arm to reach for the door. The movement immediately sent flashes of pain shooting up her arm. Wincing, she pulled her arm back, reached over with her left, opened the door and stepped one foot out of the car.

"I'd offer to help with the luggage…"

"But I don't have any. Good thing with this injured shoulder."

"You have my number at the hotel," Grimaldi said. "Call me tomorrow. Let me know if you have running water. We can have breakfast before I leave town."

She smiled. "I'll do that."

Rodrigues exited the car, shut the door and gave Grimaldi a short wave before moving up the curved walkway leading to her front door. Her right arm continued to ache and she thought of the painkillers the doctor had given her. She still had a couple hours before she could take her next dose and she'd ridden out much worse in her career.

Her purse was looped over her left shoulder. She dipped her hand into the bag and dug around until she found her keys at the bottom. Slipping the house key into the lock, she waved at Grimaldi, who backed the car from the driveway as she began to turn the key.

As Rodriguez heard him drive away, she felt a sense of foreboding creep over her and she wondered whether she'd done the right thing in staying at the house. It wasn't the aftereffects of being involved in a firefight. That adrenaline rush had died away hours ago.

She just didn't want to come home. She'd been working undercover so long, she wasn't sure she even had a home anymore. It was more like she had a 1,000-square-foot, climate-controlled box to store her stuff. Once she'd lost her husband, she'd thrown herself into her work, trying like hell to forget him, forget her old life. Undercover work had been a perfect way to do it. She adopted and shed new identities with each mission.

She'd found refuge in being someone else.

Turning the knob, she pushed open the door. She was

so caught up in her thoughts she didn't notice the traces of cologne wafting on the air inside her house until the door slammed shut behind her.

RODRIGUEZ OPENED HER fingers and let her keys fall to the ground. Her hand dropped to the Glock holstered at her waist. In the same instant, an arm wrapped around her neck and pulled tight, partially cutting off her air. She felt her feet get jerked off the floor. She was kicking her legs, but as she struggled to breathe, her limbs quickly were growing heavy.

Another hand grabbed her left wrist and pushed down on it, pinning her gun in its holster.

A shadow emerged from the darkness and stalked toward her.

CHAPTER TWENTY-NINE

Something nagged at Grimaldi as he drove away from Rodriguez's house.

The FBI agent had been concerned about something when he'd dropped her off, preoccupied, maybe. That didn't bother the pilot. She'd been through a lot in the past couple of days. Between the stress of the firefights and her captivity, he guessed she was exhausted. She obviously was a tough woman and an experienced agent. He had no doubt she could handle that sort of thing, though it might take time.

As he approached a stop sign, he tapped the brake and the car slowed.

Something else was bugging him, though. His gut told him to go back to her house and check on her. It was the same instinct that on the battlefield told him when someone was aiming a rifle at his back or preparing to attack him from around the corner.

It was one of those things he could neither explain nor ignore. Over the years he'd learned that he ignored his instincts at his peril.

If he went there and found she was okay, fine. She probably would write him off as overprotective, sexist or something else. He could live with that much more easily than if he ignored his combat senses and she ended up dead. Making a U-turn at the stop sign, he started back for the house.

He decided against pulling directly into the driveway.

Instead, a few dozen yards from the house, he wheeled the car to the curb, parked it and killed the lights. He popped open the door and went EVA.

Despite the hour, it still was warm outside compared to the Ford's air-conditioned interior. He wore a long-sleeved black button-down shirt over a navy-blue T-shirt and immediately he began to sweat. But he needed the long-sleeved shirt to cover his Browning Hi-Power. The weapon was holstered on his left hip in a cross-draw position. He also had a couple spare magazines for the weapon and a folding knife.

As Grimaldi approached the house, he saw that Rodriguez still hadn't turned on the lights and he scowled.

It had been only a couple of minutes since he'd left her at the house. There was no way she could have walked inside and plopped into bed so quickly. After a month or two away from the house, she'd want to check the place over, maybe wash her face or go through any letters or magazines that had collected there. Maybe her power wasn't working, but he saw no flashlight beams or anything else.

It was late enough, at least by suburban standards, that most residents had sealed themselves inside for the night. Grimaldi could hear a rock tune blaring in the distance, along with an occasional shout followed by the splash of someone jumping into a pool.

Otherwise, things were quiet.

The pilot approached the house at an angle, walking through Rodriguez's yard and up to her garage door. This allowed him to bypass the driveway and shielded his approach from anyone looking out the window. Again, he was acting on instinct and his instinct told him to avoid the windows until he knew what he was dealing with.

The deep rumble of someone clearing his throat followed by a cough reached Grimaldi and caused him to freeze. A couple of seconds later he caught a whiff of cigarette smoke.

Turning, he crept to the sidewall and glided along it. When he reached the edge of the house, he slipped the knife from his pants' pocket and unfolded it. He left the Browning in its holster because he didn't have a sound suppressor for it. Chancing a look around the corner, he saw a skinny, middle-aged man dressed in jeans and a polo shirt. The tails of the shirt hung loose over the guy's waist, probably to hide a weapon.

Grimaldi switched the knife to his left hand and emerged from behind the house.

He held the knife against his leg, blade pointed toward the ground, to keep it out of sight.

He wanted to know for certain the man was a threat.

The guy obliged him. Apparently seeing Grimaldi from the corner of his eye, he whirled toward the Stony Man warrior and began clawing at his hip for a gun. Grimaldi rushed forward and landed a hard right hook on the guy's jaw that sent him reeling. He kept up the pressure, landing another blow on the guy's mouth. He followed it with a hard kick to the groin with his left foot. Air exploded from between the man's clenched teeth and he sank to his knees. Grimaldi yanked his Browning from the holster and used it to club the guy into unconsciousness.

Swift and brutal, but not lethal.

A quick pat-down of the guy revealed a wallet with an Arizona driver's license issued under one name, David Wesley. He had three platinum credit cards, one issued under the Wesley handle and two others under other names. Whoever David Wesley was, he wasn't one of Rodriguez's Bureau colleagues or anyone else legitimate. While he didn't have a badge, the guy did have a .40-caliber Glock 22 clipped on his right hip. Grimaldi slipped the holstered weapon from inside the guy's waistband and hooked it onto his own belt. He also found spare magazines in the guy's pants and he pocketed those, as well.

Rising to his feet, Grimaldi moved to the sliding-glass door leading into the house and pushed it aside. Rolling the unconscious man onto his back, the pilot grabbed a handful of his shirt, dragged him through the doorway and quietly lowered him facedown to the ground.

Grimaldi heard voices almost immediately. He stowed the knife and drew the Browning.

"Stuff in the needle will keep her unconscious for hours," said a man with a scratchy voice. He spoke English with a heavy German accent.

"She won't live that long," another man said.

Grimaldi moved through the darkness, the Browning pointed in front of him, and followed the voices. He guessed the men were somehow associated with Geiger and the men behind the raid. Apparently the people behind that bloodbath wanted some payback. Getting it wouldn't be easy. Brognola already was on a plane back to Washington. Bolan had gone back to the hotel to look over some information forwarded to him by the Farm so he could nail the people behind the raid. They knew Rodriguez because she'd tried to infiltrate their organization. Grimaldi wasn't even sure they knew of himself, Bolan, or his Matt Cooper alias.

"Seems like taking her with us is more trouble than it's worth," the man with the scratchy voice said.

"Seems like you're not paid to think," the other man snapped.

"It would be easier to kill her here," Scratchy said. "That's my only point."

"Our boss thinks otherwise. We were hired to grab her."

"Fair enough."

Grimaldi rounded the corner.

He could see a pair of shadows. Their bodies silhouetted

by the moonlight filtering through the front windows. He saw at least a partial outline of Rodriguez's slender form stretched out on the floor. He guessed they'd kept the lights off to deter any passersby from looking into the windows. Grimaldi considered flicking a light switch, but dismissed the idea. The sudden infusion of light would temporarily blind the thugs, sure, but he'd need precious moments for his eyes to adjust, too. As best he could determine, they weren't wearing night-vision goggles.

He'd have to use the darkness to his advantage.

The guy nearest to him stood almost a head taller than Grimaldi. The pilot edged into the room, trying to merge with every shadow he could find, until he got within striking distance of the guy. He raised the pistol and slashed down violently on the guy's head.

Steel struck bone with an audible crack. The guy wavered for an instant before his knees gave out and he began to sink to the ground.

The other man swung into action, lunging at Grimaldi. The pilot swung the pistol as a club, but his opponent threw up his hand to block the move. Grimaldi had closed the gap between them. He jerked his head forward and struck the other man in the face. The guy groaned, took a step back and threw his hands up to protect his face. Grimaldi used the opening to deliver a roundhouse to the man's cheek that snapped his head to one side.

The Stony Man pilot moved in.

Pain suddenly surged through the back of his head and a white light exploded behind his eyes. Even as he willed his body to stay up, his legs went wobbly and he felt himself plummeting to the floor, first on his knees and then his hands.

The sole of a shoe ground down on the hand holding the Browning. *Hold the gun,* his mind screamed. *Hold the damn gun!*

Something hammered against his ribs and he belched air from his lungs. Even as he struggled to regain his breath, he was struck in his midsection again. His grip on the pistol slipped.

He saw a shadow coming toward him. He struck out feebly and the hand was slapped aside. The sensation of something heavy pressing on his chest, like someone's knee, registered with him before a final blow to the head plunged him into blackness.

BOLAN DROVE HIS rental car into the hotel's underground parking garage and eased his vehicle into a narrow parking space. Grabbing his duffel bag from the passenger's seat, he climbed from the vehicle and slammed the door. He thumbed a button on the key fob and the locks snapped into place, the car emitting a quick chirp.

When the soldier reached the front desk clerk, a pretty Asian woman greeted him. He handed her a credit card listed under his Matt Cooper alias and waited while she checked him into his room.

The desk clerk handed back his credit card and gave him another smile.

"Is there anything else I can do for you, Mr. Cooper?"

Bolan turned his attention back to her. "Sure. I have a friend checking in. I'd like to know whether he's arrived."

"Of course," she replied. She poised her fingers over her keyboard. "What's his name?"

"Jack Williamson."

She tapped in the name and stared at the screen, occasionally clicking a button on the computer mouse. After several seconds, she shook her head.

"We have a reservation for Mr. Williamson," she said. "But he apparently hasn't checked in yet."

Bolan felt concerned, but kept his expression pleasant. "Really?"

She nodded and dropped her eyes to the screen again. "And he hasn't called in, either."

Bolan nodded and gave the woman a tight smile. His key card lay on the counter. He pressed his hand down onto it and pulled it to him.

"Jack likes to run late," he said, forcing a lightness into his voice.

"I can have him call your room when he gets in."

"Tell him to call my cell," Bolan said. "He has the number."

Once the soldier had put a few yards between himself and the desk, he dialed Grimaldi's number and waited. After two rings, someone answered, but said nothing.

Bolan let a few seconds of silence pass. "Hello?" he said.

The line went dead.

Muttering a curse, Bolan turned and headed back for his car.

As HE WHEELED the car up the garage's exit ramp, Bolan tried calling Grimaldi again, but got no answer.

He thumbed in a code for Stony Man Farm. He heard several clicks as the call was routed through a series of cut-out numbers before it finally began ringing. Barbara Price answered.

Her voice sounded weary.

"It's Striker," he said.

"Are you bedding down for the night?"

"Negative," he said. "We have a problem."

The change in her tone was immediate.

"What happened?"

Bolan quickly told her that he'd lost contact with Grimaldi, who'd been transporting Rodriguez to her house.

"You don't think they, um, hooked up, do you?"

"Negative. I know he has a girl in every port. But I don't think that's the case here. He'd never ignore my call."

"True."

"And someone answered, said nothing and hung up."

"You're right. Something's wrong," Price agreed.

"I'm going to her house."

"Okay. What do you need from me?"

"Can you get Rodriguez's phone number?"

"Sure."

"Do that. Make a call and see if she answers. If she's okay, we need to figure out where Jack is."

"I can locate his phone, too."

"Do it, then. Call me back."

"Right."

His expression grim, Bolan disconnected. He'd plugged Rodriguez's address into the onboard GPS before leaving the hotel.

His mind began to roll through the possible scenarios. Unless Grimaldi had a bullet hole in his throat, he wouldn't answer the phone without speaking. If he was going to stay with Rodriguez, he still would've answered the phone and probably would've let Bolan know he wasn't going to be at the hotel. Grimaldi was a pro. They were in a strange town, in the middle of a mission. He wouldn't disappear without a good reason. Bolan's phone vibrated on the passenger's seat and he picked it up.

"Go."

"I tried Rodriguez's phone," Price said. "She didn't answer, either."

"Okay."

"What next?"

"I'm heading over to Rodriguez's house," the Executioner said.

CHAPTER THIRTY

Bolan stared down at the dead man who lay on the floor at his feet. The corpse was resting on his right side. Blood had seeped from the ragged, fist-size opening in the guy's forehead and had formed a dark sunburst on Rodriguez's living-room carpet. Two other men, apparently killed by gunshot wounds to the chest, lay a few feet from the first guy.

Bolan didn't recognize any of the men. However, using his phone, he snapped their pictures and sent them to the Farm's cyber team to look for a match.

He'd arrived at the house less than two minutes ago and sneaked in through the backyard. Along the way, he'd nearly stepped in a dark spot on the concrete patio. Producing a flashlight, he'd studied it and found it was a small puddle of blood, some of which had been smeared along the concrete. Alive or dead, the bleeder had been dragged inside for some reason.

Once he'd found the bodies in the living room, he'd drawn the curtains and turned on the lights.

What he'd learned had been a mixed blessing. He was glad to see that none of the corpses was Grimaldi or Rodriguez. But it also left him with the problem of finding them.

While he waited for a reply from the Farm, he searched the rest of the house and the attached garage, but found nothing helpful. After a few minutes he came across Grimaldi's and Rodriguez's phones. They'd been set neatly on a countertop, one next to the other.

Bolan assumed they'd been left behind in case someone tried to trace them. That much made sense to him. More mysterious was the decision to leave behind the bodies.

Bolan had eyeballed the entrance wounds and the men seemed to have been shot at close range, one of them execution style in the back of the skull.

The soldier knew Grimaldi wasn't squeamish about killing the bad guys. However, he had a hard time imagining the pilot shooting someone in the back of the head at close range, except under the most dire of circumstances.

Three more minutes passed when Grimaldi's phone began to vibrate against the countertop. Scowling, Bolan went to the phone and picked it up. The word "Restricted" flashed on the screen.

Bolan answered the phone.

"Yeah?"

"You're looking for your friends, I assume?"

The man's English was good, though Bolan detected a trace of a German accent.

"Stupid question," the Executioner said.

The caller chuckled. "I assume you're distressed. Good again. Perhaps you can appreciate my own distress."

"I feel you," Bolan said, just to keep the guy talking. At the same time he sent a text message to Price telling her to trace the call on Grimaldi's phone.

"Your behavior in Arizona has put me in an awkward position."

"Yeah."

"And now you're in an awkward position."

"Meaning?"

"I think you know."

"Try me," Bolan said.

"I have your comrades. I have plans for them."

"So what do you want from me?"

"I want you to join us, Mr...."

"Cooper. Matt Cooper."

"Ah, Matt Cooper," the man replied. "Very good. And you are an FBI agent, like your friend, Ms. Rodriguez?"

"Something like that," Bolan lied.

"Then you probably wouldn't come alone."

"I'll come alone," Bolan said.

"Good, here's the address," the man said, reciting it.

"WE COULDN'T TRACE the call," Price told him four minutes later. "Whoever it was had equipment and knew what they were doing. We tried to follow the call, but it lead to a dead end."

"He gave me an address," the soldier told her. The Executioner still was standing in the kitchen, next to the counter, staring down at the phones as he spoke. He recited the address for Price. "Give me any kind of background you can on this."

"You know this is a trap, right?" Price asked.

Bolan ignored the question. "The pictures I sent—were you able to ID them for me?"

"One of them is of Wolfgang Kesselring. At least that's the name he was given at birth."

"He has another name?"

"Several of them. As in at least a half dozen known aliases, all of different nationalities, according to Interpol. Chances are he has even more that the authorities don't know about. I can email you his Interpol file."

"Just give me the highlights," Bolan said.

Phone still pressed to his ear, he flipped off the lights inside Rodriguez's house, exited the structure through the rear door and walked in the direction of his rental car.

"Kesselring's a mercenary," she said. "At least that's how he's spent the last dozen years or so. Before that he was a member of the German military for a decade." She paused.

"Notice I didn't say a 'decorated' or 'respected' member of the military. Wolfgang had a few personality problems."

"Such as?"

"He hated authority. That's obviously a strike against you when you're a soldier. Had a gambling problem and, oh, he was a vocal racist and an anti-Semite. He wasn't respected or wanted for obvious reasons. The other soldiers feared him, especially since he seemed volatile."

"So he got drummed out."

"Right. Unfortunately, for all his problems, he was enterprising. Once he got kicked out, he began selling his services on the open market. Obviously, he was willing to work in Africa as a security person, so long as the client was white. When he'd made enough enemies there, he made tracks back to Europe. Since he was good with a gun and pretty fearless, organized crime groups there hired him as muscle. His specialty was going into ethnic neighborhoods and shaking down businesses. Once they figured out how ruthless he was, he moved on to bigger things—like killing people."

Bolan got the picture.

"So what's he doing in the U.S.?" he asked.

"This is where things get a little weird," Price said. "A year or so ago, he got picked up by a security firm based in Berlin. At least that's according to the CIA's Berlin station chief. Kesselring came across the CIA's radar because he'd been roughing up a couple of their best sources. The Agency was about to deal with it when he disappeared. A little while later, they learned he'd run to the U.S."

Price paused and Bolan could hear her tapping at her keyboard for a couple of seconds.

"Apparently this security firm has offices in Washington, D.C., and Los Angeles. Kesselring came over here to work in the L.A. office. After that, his trail goes cold."

Bolan fell silent for a few seconds and thought it over.

"What about the security firm? Any information you can dig up on it?"

"Hang on."

Bolan heard Price working the keyboard again. Probably a minute passed before she spoke again.

"A year ago, the Los Angeles *Times* carried a brief item about the office being opened here. It supposedly was aimed at European executives and tourists who wanted security while they were in the United States. I won't read you the whole article, but the firm stresses that it focuses on being discreet. I can have Bear and the others background this company, see if they can follow the paper trail a little deeper."

"Good," Bolan said.

"In the meantime, I have someone else you can track down," Price added. "The article quotes a man called Thomas Denver. Apparently, Denver was in charge of the L.A. office. Hang on a second." She went silent again for a few seconds. "I'm emailing you an address," she said. "We'll try to get more information to you ASAP."

"Make it quick," Bolan said. "Denver may have no idea what he's involved in. If he's clean, I'll go easy on him."

"And if he's dirty?"

The soldier didn't bother to answer.

CHAPTER THIRTY-ONE

Denver lived outside Phoenix in a gated neighborhood populated with cookie-cutter luxury homes. Bolan parked his rental at a gas station near the development. He pulled himself over the fence and dropped to the other side, hitting the bare earth with a thud.

The guard shack was lit but empty. A white Ford with a light bar fixed to the roof and a star fixed over the word Security on the driver's-side door was parked next to the guard house. As he passed the car, he let his fingertips graze the hood. It felt cool to the touch. The soldier assumed the security was only on the scene during the day to give the residents a sense of safety.

A false sense of safety, it turned out.

From what Price and the cyber team had turned up, Denver had a long criminal history, one accrued under multiple identities. The child of a wealthy parents—his mother was estate developer and later a state senator, his father a respected heart surgeon—Denver had decided to tread a dark path. By the time he reached eighteen, he had been implicated in two rapes, though his parents' influence and wealth had made sure neither went to trial. He'd burned through a series of private schools and colleges, racking up several assault complaints along the way. Though it wasn't immediately clear how it happened, Denver caught the attention of a Phoenix crime boss who brought him on first as an enforcer and later as part of his inner circle. Knowing the Mafia as Bolan did, he guessed the Don had been drawn to Denver's connections as well as those of his family. Why Denver had severed his ties with the crime boss and how he'd been allowed to walk away with his skin intact wasn't entirely clear.

At this point, Bolan didn't care. He had other questions for Denver.

A block away the sidewalk ended at a four-way stop and across the intersection stood Denver's house. The house was mud-brown and looked like two cracker boxes laid on their sides and joined together to form an L. Curved red tiles covered the roof. A black BMW convertible stood in the driveway, the top folded down. Lights burned on the first floor and Bolan could hear muffled music through the walls.

Bolan veered off the sidewalk, crept through Denver's front yard, melted into the inky shadows running along-side the house and, drawing his Beretta 93-R, made his way to the back door. Apparently, Denver was one to leave his work at the office. The alleged security consultant had outfitted the house with mediocre locks that Bolan was able to pick easily.

As the door swung inward, the music grew louder and Bolan could make out the chunky guitar riffs of a heavy-metal song. He shut the door and moved through the house. As he exited the kitchen and moved into the dining room, he heard glass break followed by a distinctly feminine laugh.

Following the music, he wound his way through the first floor until he reached a set of double doors. One of the doors was ajar. He heard more laughter, this time both a man's and a woman's.

The soldier raised the Beretta, gently pushed the door open and moved through it. He found Denver seated on the floor with a woman straddling him. The guy was shirt-less and his back was pointed at Bolan. The woman's shirt was unbuttoned, her skirt hiked up around her waist. An open bottle of whiskey stood on the floor, a glass next to it.

The woman's eyelids were half closed and she was undulating her upper body in time with the music. Her eyes drifted in Bolan's direction, and he steeled himself for her to scream. Instead she looked away, shut her eyes and continued moving to the music.

Bolan came through the door. His right arm flew up, aimed and squeezed off a burst from the Beretta. The bullets drilled into the MP3 player. It sparked and silence descended over the room. Denver gave the woman a hard shove and twisted to look for the source of the shots. As he locked eyes with Bolan, he lunged across the floor where a pistol sheathed in a shoulder holster was looped around the back of a chair. The Beretta coughed again and the bullets chewed into the floor.

The woman screamed. Bolan crossed the room, drove a booted foot into Denver's midsection and the guy dropped to the ground. Though he had no intention of shooting the woman, Bolan wagged the pistol in her direction and said, "Shut up."

He had to repeat himself twice more before she finally complied. Bolan gestured at a closet with the Beretta's muzzle. "Get in there," he said.

"What's going to happen to me?" she asked, buttoning her blouse.

Bolan shook his head. "Nothing. Just get in the closet. Don't come out until I say so. I'm not here for you."

"What about me?" Denver asked.

Bolan looked in the guy's eyes and saw fear in them.

"I have money," Denver said. "I've got some jewels, too. It's all upstairs in the safe. Let's go up there and I think we can work something out."

Bolan gave the other man a hard look.

"If you want to save your miserable skin, then shut up.

I didn't come here for your money. And I'm thinking you
have a gun in the safe." Bolan saw something flicker in the
guy's eyes and the corner of his mouth twitched.

"Bullshit," Denver said. "I don't know what you're talking about."

"I don't want your money," Bolan repeated.

Denver smiled and spread his hands. "C'mon," he said.
"What else could you want from me?"

"I have questions."

The guy nodded. "You mind if I sit down?" he asked.

Bolan shook his head. Denver backed into a couch,
dropped onto the middle cushion and crossed his left ankle
over his right knee. "So," Denver said, "what do you want
to know?"

"Wolfgang Kesselring."

"Yeah?"

"He a good friend?"

"Wolfie? He doesn't have friends. The guy is…" Denver searched for the word. "He's socially awkward. Unless
you lube him up with a few drinks."

"He still work for you?"

Denver licked his lips. "No."

"Try again."

"Yes."

"Better. You know where he was tonight?"

The guy shook his head. "He works for me. We don't
sleep together."

Bolan nodded toward the room where Denver had been
partying. "Obviously."

"Look man, you want to get to the point? What happened? You're obviously not a cop. Or if you are, you're
crooked as hell because you came alone and you haven't
shown me a badge. What's your game?"

"Kesselring's dead."

"How?"

"Gunshots."

Denver crossed his arms over his chest. "You the shooter?"

"I knew he was dead, right?" Bolan said. He figured the other guy might get more talkative if he thought Bolan had killed one of his associates.

"So what was the issue? Did the idiot owe you money? Don't feel special. He owes everybody money."

"Owed."

"Yeah, owed. Look, if you're thinking you can get the cash out of me, forget it. It's not going to happen."

"Two of my friends, a man and a woman, came up missing tonight. I found your buddy—the one who's now leaking brains all over someone's carpet—at the scene. There was a second guy there, too."

"Dead?"

Bolan nodded.

"Shit, man, I've met some stone-cold killers before, but you're insane."

"And yet you want to jerk me around."

Denver held up his right hand, palm facing Bolan, as though ordering him to halt.

"I'm not jerking you around."

"I repeat, I had two friends disappear tonight. Do you know anything about it?"

Denver locked eyes with Bolan and shook his head. "No."

Bolan took a step forward and pointed the Beretta at Denver's forehead. The man stared at him for a few seconds, trying to gauge whether the soldier was bluffing and decided he didn't like what he saw. He put up both hands this time.

"All right," he said. "I knew something was going down. I had no idea it was a snatch and grab, though."

"You thought it'd be a murder."

"I had no idea what it'd be."

"What did you know?"

Lowering his hands, Denver heaved a sigh and lowered his head, appearing beat down by the exchange though Bolan couldn't be sure.

"Look, there's this crazy woman…"

"Named…?"

"Her name's Dagmar Gabriele, Okay? Jesus. Anyway, as I was saying, she's crazy as hell. Not exactly sure what her deal is, but it's like she has no conscience, you know what I'm saying?"

"Unlike you."

"Screw you, man. You want to hear what I have to say or not? Technically, she works for me, but I never see her or hear from her. Maybe once or twice a year she calls me and asks for something. And I've already been told in advance to never tell her no. I'm just supposed to shut up and supply her with anything she wants—people, guns, forged documents, cars. I have lot of contacts who can provide those things, so long as the money is right."

"So she's an assassin."

"I don't know. I just supply her with things. I don't ask questions."

"You're a bad liar," Bolan said.

The other man's neck and cheeks flushed red and he pressed his lips into a tight line.

"She kills people," Bolan said. "Am I right?"

The other man nodded in agreement.

"So she called and asked for some people…"

"Would Gabriele have killed my two friends at the house?"

"Depends on her orders."

"And the orders come from Vogelsgang."

Denver exhaled as though he'd been kicked in the gut.

"I'm not going down that road," he told him.

"I'll consider that a yes. Where would she take them?"

"Hell if I know," the guy said. "Seriously, I don't know. Like I said, she calls me a couple of times a year and asks for stuff. Once in a while someone will send her packages at my office and she'll stop by to pick them up. She's a beautiful woman. Short black hair. Pretty face. Long legs."

"So you have no idea where she lives?"

The other guy shook his head no. "I was told not to get too interested in her. I did as I was told."

"Because you're all about following orders."

"Screw you."

Bolan ignored the guy and considered his options. Finding her without an address would take too long. And, even if he or the Farm could track down an address, there was no guarantee she'd be there. He was silent for a few seconds, considering his options when an idea occurred to him.

"What's her number?"

Denver's brow furrowed and he seemed to be thinking about it.

"Yeah, I have the number."

"What is it?"

"Hold on a second," the other guy said. "I've been telling you everything you want to know. Now it's my turn."

Bolan said nothing.

Denver continued. "I want to make a trade. You want the number. I want to live. I'll give you the number and you let me live. I'll forget I ever saw you or that we had this conversation. I have to. If the Germans find out I told you something, they'd bury me up to my neck in the desert and slather my head with honey."

"Seems reasonable," Bolan stated.

"So you see where I'm coming from? Good. I don't want any trouble. If you want to go find your friends, fine. You and I don't have a beef with one another, right?"

"The number."

Denver said it once then, at Bolan's prompting, repeated it.

Bolan raised the pistol and aimed it at the other man. Denver's jaw gaped.

"What the hell?" he said, his voice taut with fear. "We had an agreement! You said if I gave you the number, you'd let me live."

"No," Bolan said. "I said it was a reasonable request. I never agreed to it."

"Son of a..."

"You hear those sounds coming from the other room?" Bolan asked. After a couple of heartbeats he continued. "Yeah, me neither. The woman in there was terrified, hysterical. But after a few minutes she went completely silent. That should seem odd except that I saw the small glass vial under the couch. I'm guessing you put that in her drink, right?"

A bewildered smile tugged at Denver's lips.

"Hey," he said, "I'm just looking to have a little fun. Hell, c'mon man. She's a hooker." He forced a laugh. "I'm just trying to get my money's worth."

"Wrong answer," the soldier said quietly.

Denver made a desperation play. He grabbed up a glass and tossed it at Bolan's head. The soldier jerked his head to one side to avoid the projectile. A microsecond later Denver was on his feet and lunging for Bolan.

The Beretta sneezed a single Parabellum round, opening a hole in the Denver's left temple.

CHAPTER THIRTY-TWO

Grimaldi cracked one eye open and tried to size up his situation. He was lying on his right side, on bare concrete, where he'd been dumped while unconscious. He was surrounded by stacked shipping crates. Moving with deliberate slowness, he tried to move his hands and feet and found them bound with something. For some reason, they hadn't bothered gagging him. Pain throbbed at the back of his skull.

From behind, he heard two men speaking German. He had no idea how long he'd been unconscious. He had fleeting memories of being thrown in a van, followed by more darkness.

He wasn't sure whether Rodriguez was in the room with him. At this point, he was trying to remain as still as possible. Right now, they assumed he was out cold and probably paid him scant attention, which gave him time to think. Once he started moving, they'd descend on him, maybe move him somewhere else or torture him. He doubted they were going to kill him—yet—otherwise, why drag him here?

The squeak of a door swinging on its hinges sounded from somewhere else in the building. An instant later the pilot heard the clicking of shoes against the floor. The clicking grew louder with each passing moment until it sounded loud enough to be within a few feet of him.

The two men muttered greetings. A female voice rattled off something in German and, sounding like chastened children, the men replied, "Jawohl." More footsteps came in his direction. Grimaldi caught a trace of perfume followed by a fiery pain in his lower back. He inhaled sharply, groaned and rolled onto his back, both eyes now wide open.

He saw a woman staring down at him. She was pretty except for the glint of psychosis in her eyes. He glanced over behind her and saw Rodriguez also lying on the floor, her hands and feet secured with duct tape. With her face turned in his direction, Grimaldi could see her eyes were closed and her lips were parted slightly.

Two big men—both dressed in blue denim jeans and black T-shirts—were walking away from Rodriguez's inert form. One of the guys, Frick, had blond hair combed back off his forehead, while Frack had field-mouse brown hair, the bangs cut straight across his bulging forehead. The blond guy carried a Benelli shotgun while the other guy had a pair of pistols stowed in a dual shoulder rig.

"Bitch," he gritted.

She smiled.

"You should have killed my hirelings instead of merely knocking them out," she said. "It would have saved me from having to tie up that loose end. Be happy I haven't killed you."

"I'm ecstatic," he said. "Sorry, should I call you Ms. Bitch?"

A lopsided smile formed on her lips.

"Dagmar is fine," she said.

She slid a hand into the pocket of her shorts and pulled out a folding knife. She held it up, shook it just slightly. "You know what this is?"

"Hey, my knife," Grimaldi said. "Thanks for finding it."

Unfolding the blade, she turned, walked a few steps and knelt at his hips. She raised the knife over her head like some psycho from a grade-B movie and plunged the blade at his crotch. Grimaldi tensed his body and clamped his jaws shut.

The point of the blade stopped an inch shy of his body.

She turned her head. With her eyes half closed, she ran the tip of her tongue over her teeth. "So close," she said. "Perhaps next time I will not stop."

"If you really want it," Grimaldi told her, "you could just ask."

"You think you are funny, yes?"

"No," the Stony Man warrior said, "I think you're crazy." He jerked his head at the two men who were standing behind her. Their bulky bodies seemed to block out the glow from the overhead lights. "Frick and Frack think you're crazy, too. They're just too scared to tell you."

She pursed her lips at him and her eyes narrowed.

Hopped up on adrenaline, Grimaldi decided to push the needle a little further.

"They're too nice to say anything," he said. "But I heard them talking before you arrived."

She pushed the point of the knife gently into the fabric of his jeans and traced a small circle around his crotch.

"We'll see about that," she said.

She drew herself to her full height, maneuvered the knife blade in the air in a small circle before spinning on her heel and crossing the floor. She stopped halfway between Rodriguez's body and Grimaldi, threw him a look over her shoulder and smiled.

"Obviously, I can't break you. You're too tough." She turned her gaze from him and started again for the unconscious FBI agent. "Your friend here's tough, too. But it's much harder to fight back when you're unconscious."

She stopped a foot away from Rodriguez. Pulling her foot back, she fired off a kick that hammered against Rodriguez's ribs. The woman moaned, her face contorting in pain, but her eyes remained closed.

"We drugged her with a very powerful tranquilizer. I could cut her hand off and she wouldn't wake up."

"Wow. Look, I'm sure a psychologist would have a field day with you. More fun than me, if that's possible. But how about you spare me the 'Hey, I'm homicidal' act?"

The lopsided smile came back and Grimaldi wondered if he'd pushed her too far.

He got his answer.

She knelt next to Rodriguez.

"Hey, now..." he said.

She pulled her hand back and drove the knife into Rodriguez's thigh, then gave it a twist.

The agent moaned again, and he thought he heard a small sob gurgle up from her throat, almost like a sleeping person reacting to a bad dream.

Gabriele yanked the knife from the agent's leg, leaving a ragged line of blood drops along the concrete. She raised the blade in front of her face, turned and studied it, seemingly fascinated with the light gleaming on the blood-covered blade.

"Nice," she said.

The blade stabbed down a second time. A protest welled up in Grimaldi's throat, but he held back when he saw she just was wiping the blade clean on Rodriguez's pant leg. She reached for Rodriguez's face and grazed her fingertips along the other woman's cheek.

"So much fun I'm going to have with you," she said.

She rose again and returned to Grimaldi's side, knelt and poised the blade an inch from his right eye.

"Let's chat," she said.

"The people who hired me," Gabriele said, "know so little about you and your friends. They want me to change that."

"We're kind of a secret society," Grimaldi replied.

She nodded. "Of course, you are. But as you've seen, I

can get people to open up to me. Now, who are you with? Are you FBI like this woman?"

Grimaldi shrugged. "Something like that. Look, she's bleeding over there."

"I know. It's terrible, isn't it? If only someone would do something about it. Maybe like you. Who are you with?"

"You said it yourself. We're FBI. You searched my pockets, right? So you saw I had Department of Justice credentials."

She nodded slowly. "I saw them," she said. "But, I don't know. I'm having trouble believing you. I mean, the FBI, they are—what's the word? Boy Scouts. You and your friend—the other man. What's his name?"

"Cooper."

"Ah, Cooper. He's killed a lot of people. He moves from continent to continent. He kills with impunity. That doesn't seem like FBI behavior to me."

"He's sort of a maverick."

She hesitated for a couple of beats, then gave a weird laugh. "You, Jack Williamson, are a funny man. Very funny." Her expression morphed into a pout. "But you're not honest. If I had more time, I might want to play this game with you. But my boss is a prick and I need answers now. You understand?"

Grimaldi nodded.

His eyes drifted past the German woman to Rodriguez. The darkness around the knife wound had spread, covering the fabric with a blossom-shaped bloodstain. Blood also had begun to seep onto the floor. He tried to run things quickly through his mind. Blood wasn't spurting from the wound, which was good. But she still couldn't bleed like that forever. He turned his eyes back to Gabriele.

"Patch her up, then we talk."

"You are confused. Tell me what I want to know, then I'll patch her up."

"Call it a good-faith measure."

"Call it a nonstarter."

He knew the woman was lying, but she had more leverage than him. The longer he held out, the more blood Rodriguez lost. Gabriele wanted the information, but she had time on her side.

The pilot scowled. "Okay. Here's the real story."

CHAPTER THIRTY-THREE

Seated at the wheel of the brown van, Danny Bertke dumped his cigarette into a half-empty cup of coffee. The butt hit the cold liquid and died with a hiss. Waving the cloud of cigarette smoke from his face, he turned and studied the image on the laptop that rested on the van's passenger seat. A small camera fixed to the van's roof was feeding into the computer, allowing him to watch a squat office building at his six.

His eyes flickered to the time stamp. He frowned. The target would be here in five minutes. If he was dumb enough to show. Bertke had his doubts. If the guy was as good as everyone said, he wasn't going to walk into a trap, even to save his friends. Or he'd swoop in with a million cops and federal agents and turn the whole thing into one big cluster.

Bertke dipped his hand to the floor, grabbed up the mini-Uzi resting there and laid it across his lap. If the cops came, he'd already decided to go out in a proverbial blaze of glory. As far as he was concerned, they were his enemy. So were federal agents, judges, prosecutors and anyone he believed was looking to infringe on his freedom.

He'd spent two years in the Army as an infantryman. He'd joined for the combat training, but had been okay with going to Afghanistan to take out the Taliban. The way he saw it, shooting those bastards would be good training for when the blacks went crazy in America and launched an all-out race war on the whites. Unlike some so-called

"Americans," he knew a war was imminent and wanted to be ready to kill the enemy.

Then the government had assigned him to work with a black sergeant. He'd tried to put up with the bastard person yelling at him and ordering him around. But a proud man such as himself could take only so much shit before he lost it. One day the sergeant had caught him sleeping on guard duty, had screamed at him and said maybe he should "crawl back home to his momma."

Bertke could tolerate a lot, but not a black man speaking of his mother. Once the sergeant had turned away, Bertke had thrown a punch that had caught the other man in the jaw and knocked him to the ground. After that, things got a little hazy. The guy had hit him back more than once, landing blows on his abdomen. To this day, Bertke swore someone had held his arms, they'd had to have. Otherwise, he would've fought back.

The whole thing ended with Bertke being tossed from the service. With a dishonorable discharge on his record, he'd found it hard to score a job. Then he'd met Thomas Denver and considered it a gift from the Almighty. The guy had hired him for some uniformed gigs first, guarding warehouses or office buildings. After a while, though, Denver had seen Bertke was made of bigger stuff. Denver had spotted the swastika tattooed on his upper right arm and asked him about it. At first, Bertke assumed he was going to lose his job, but Denver had seemed more interested than incensed, asking him several questions and agreeing with him on most of the points he made.

The next thing he knew, he was hired full time and being shuttled off to the desert for weeks of training, nearly all of it by German nationals.

The trainers were tight-lipped most of the time. However, they had told him he was going to "take the fight to the enemy." That was all he'd needed to know. He'd stopped asking questions and doubled down on his work.

Being barred from the raid had burned his ass. Seeing how it turned out so badly, though, he now considered it a good thing. He could've been among the patriots slaughtered at the ranch. Now, he was going to avenge his comrades. He'd be a hero.

Someone tapped on the driver's window, startling him. He turned to see to a man standing outside the vehicle, his upper body wrapped in a tattered coat. A misshapen fedora was pulled over his head, covering his eyes. His face, smeared with black dirt, was filthy.

Bertke was so mad he could spit. A bum. Probably a kook, too, since he was wearing a trench coat in the 90-plus-degree heat.

He tried to ignore the guy, but the ragged son of a bitch kept rapping on the glass. He rolled down the window and immediately smelled a nauseating mixture of alcohol and excrement.

"Get the hell out of here," he ordered.

"I ran out of gas," the guy stated. He pointed east. "It's on the highway. Dead. I got no money."

"Get the hell out of here," Bertke repeated.

"I need gas."

"Oh, yeah? Where the hell's your gas can?"

The guy weaved on his feet. "My wife and kid are on the highway. They need help."

"Well, go help them."

"I need money."

"I said go. What's the matter with you?"

Bertke felt his face and neck burning hot and his left hand was clenching into a fist.

"Are you deaf? I said go."

"My wife and kids…"

That tore it for Bertke. He set the Uzi on the floor, thrust open the door and extended one leg outside, ready to set it on the cracked asphalt.

In a heartbeat the bum straightened, came around the open car door and jammed a pistol under Bertke's jawline.

He froze.

"Move," the bum said.

As the guard backed into the van, Bolan followed him inside. With the Beretta's muzzle, he gestured toward the back of the windowless vehicle. Fortunately, his target was portly and had pushed his seat as far back as possible from the steering wheel. That gave Bolan the room he needed to slide into the seat, slam the door and grab the Uzi lying on the floor and train it on its owner.

"Turn and go to the back of the van," Bolan said.

Sliding out of the seat, the soldier ducked his head and followed the other man deeper into the van. Along the way, he relieved the guy of a Glock 19 that was holstered in the small of his back. He slid the handgun into the pocket of his ragged overcoat.

"If this is a robbery…"

"Shut up," Bolan said.

"I don't have any money."

"It's not a robbery," Bolan replied. "I was invited here. Maybe someone mentioned I'd be coming."

Bolan heard the other man swear under his breath.

"Exactly," Bolan said. "You're screwed."

"Uh-uh. You're screwed, buddy. You know how many people they have waiting inside the building for you?"

"No," Bolan said. "You're going to tell me, though."

"I'm not telling you…"

The Beretta dispatched a single round that drilled into the man's thigh. He screamed and rolled onto his butt, grabbing protectively at his leg.

"Fourteen," the guy said through clenched teeth.

"Now we're off to a good start," Bolan replied.

MINUTES LATER BOLAN slid open the van door and stepped from the vehicle. He'd shed the hat and the overcoat, using the latter to cover the body of the man inside the van. Bolan had gotten a few answers, but the guy had pulled a knife and lunged at Bolan, forcing the soldier to open a third eye in the guy's forehead.

Stepping onto the sidewalk, Bolan took a frag grenade from one of his pouches, pulled the pin and tossed the bomb inside. Slamming the door, he ran into a nearby alley.

A couple of seconds later he heard a muffled explosion as the grenade blew, followed by a second blast as the flames burned into the gas tank.

A pair of small industrial buildings stood next to the building where Bolan was supposed to meet with the caller. He ducked into an alley that stretched between them and jogged through it. He then glided along the rear of the building closest to his target, occasionally ducking underneath windows along the way. He guessed the explosion would attract the attention of the gunners waiting for him. Most would move to the front of the building to get a look at the flaming van.

At least one or two might even rush to it to see whether the driver could be helped.

Bolan hit the throat mike.

"Striker to Base," Bolan said.

"Go, Striker," Price replied.

"The Phoenix Fire Department might get a call from my location."

"Okay."

"I blew up a van."

"Okay," Price said. Bolan thought he heard a hint of amusement in her voice.

"Tell them to hang back. Same goes for the police. Best I can tell, the neighboring buildings are empty. There's no reason for them to get close."

"Understood," Price replied.

"Did you get a satellite window?" Bolan asked.

"Right," Price said. "It's running an infrared scan on the building. It looks like you have three guys on the roof and six more on the top floor."

A fire escape ran up the side of the building at Bolan's back. He jumped, grabbed the bottom rung of a ladder and climbed up, relying on the steely muscles of his back and arms to pull him up until he could set a foot on the bottom rung.

He continued to climb until he reached the third-floor landing. Bending at the knees, he sprang up until he could reach a parapet bordering the roof. He grabbed it and pulled himself up until he could hook his left leg over the edge of the roof.

He went over the side and landed on the rooftop in a crouch.

On the neighboring building, Bolan saw three men on the roof. Two of them had moved to the edge to see what was happening. The third guy, an assault rifle canted at a downward angle, hung several yards back from the other two and was scanning their surroundings for threats.

Bolan brought around the M-4 and lined up a shot at the guy watching for problems, since he seemed the most alert. Once gunfire rang out, the other two men would have to switch their attention from the fire, wrap their minds around the idea they were under attack, locate Bolan and begin firing on him. If they were pros, it might take them a second or two, time Bolan could use to his advantage in a firefight.

The M-4 cracked and a bullet punched into the right eyeball of his target, spinning the man. The soldier whipped the rifle to his left and took down the second man with two shots to center mass. As that guy folded to the ground, the third shooter was watching his partner crumple to the ground and raising his machine pistol. The weapon cracked one more time, catching the guy in center mass and killing him.

Bolan moved up to the edge of his building and checked the distance between it and the other structure. Even with a good running start before he jumped, he'd still only bridge about half the distance between him and the other roof. Instead, the soldier went down the fire escape, ran to the other building and moved around back. While the fire had provided a distraction, Bolan guessed the sound of gunshots would cause the people in the building to react. A team leader would try to raise the roof sentries on his radio, fail and send a couple of guys up to check it out, unless they had a video feed from the roof team.

Maybe they'd redeploy to the entrances.

That meant Bolan had to get into the building first.

The building had two back doors. The soldier moved to the nearer one and tried the handle, but found it was locked. A card reader was attached to the wall next to the door. From his pants' pocket, he took out the security card he'd liberated from the guy in the van, slid it through the reader and the bolt snapped back with a thunk.

Stowing the M-4, he fisted the Beretta and slipped inside. Just as he finished easing the door closed, a hardman appeared. When he saw Bolan, his mouth opened with surprise and a lit cigarette tumbled from his lips. If he had something to say, it died in his throat. The Beretta pumped three shots into the man's chest. The bullets punched through the man's sternum and ribs, rent his internal organs and tapped red geysers of blood.

Four down, ten to go.

Assuming Bolan's friend in the van had told him the truth.

From what the guy had said, the whole idea had been
to draw Bolan here to kill him. The guy footing the bills
wanted to know more about the people who'd derailed his
plans. But he'd decided Bolan—or Cooper—was too dangerous to try to take alive. He'd sent a hastily assembled
kill squad here to assassinate Bolan. Apparently he had
assumed correctly—that Bolan would go anywhere, put
himself in peril to help his friends.

Score one for the bad guy.

Unfortunately for him, though, he'd missed the other
lesson—luring Bolan somewhere and killing him were
two different things. So the guy pulling the strings had
Bolan. Lucky him.

The soldier moved through two more rooms, gunning
down two hardmen as he moved along. Feeding a fresh
magazine into the Beretta, he holstered it and took up
the M-4 again. The soldier reached another interior door,
pressed himself against a wall and hesitated. Peering into
the room at an angle, he could see a large cabinet with
glass doors. It was set at an angle and he could see the
faint reflection of a man in a red shirt pointing a rifle at
the doorway.

Reaching into a pouch, Bolan pulled out a flash-bang
grenade, yanked the pin and tossed the bomb into the other
room. It banged against the floor, catching everybody's
attention. An instant later it burst with a white flash and
a loud crack.

Bolan moved into the room where he found three men
waiting for him. Red Shirt had turned a heavy wooden
table on its side to use for cover. His head was visible
over the edge of the tabletop, his hands over his eyes as he
waited to regain his senses. Bolan burned the guy down
with a spray from the M-4. He wheeled to his left and took
down a second guy with a burst to the chest. A third guy,
this one holding a machine pistol aimed at nothing, took

a step forward. He was rewarded for his initiative with a punishing burst from the M-4 that shredded his chest and tore apart his heart muscle.

Nine down.

He searched the rest of the lower floor, but found it was just him and the corpses.

The shooters upstairs apparently thought it was best to wait for him. Bolan saw no option but to oblige.

He found an elevator, stepped inside and pressed the button for the second floor.

JAMES MILLER HEARD the elevator doors close on the floor below.

Turning, Miller, the team leader, gestured for the others to fan out and wait. They complied, spreading into a ragged line and aiming their weapons at the elevator doors.

Miller watched the first floor light go dark. His mind was racing and he was fighting like hell to stay focused. He'd been warned their target was a damn war machine. Initially he'd thought it was an exaggeration, maybe a way for those German pricks to rationalize how badly they'd screwed up the last operation. Now he was convinced they'd told the truth. The guy had gotten past several of his men, but Miller and the rest of his team were experienced gunners, ready to rain down death on the guy. They had him outmanned and outgunned.

Still, Miller, a former U.S. Army Ranger who'd turned mercenary, could feel his heart slamming in his chest. He was scared and it felt like hell.

The doors slid open.

"Fire!" he yelled.

Gunfire erupted in the large waiting room. Swarms of steel-jacketed slugs stabbed through the space between the doors and into the elevator car. Brass shell casings rained to the floor while bullets chewed apart the elevator's interior, fouling the air with shards of particle board, plastic and gun smoke.

Even before the last shooter emptied a magazine, Miller saw something that made his blood run cold.

The car was empty.

Son of a bitch. It was a distraction. He was probably using the stairs.

He ejected the Steyr's magazine and grabbed for a fresh one. A glance right told him the other guys were pawing through their pockets or snapping fresh magazines into their weapons.

As he pulled the magazine free, he peered through the haze of gun smoke and saw a dark figure fall from the top of the elevator and land in a crouch.

Then something hot drilled into his eye socket and everything went black.

THE EXECUTIONER SWEPT the flaming M-4 back and forth in a tight arc. His weapon churned out an unforgiving blast of bullets. The rounds lanced through the veil of smoke hanging between Bolan and his targets, chopping down two shooters in the span of a heartbeat.

Coming through the door in a crouch, the soldier whipped the M-4 at a shooter and tapped out a burst that took the guy down with a clear shot through the eye. Gunshots whistled over Bolan's head, missing him by inches. He threw himself forward just before another volley of bullets tore through the air where he'd crouched an instant before. The soldier rolled onto his side and raised his weapon. It rattled through the last few rounds in the magazine. The bullets caught his opponent in the arm, forcing the guy to release his hold on his submachine gun.

The wounded man began clawing at a pistol holstered on his hip. At the same time, Bolan tossed aside the M-4 and grabbed for the Desert Eagle stowed in a thigh holster.

The Executioner cleared leather a microsecond before the hardman. The Desert Eagle thundered. The .44 Magnum slug punched into the man's shoulder and the joint seemed to disintegrate in a spray of red. A mercy round from the Israeli-made pistol slammed into the man's chest and took him out of the fight forever.

Holstering the Desert Eagle, Bolan fed a new magazine into the M-4 and charged the weapon.

He'd taken down twelve hardmen. Moving to the stairs, he climbed them slowly. If any more of Vogelsgang's troops were roaming around, they'd apparently decided staying put was the best option.

The Executioner paused on the third-floor landing, the M-4 clutched in both hands. He waited a half minute or so for any sounds, but heard nothing on the other side. A small rectangular window on the door offered him only a limited view. Pressing his hip against the door's release bar, he pushed it down and used his body weight to fan the door inward. The opening led into a small lobby that was almost identical to the one found on the second floor.

He let his hand fall away from the M-4's foregrip and used it to ease the door closed behind him. The lobby was empty of furniture. The medium blue carpet was ripped in places. Black circular stains had formed on the carpet, and the faint smell of mildew hung in the air. Considering Phoenix's dry climate, Bolan had to assume the water damage had come from a burst pipe instead of from a leaky roof.

The soldier brought the M-4 to his shoulder and crept through the lobby, past a built-in reception station and into a hallway. Mixed in with the mildew, Bolan smelled traces of cologne in the air. The smell was strong enough that Bolan guessed the person wearing it had been there within the last few minutes.

Bolan had studied the building's plans before ever stepping foot into it. He knew there was a second stairwell and elevator on the opposite side of the building from where he was standing. It was possible the last couple of shooters had decided to skip their payday and retreat. Possible, but Bolan wasn't optimistic. More likely he was going to have to take them out, too.

Bolan had walked a dozen steps when his combat senses started nagging him. He turned and saw a man poking out from a doorway behind him. The guy's arm was extended, and he was lining up a shot at Bolan's back.

The weapon roared once. In the same instant the Executioner threw himself to the side. He felt the slug tug at his shirt sleeve, but miss flesh. The M-4 in his hands ground out a short burst. The rounds caught the guy in the hip and chewed a vertical line up his torso. He stumbled back a step, a shocked look etched on his face, and hit the other side of the door frame before collapsing.

More bullets sizzled just past Bolan's ear.

He wheeled. Another shooter had emerged from behind one of the other doors and was trying to nail Bolan with a pistol. The Executioner's assault rifle ground out a line of 5.56 mm ammo that hammered into the wall near where he had seen the shooter. The man had slipped out of sight. Bolan kept up the pressure, hosing down the walls with short bursts from his rifle while he moved toward the last shooter's hiding place.

Bolan dropped one hand from the M-4 and snagged a frag grenade from one of his pouches.

Pulling the pin with his teeth, the soldier moved up to the door and tossed the weapon into the room, spun on his heel and ran.

Bolan counted the seconds. When he had run out the clock, he threw himself to the floor and slid several more feet from the blast site.

The grenade blew with a loud whump. The blast unleashed a swarm of bits of razor wire. Bolan heard the man inside the room cry out, but then go silent. The soldier hauled himself to his feet, moved to where the grenade had exploded and peered inside. He saw a man's remains sprawled on the floor. The skin of his neck, face and hands had been carved away by the blast, his clothes had been shredded. What remained was soaked in the man's blood.

CHAPTER THIRTY-FOUR

Three minutes after the final hardman died, Bolan was back on the street and walking past the twisted remains of the still-burning van.

On his way out of the building, the soldier had grabbed wallets and cell phones from a few of the dead men. He carried them in a small pouch. He could go through the wallets himself. He'd pass along the cell phones to the cyber team to download numbers called and received, contact lists and other information. Whether it would produce any useful intelligence was another matter.

He climbed into his rental car, fired up the engine and called Price.

Once they'd finished their greetings, he said, "It would probably be best to send in a clean-up crew."

"How many dead?" she asked.

Bolan told her fifteen, including the driver of the van.

"They may have to get creative," she said. "I don't think they can cart that many bodies out of there without anyone noticing."

"Understood," Bolan said. "We have some time before daylight. I'm guessing they'll want to make all this go away before the work crowd starts rolling in for the day."

"I'm on it. What's next?"

"Finding Jack and Rodriguez."

"A couple of prisoners might've helped on that score," Price said.

"Maybe," Bolan said. "The guy I questioned had no idea

what I was talking about. He said this whole thing had come together in a matter of hours. Most of the shooters here had trained for the raid on the ranch. The guys putting it together put a cap on the number of fighters. Some of these guys got left on the sidelines."

"Apparently that's where they should've stayed."

"Apparently."

"I may have a lead for you, though," Price said.

"I'm all ears."

"I have an address for you to plug in to your GPS."

"Go."

Price recited the address and he programmed it into the onboard GPS system.

"Where did this come from?"

"We ran Gabriele's name and came up with some background. Here in the United States, she really has no record at all. There's probably some analyst in the bowels of the CIA or NSA who tracks her. But she's not even a blip on the radar for the other alphabet soup agencies in our country, especially on the law-enforcement side."

"Okay."

"In other countries, especially Europe and Africa, our girl gets around. We're compiling a dossier on her..."

"Better just give me the highlights," Bolan said.

"Of course. She grew up in Berlin. Father was high up in the country's intelligence establishment. For a long time he was highly respected by the Americans and the Brits as a cold warrior. A lot of the work he did at the time still remains classified. I glanced through it. His record was impressive. He ran a lot of operations in East Germany against the Communists.

"Gabriele's mother came from wealth and was well connected within Europe's elite. Her status is surprising when you consider how the family made its money."

"Adult films? Brothels?"

"Very funny. No, apparently her father and grandfather had been industrialists in Germany for decades. They'd started with a small machine shop and built it into a major manufacturing concern that generated big money for them. During World War One, they lost a big chunk of the business, especially when it came to exporting goods. They took another hit with the Great Depression. When Hitler's rise to power began, the family saw the writing on the wall and decided to cover their asses by throwing their support—especially their money—behind Hitler and the Nazis. The great-grandfather even acted as an unofficial consultant for the Nazis when it came to industrial policy, especially building the manufacturing capacity necessary to fuel a war machine."

"Good old grandpa," Bolan said.

"He was a survivor," Price replied. "After the war, the same guy who'd been licking Hitler's boots offered up his services to the Allies when it came time to rebuild Germany. Here's a shock. His motives weren't altruistic. A lot of the policies he suggested ended up benefiting his own interests. There was suspicion of graft and a few inquiries, but nothing ever stuck. Make of that what you will. Of course when the Russians came on strong after the war, he was willing to fight back both because he held a grudge from the war and, to his credit, he opposed communism. It was his clout that helped his son-in-law move up in the country's fledgling intelligence network."

"Was Gabriele's father a Nazi?"

Price paused and Bolan could hear her tapping some keys on the other end of the line.

"No," she said. "He was a child during the war, the son of a ghetto tailor and a stay-at-home mother. He was extremely intelligent, a natural-born engineer. He ended up working for his future father-in-law while going to night school to become an engineer."

"And he married the boss's daughter."

"Right. They stayed childless for a long time. Apparently she couldn't get pregnant for some reason. But they did adopt Dagmar late in life. She had been moving through the foster-care system for years. According to the intelligence reports we tapped, she had some, um, anger issues. She stabbed one of the workers and tried to smother a crying baby. The orphanage neglected to mention those issues to Momma and Poppa Gabriele when they went to adopt her. Once the proud patents discovered her problems, they decided to stick with her and try to get her some help. It never took, obviously."

Bolan saw a red light ahead and tapped the brake to slow the car. A quick glance at the trip counter told him he'd put about two miles between himself and the industrial park.

"Since we're talking about her, I'm guessing she only got worse," Bolan said.

"Yeah, our lives don't intersect with the sane ones too much, do they?"

"Not too much." The light turned green and Bolan stomped the accelerator.

"While the parents didn't exactly desert her, they did spend a lot of time doing other things. He worked like crazy, while she spent a lot of time on philanthropic causes. That meant little Dagmar was left with hired caregivers a lot. And, unfortunately, her great-grandfather."

"The Nazi sympathizer."

"That's the one."

"Perfect."

"Grandpa wasn't a prize when he was young. As an old man, he apparently spent a lot of time ranting about how much better things were in Germany under Hitler, about the inferiority of non-whites and non-Christians, all the usual crap these people spew. Complicating matters,

Grandpa also was a pedophile who made a habit of sexually abusing Dagmar as a young girl."

"That proved to be the old man's downfall," Price said.

"They threw the old bastard into a home away from kids?"

Bolan heard Price sigh wearily. "Unfortunately, no. The parents stayed so busy, they were unaware of what was happening in their mansion. And once they learned the truth, they didn't do anything. Two of Dagmar's caregivers blew the whistle over the years. The first used the information to blackmail the family. They paid and the secret stayed under wraps until she got busted for blackmailing another employer years later.

"A second nanny tried to do the right thing. She threatened to go to the authorities. The mother—Mrs. Philanthropy—conked the woman in the head with a vase, knocked her unconscious in front of Dagmar, panicked and fled the room. This little attack on her mother's part apparently mystified the girl. She picked up two more vases and finished the job. When her mother returned, she found little Dagmar kneeling next to the corpse. Her hands, arms, face and clothes were smeared with the woman's blood."

"And we know all this how?"

"She told the story to a prison psychologist years later—after she'd been picked up for two more homicides, each messier than the last. Here's where it gets weird," Price said.

"Because the rest of the story's so pedestrian."

Price ignored the comment. "She was extremely smart and had a gift for languages. When she wasn't braining people, she learned four different languages, including Russian and English. This caught the eye of some intelligence bureaucrat in Germany who thought he had a great idea—a beautiful young woman who likes to kill people and speaks multiple languages."

"Why not make her an assassin?"

"Bingo."

"Because psychopaths are so easy to control."

"The project failed, obviously. It blew up in the guy's face. Dagmar Gabriele was happy to kill people. She didn't even mind being told which people to kill. But a girl sometimes can't help herself. She'd go rogue and kill someone just because she wanted to. Eventually, the government gave her the boot. It was a no-fault divorce where everyone went their separate ways—sort of."

"Sort of?"

"The bureaucrat who started this whole project? It was Friedhelm Geiger. He'd been brought in from the field to create the perfect assassin. He didn't want to see his little creation just disappear into the world. He kept in touch with her. I don't have good confirmation on this, but supposedly she helped on a couple of his mercenary gigs. Her specialty was getting close to high-value targets, like generals or politicians, and taking them out."

"And now she has Jack and Rodriguez."

"Yes, I'm sorry, Striker."

"I know. Where did the address come from?"

"Dagmar has a couple of guys she travels with. They're on some watch lists in the U.S. and other countries. They know that, so they travel under aliases. What they didn't realize is NSA figured out one of their aliases a few months back. They have the cell phone number, credit cards and other information for that alias. The guy fired up his phone about an hour ago, a few blocks from your present location."

"Send me any other information you have," Bolan said.

"Already did."

The pouch of phones Bolan had taken from some of Vogelsgang's other fighters lay on the front passenger's seat. One of them began to ring.

"Gotta go," he said, ending the call with Price.

Grabbing the pouch, he turned it upside down, dumped the contents on the seat and searched through the phones until he found the one ringing.

The word "restricted" flashed on the screen. Bolan pushed the Talk button and brought the phone to his ear, but stayed silent.

"Hello?" a man said. Bolan recognized him as the guy who'd called him at the hotel.

"Hello," the soldier said.

The guy went silent for several seconds.

"You're alive," he said.

"Yeah," Bolan said.

"My people?"

"Dead. All of them."

"You're formidable," the other man said. "I'll give you that."

"I'm formidable and you're screwed," the Executioner repeated. "You had a bad idea, you took a shot at it and you failed. Pretty soon half the world's going to be looking for you. You're going to end up with a bullet in the brain."

"You sound confident."

"You're going to end up dead," Bolan said. "But here's the beauty of it. That's just the end game. Hell, that will be sweet relief for you."

Bolan paused, but the other man said nothing. After a few seconds the soldier started up again, his voice calm.

"You think you got at me by taking my friends? I can get at you, too. Take your money? Kill those around you? Destroy every building you own. Take your pick, I can do it."

"You would do these things, even with your friends at risk?"

"No," Bolan said. "Before I would've just killed you.

Now I'm going to destroy you. Enjoy the wait. You'll never see it coming."

Vogelsgang started to say something. Bolan terminated the call. The phone rang and he ignored it. It was a risky gambit on his part. From what he could tell, Vogelsgang was thin-skinned and privileged, a man used to wallowing in unearned respect.

Bolan didn't shoot off his mouth for bravado or to make himself feel better. He did it with a specific goal in mind. Treating Vogelsgang like dirt would unnerve him; probably make him wary of Bolan. At some level, it might even make him full-on afraid of the warrior. Unnerve or scare him enough and the guy would do something stupid. The play wasn't without risks. Would it piss him off enough that he'd kill Grimaldi and Rodriguez? Bolan hoped not. Though there'd been many casualties on Bolan's side in his War Everlasting, at his core he would rather have taken a bullet than let harm come to someone else.

Life didn't always work that way, especially on the battlefield. The soldier could hope for the best, but he had to keep moving forward.

"HELLO?" VOGELSGANG SAID into the phone. "Hello?"

No one answered. The son of a bitch had hung up on him. On him. The German felt his stomach clench and his face grow hot with anger. Goddamn American. He called Cooper again, but the damn guy didn't bother to pick up.

He dialed Gabriele, who answered quickly.

"It's me," he said.

"Okay."

"Gather up your new toys," he said. "You're bringing them here. Things have changed."

"Changed? How?"

"The American is alive."

"I thought your people were going to deal with him."

"He dealt with them instead. Look, don't argue with me. I have people arranging a flight out of there for you. Just sit tight for a few hours and I'll call you."

"A few hours? Why so long?"

"I need to line up someone I trust to fly you out. I know a couple of charter services that are used to moving illicit cargo."

Gabriele giggled at that.

"I've certainly never been called that before."

"Shut up. Shut up and listen. I'll line up the transportation. You stay put. And I want those two kept alive—at least for now. They may come in handy if we need to bargain with this man."

CHAPTER THIRTY-FIVE

Grimaldi watched as the woman turned off her cell phone and set it on a nearby table. She turned toward him and flashed a smile that made an icy sensation race down his spine.

"We're going to travel, my friend," she said.

"Yippee," Grimaldi replied.

The German woman pouted and moved closer to Grimaldi. "Now, now. It will be fun. We're going to the beach." Her eyes dipped from his and roamed over his body. "If you're good, maybe you can see me in my swimsuit."

"Enticing. Does it have cartoon animals on it, crazy lady?"

The lust evaporated from her eyes. They narrowed and radiated cold rage. Her full lips morphed from a smile into a thin, red gash.

"Oops," Grimaldi said brightly. "Wrong thing to say?"

She buried a fist into the pilot's stomach, driving it upward at an angle. It collided with his diaphragm and knocked the air from his lungs. She followed up with a left roundhouse that struck his jaw, whipping his head to one side even as he struggled to catch his breath. He never saw the leg sweep she used to put him on the floor. He just felt his body plummet to the floor. She stared down at him for several seconds before the smile returned, even if the eyes continued to beam hatred at him.

"Sensitive topic I guess," Grimaldi said.

She knelt next to him. Pressing the tip of her index finger gently against his chest, she again began tracing random shapes on his chest and abdomen. Her stare reminded him of a dog eyeing a steak, ravenous and focused.

"You said the wrong thing."

Reaching into a pocket, she pulled out the knife she'd used to stab Rodriguez, unfolded it and waved the sharp edge inches from Grimaldi's face.

"I'm going to make you wish you'd never said that."

"I think I'm already there."

"No, you're not even close. Not yet."

One of her hardmen cleared his throat. She paused and threw him an irritated look.

"What?" she snapped.

"We need to bring them alive."

"He'll be alive," she said. She turned her gaze back to Grimaldi. "You'll be alive," she said. "You might be missing some pieces, but you'll be alive."

A CHAIN-LINK fence ran along the back of the property. Bolan moved up to it and dropped to one knee, looking around for any signs of motion sensors or other alarms. When he didn't see any, he climbed up and over the fence in a matter of seconds. He'd already driven around the block once before parking the rental car out of sight. He spotted one guy walking around the grounds. He assumed the man was a sentry, though he couldn't see any weapons.

He rose to his feet and, moving in a crouch, crossed the faded asphalt parking lot that surrounded the warehouse. Just before he reached the building, he heard the footsteps of someone moving along the warehouse's perimeter. Blending into the shadows, he pressed his back against the building and waited as the footsteps grew louder. Bolan already had the Beretta in his left hand. With his right hand, he withdrew a Taser stun gun and aimed it at the corner of the structure.

He guessed whoever was patrolling the grounds was one of Vogelsgang's people, but he couldn't be sure. Since the German tycoon owned the building, it was possible he employed a night watchman at the grounds to protect the place from vandals. It could even be a cop moonlighting to make a little extra money.

Just in case, he'd decided to use non-lethal force until he entered the building.

After that, all bets were off.

The man rounded the corner, a flashlight clutched in his right hand. Since his eyes were focused on the space between the building and the fence, he didn't see the Executioner hiding in the darkness. The soldier triggered the stun gun. The probes buried themselves in the guy's chest and the weapon churned out enough volts to knock the guy unconscious.

Kneeling next to the guy, the soldier sifted through the man's pockets, where he found a wallet, a half-empty carton of cigarettes and two pistol magazines. The guy was wearing a black short-sleeved sport shirt over a dark red T-shirt. The tails of the guy's shirt had fallen away to reveal a pistol holstered on his belt. Bolan stowed the pistol and magazines in one of the extra pockets of his combat blacksuit, figuring Grimaldi might need a weapon. He also found a ring with three keys on it in the guy's shirt pocket.

Bolan went around the corner until he reached a single door on the side of the building. The first key he tried didn't fit the lock, but the second one worked. He was inside the warehouse in seconds.

From where he stood, he saw Rodriguez lying on the floor. Her pant leg was stained dark, and he saw a bandage on her leg. He heard another woman's voice, the tone shrill, and assumed it was Gabriele.

Grimaldi was nowhere to be seen.

The soldier crossed the room, his eyes sweeping around for other guards. He heard the woman say, "You might be missing some pieces, but you'll be alive," and assumed she was speaking to Grimaldi. Bolan got his confirmation a second later when he heard the pilot reply, "Sweetie, if you want that body part, you're going to need a bigger knife."

Even under the circumstances, Bolan grinned. If the lady was waiting on Grimaldi to beg for mercy or to break, she had a hell of a long wait. The guy just didn't roll that way. An uneven line of stacked crates stood between Bolan and his quarry. He kept the crates between himself and the others while he moved in so they couldn't see him. Glancing around the corner of the crates, he took in the scene. Gabriele knelt next to Grimaldi, one hand flat on the pilot's chest, the other holding a wicked-looking knife. Her eyes shone with madness and her lips were peeled back in a menacing smile. Since Grimaldi was lying on his hands, Bolan assumed his wrists were bound in some way.

Gabriele's two thugs stood several feet away from her. One had his arms crossed over his chest. He was watching things unfold with a blank look on his face. A Benelli shotgun was leaning, muzzle up, against a crate.

The second guy was facing away from the others, studying the nails of his right hand. He was carrying a pistol of some kind in a shoulder rig.

Bolan emerged from cover, the Beretta extended in a two-handed grip, and went to work. The first triburst caught Mr. Nails in the side of the head. The second hardman saw his buddy's corpse weave back and forth, and dived for the shotgun. Bolan had anticipated the move. Moving just slightly at the waist, he tapped the Beretta's trigger and it unloaded a second burst. Two of the rounds opened small red holes in the guy's shirt as they drilled through his ribs and tore open his heart, killing him. By the time his corpse slapped against the floor, Bolan already was swinging the Beretta at Gabriele.

She froze.

"Stand up," Bolan ordered, "and drop the knife. Otherwise, I'll put you in the ground."

She pressed her lips together tightly and for a stretched second stared at Bolan. Finally she stood and tossed the knife.

Bolan wagged the Beretta's muzzle.

"Back away from him," he said. "Turn around and keep your hands up."

"Do it," the pilot said. "He's really possessive."

She took a couple of steps back, turned and kept her hands in plain sight.

Bolan moved to Grimaldi. Scooping up the knife along the way, he used it to cut his friend's wrists loose. The pilot brought his hands around and rubbed his wrists. Bolan handed him the knife so he could cut his legs loose.

Bolan nodded at Rodriguez. "Why is she so still?"

"Drugs," Grimaldi said. Hauling himself up from the floor, the pilot started for the injured FBI agent. He was limping slightly, and Bolan assumed the restraints had caused his feet to go numb.

"We're going to need an ambulance," Grimaldi said. "She lost some blood."

Bolan pulled the cell phone from his belt and slid it across the floor to the other man before turning his attention back to Gabriele.

"Where's Vogelsgang?" he asked.

She shrugged. "No idea."

"She's lying," Grimaldi said. "I heard her talking to him on the phone. He was going to send a plane for them, um, I mean us."

"Flight to where?" Bolan asked.

She shrugged. "No idea."

"We're going to find him," Bolan vowed.

"Good luck with that," she replied.

Gabriele wheeled left and dived for the Benelli shotgun propped against the crates. The Beretta chugged out three rounds, one of which caught her in midair, coring through her temple. She hit the ground in a heap, eyes locked open. Blood and brain matter leaked from the exit wound, staining the concrete.

"I'm not cleaning that up," Grimaldi said.

CHAPTER THIRTY-SIX

The Caribbean

Vogelsgang could hear ocean waves crashing against the beach through the open window of his office. Normally he'd enjoy the soothing sound, rhythmic and predictable, of the surf, along with the occasional screech of sea gulls. He'd mix himself a drink, take it to the window and enjoy deep breaths of the salt-tinged air.

This day was another matter.

This day, he was breathing the stench of defeat, tasting the bitterness of rage.

The American had derailed his efforts and had destroyed much of his infrastructure. The German glanced at the screen of his PC and re-read the headline.

German officials had raided his factories, shuttering them indefinitely. The newspaper indicated Vogelsgang had been targeted because of tax problems.

A nice cover story, he knew, and one he couldn't publicly repudiate. He was on the run from the Americans, the Europeans and probably the damned Israelis, too. Even though he'd never threatened the Israelis, he knew the Jews would come for him, given his connections with neo-Nazi groups. His persecutors could say anything they wanted about him and he'd have to take it. If he stuck his head up, he'd get it taken off, figuratively if not literally.

So here he was hiding in a beachfront property in the Caribbean. He'd bought the property a couple of decades ago. A long string of shell companies shrouded his ownership. He'd originally set it up that way for tax reasons, along with a network of overseas bank accounts. Now he was grateful to have a shield from the prying eyes of the world's intelligence and law-enforcement agencies.

It was a weak shield. When he'd established the elaborate networks that obscured his wealth, no one had been looking at him. Now he'd attracted all the wrong kinds of attention.

But he was changing things. Right now he had his accountants working hard to grab and move whatever of his money they could before someone else could snatch his assets. He'd likely lose some in the process, a fact he'd reconciled with. But he needed as much as he could get.

He was about to fund a war.

Of course, he'd set aside his notions of changing the world. Apparently the status quo was too strong, the people too stupid to want the same things he wanted.

Fine, he could live with that. He'd set his sights much smaller.

He was going to wage war on Matt Cooper.

Vogelsgang leaned back in his desk chair and massaged the bridge of his nose with his thumb and index finger. A glance at his watch told him he'd been awake for twenty-four hours.

He'd downed a half bottle of whiskey, occasionally lacing it with pink powder from crushed amphetamines. The speed had helped focus his mind while the whiskey insulated him from the concerns of watching a fissure open in the earth and swallow his entire empire.

He'd been able to do what mattered. A phone call to one of his South African contacts had led to him hiring a dozen or so mercenaries willing to spill blood for a couple of bucks.

It was a small force compared to what he'd had a week ago. But it would be enough for now.

He needed some time to think things through and plan his next move. Cooper, if that even was his name, was a high-level operative. He probably had no address, no family and few friends. Tracking him down wouldn't be easy, Vogelsgang realized. But he considered himself highly motivated to make it happen.

Filling his glass to the rim, he moved to the window and fixed his stare on the ocean waves rolling in. Further inland, a couple of guards armed with submachine guns stood on the beach. One was smoking a cigarette and kicking the sand with his booted foot. The second was lowering a pair of binoculars from his eyes and turning toward the house.

When he spotted Vogelsgang looking at him, he acknowledged him with a nod.

The German ignored him and cast his gaze to the right, not wanting to interact with his hired hands. A couple of seconds later a voice from below caught his attention. He felt his irritation rise. Was the guard yelling at him now, trying to get his attention?

He turned back toward the guards. He found the one who'd nodded still looking at him. Now he was pointing at Vogelsgang with one hand, grabbing for the machine pistol that hung from his shoulder.

What the hell? Vogelsgang opened his mouth to shout at the guard, but before he uttered a word, a large, dark shape zipped past his vision. A second later he heard something thud against the ground below. Acting on instinct, he hurled himself backward. A heartbeat later he heard the rattle of a submachine gun from down below, heard bullets smack into the building. Chatter from a second weapon joined in with the first.

Cooper was here!

His face a grim mask, Vogelsgang spun and returned to his desk. An MP-5 lay on the desktop. He scooped it up, clicked off the safety, aimed the weapon at the ceiling and squeezed the trigger. The weapon's steady rattle echoed throughout the chamber as the weapon churned out a blistering stream of autofire. Spent shell casings cascaded to the floor. Bullets punched through the ceiling and Vogelsgang hoped they'd pierce the flat roof and hit someone. Hunks of drywall and dust fell to the floor.

He kept spraying until the magazine cycled dry. He switched out magazines and emptied the fresh one into the ceiling, too. At the same time, he could hear more shouts and gun shots coming from elsewhere in the compound.

Ejecting another empty magazine, he tossed it aside and loaded the weapon again. He cast his gaze upward and saw sunlight peeking through the holes in the roof. He guessed his wild shooting had killed some of his own men. Vogelsgang could live with that. Mercenaries such as the ones around him were easy to come by for a man of his means. The only thing that mattered was killing Cooper.

BULLETS DRILLED THROUGH the rooftop at Bolan's feet. The fusillade splintered wood and shredded rubber roofing materials.

As the first slugs pierced the rooftop, Bolan, teeth gritted, wheeled around and launched into a dead run.

If he could outlast the initial burst of fire, he'd buy himself a few seconds while his attacker reloaded. That would give him enough time to cross the rooftop and dive through the doorway leading into the building. Not a great plan, but it was the best he had for the moment. He hadn't anticipated someone unloading a submachine gun into the roof.

The bullets sliced upward, missing his feet and legs by millimeters. He felt them tug at his pant legs. As he closed in on the door, it swung open. A squat man with black hair filled the doorway, a shotgun held close to his body. The Executioner triggered his FN SCAR assault rifle. Flames lashed out from the muzzle as the weapon spit 7.62 mm rounds. The barrage caught the guy in the torso, cutting a short, diagonal line across his upper body. He jerked under the onslaught, a strangled cry escaping his lips.

When the SCAR stopped spitting bullets, the guy's body collapsed to the rooftop. The shotgun fell, struck the ceiling and cut loose with the blast of a 12-gauge shell. The soldier stepped over the guard's corpse, through the door, over the landing. Aiming the SCAR down the stairs, he descended into the building. From below, he could hear raised voices and the slap of shoe soles striking bare floors. The sounds were muffled, he assumed, because a second door stood between the stairs and his targets.

By the time he reached the middle of the staircase, the door ahead of him cracked open, allowing a sliver of light into the darkened area, followed by the barrel of an assault rifle.

Bolan flattened against the wall and, gripping the SCAR in one hand, aimed it at the door. One of Vogelsgang's thugs poked his head through the space between the edge of the door and the jamb. The soldier couldn't see the guy's face, but judging by the angle of his head, he guessed his adversary's eyes were fixed on the wall opposite him.

The guy was pushing open the door with his elbow as he began to move through it.

Bolan could see another silhouetted form right behind the guy.

The soldier fired off a fast volley. Muzzle-flashes exploded and extinguished with a strobelike effect, illuminating the guy's surprised face. Bullets chewed into the man's chest. His body went limp and pitched forward.

Bolan continued down the stairs. The dead thug's body had fallen forward, wedging the door open. Two more silhouettes edged toward the stairwell entrance. Bolan snapped off a couple of quick bursts through the opening, the spray of bullets forcing the hardmen to scatter.

When Bolan reached the final step, he tapped out another fast burst before he went through the door in a crouch. One of the guards was pressed against a wall, his shooting hand extended forward. Flames and steel-jacketed slugs spit from his machine pistol. The line of bullets cut through the air just above Bolan's head. A second shooter had dropped to one knee and was trying to line up a kill shot at the warrior.

Bolan swept the rifle in a horizontal arc, hosing the guards with a torrent of blistering autofire. The assault rifle cycled dry. The Executioner released his grip and let it fall on its strap. Instinct told him to turn. In one fluid motion, he yanked the Beretta free from his shoulder holster and wheeled. Before he had turned more than a few inches, he heard thunder peal and felt something pound into his ribs.

The force of the impact stole his breath and shoved him off his feet. He found himself staring up at the ceiling. His mouth open, he tried unsuccessfully to refill his lungs, a slight wheeze escaping his lips. His ribs screamed with pain.

He lifted his head to see his attacker. He saw a dark form ahead of him, but his gaze was unfocused. Fortunately the Beretta had remained in his grip. The pistol came up and coughed out a trio of 9 mm stingers, followed by a second burst.

From what Bolan could tell, the rounds had missed his target. But he did cause the guy to duck and run away.

The soldier attempted another shallow pull of air. This time his chest had opened enough to allow in some breath. He propped himself up onto an elbow, his teeth clenching, to hold back the pain.

Bolan swept the Beretta across his field of vision, but saw no one. A steel security door pocked by several bullet holes stood closed in front of him. Whoever had attacked him had apparently fled through the door. Damn. Bolan raised himself from the floor.

As he got to his feet, he probed his rib cage under the trauma plates of his threat level III vest with the first two fingers of his left hand. In response, bolts of pain seared his midsection. Wincing, he pulled his hand away. He guessed he'd have one hell of a bruise on that side of his torso, but no broken ribs. Things had happened too quickly for him to know whether Vogelsgang was the shooter, though he guessed so. A mercenary, at least a trained one, would have sought cover from Bolan's return fire.

But with a target knocked on his back and possibly injured, a trained killer wouldn't have run far.

Before Bolan could take a step toward the door, his combat senses began screaming for his attention.

He spun, the sudden movement sparking more pain in his ribs. Two of Vogelsgang's foot soldiers were coming up behind Bolan, SMGs held at waist level. The Beretta extended in front of him, Bolan fired a quick burst of Parabellum slugs at the closer of the two shooters. The slugs drilled into the guy's torso. He yelped and stumbled back, his SMG's muzzle canting up 45 degrees as he moved. Flames and steel-jacketed slugs burst from the barrel, drilling into the ceiling.

The second shooter darted away from his injured comrade. He swung his SMG's barrel in Bolan's direction, ready to cut loose with a burst. The soldier reacted by triggering the 93-R. The weapon spit two quick bursts and a ragged line of red dots opened on the hardman's chest as the weapon stitched him from the right side of his abdomen to his left pectoral. The Executioner watched as his target wilted to the floor in a boneless heap.

Ejecting the nearly spent magazine from the Beretta, Bolan fed another into the weapon and slipped it back into his holster. He then took up the SCAR, reloaded it and crossed the room to the door through which the other shooter had disappeared.

Clutching the SCAR in his right hand, he popped open the door and slipped through it. Three doors opened off the hallway; two on the left, one on the right. A fourth door stood at the other end of the hallway, and Bolan assumed it led into another flight of stairs.

The Executioner edged along the wall, his ice-blue eyes sweeping his surroundings for more threats, his ears straining for clues as to whether more attackers lay ahead. His ribs continued to ache at the point where the bullet had struck his vest. He tried his best to ignore the pain.

Bolan slipped into the first door to his left and quickly cleared the room before moving into the second room on the same side. A quick sweep turned up nothing. Maybe Vogelsgang—or whoever had shot him—had decided to run.

Just before Bolan returned to the corridor, he heard a door slam closed. Muttering a curse, he stepped back into the corridor and marched to the door at the end of the hall. Through the heavy door, he could hear the thudding of feet scrambling down stairs.

Opening the door, he went through it in a crouch, ready to take down Vogelsgang forever.

A dark shape hurtling at him registered in his peripheral vision.

FROM ABOVE, VOGELSGANG heard the door open. On the wall, he could see a shadow version of the door opening, the shadow of a crouched figure coming through it. It had to be Cooper. A second shadow burst into view, and Vo-

gelsgang heard the smack of two bodies colliding, someone grunting with the impact.

He nodded to himself and continued down the stairs.
If Cooper had thought about it all, he probably assumed
Vogelsgang was running from him. In fact, the German
wanted to confront Cooper head-on. While he hadn't expected Cooper to find him so quickly, he'd realized that it
gave him exactly what he wanted; a chance to murder the
man who'd derailed his plans. Once he took Cooper out
of the picture, he could begin to rebuild his organization
under a new identity, perhaps. Maybe he'd never return to
its previous pinnacle. But at least he could begin to amass
some power again, maybe even revive the United Front.

But first things first.

Cooper needed to die.

Vogelsgang knew just how to make it happen. He'd let
Cooper run through a gauntlet before he'd ever reach him.
By the time the bastard got within shooting distance, he'd
be exhausted, vulnerable.

He'd kill the American.

But only if he could look into his eyes and watch the
life drain from them.

BOLAN WHEELED TO his right, with less than a heartbeat to
assess the situation. A man hurtled at him. The soldier
had a vague impression of wide shoulders and a big chest,
head shaved clean.

The Executioner tried to step out of the other man's
path. The landing they were on was cramped, the sides
hemmed in by a railing. The soldier whipped sideways
and swung the buttstock of his assault rifle in an arc and
struck the guy's jaw with an audible crack.

If it hurt the guy, he gave no outward sign. Instead,
moving with a speed that belied someone of his size, he
whipped around to face Bolan. His right hand lashed out,

grabbed hold of Bolan's web gear, yanked him from the ground and slammed him against the wall.

The impact of his body striking a brick wall caused the soldier to grunt. He brought around the SCAR, planning to put the guy down with a quick blast of autofire. The hardman grabbed Bolan's wrist in one of his massive hands and squeezed the soldier's bones as if he was wringing water from a towel.

The guy moved his face closer to Bolan's. His nose was wide and flat, his nostrils flaring with exertion. His lips had curled back, exposing gritted teeth. The Executioner tipped his head back and thrust it forward. His forehead smacked into his opponent's. A white light exploded behind his eyes when their heads collided. The hardman's grip loosened and he whipped his face away.

Black dots swam in Bolan's vision and pain quickly spread through his forehead.

He cocked his right leg back, released it in a vicious arc. His shin bone smacked hard into the other man's groin, not stopping until it collided with the thug's pelvis.

A rush of air bellowed from between the other man's lips. He released his grip on Bolan and pulled his hands back, as though burned. The soldier plummeted to the ground, his hand reaching for his Ka-Bar fighting knife even as his feet struck the landing.

Bolan swung back his arm and thrust the blade at an upward angle at the other man's gut.

The Ka-Bar's steel bit deeply into the man's stomach and he yelped in surprise and pain.

The soldier tried to yank the blade free. Before he could, the massive mercenary swung one of his cinder-block fists at Bolan. It was a wild punch. But fueled by rage, pain and adrenaline, the guy was able to move quickly. Bolan threw himself to the side, releasing his grip on his knife. The bigger man's knuckles brushed the soldier's temple, knocking his head to one side and his body against the railing.

The mercenary had ripped the knife from his belly and, screaming, raised it above his head. Bolan's foot lashed out and his heel slammed into his opponent's knee.

The damage to his knee caused the man's legs to buckle, and he sank to the ground.

Bolan scrambled across the floor until he could reach his fallen knife. His hand lashed out and he wrapped his fingers around the handle, brought the knife up from the ground and thrust it into the other man's throat.

Razor-sharp steel nicked the guy's carotid artery and blood spurted from his neck.

His lips parted and he released a gurgling noise. One of his big hands slapped at his neck, desperately trying to get hold of the knife or to cover the wound that was taking his life. Bolan uncoiled from the floor and stood over the man, who bled out in seconds.

The soldier turned and moved to the stairs.

Kurtzman and the cyber team had tracked down plans to the building in one of the public databases and had forwarded them to Bolan. The plans had been simple, and the soldier guessed Vogelsgang had made countless modifications over the years. But at least from the exterior, everything had matched the original designs. Three exits—two at ground level, one in front, the other in back. The rooftop door he'd used to enter the building was the third. The rear entrance actually led into a small garage outfitted with a car elevator that lowered into an underground garage. The stairwell Bolan was using also wound down to the garage.

The soldier assumed Vogelsgang was heading to the garage so he could climb into one of his cars and escape. But he decided to check out the first floor quickly, in case the guy had panicked and tried to flee on foot. It took the soldier just a couple of minutes to clear the first floor,

where he found no one. He started back toward the stairwell, ready to go to the lower level, but halted in midstride.
Turning, he headed back to the first-floor garage.

VOGELSGANG RACED DOWN the stairs.

When he reached the bottom, he paused at a keypad
fixed to the wall next to the doorway leading into the underground garage, and punched in a lengthy numeric code.

Once he'd entered the final number, the mechanism
beeped softly, the door released and swung inward. Passing through it, he held the door open with the side of his
foot until he found an angled piece of rubber used as a
doorstop and slipped it under the door.

Returning to the keypad, he tapped in another sequence
of numbers, an override code that kept the security system
active even with the door open. He then pressed a second
set of numbers and a pair of red lights began to flash on
the keypad.

He stared at the lights for a couple of seconds and a
smile crossed his lips.

Now another unpleasant surprise awaited Cooper, the
German thought.

The first of several.

THE DINING AREA opened directly into larger room. It was
furnished with a couch, a couple of chairs and a large,
muted television that was broadcasting a soccer game. A
coffee mug stood on one of the tables. A water bottle lay
on its side at the edge of the table, a drop of water gathering in its mouth, ready to drop the floor where the bottle's
contents had gathered. A newspaper lay on the ground,
where it apparently had been tossed aside.

Bolan guessed guards or building staff had been here
passing time when taking a break when the first shots
rang out. Had they been among those he'd already killed

or were they still in the house? He edged into the room, scanned the area and found it was empty. While he crossed the room, he noted traces of cologne in the air, mixed with food smells from the kitchen.

When he reached the other side of the room, he moved cautiously through a second door and found himself in a short corridor.

The front door and a small entryway stood at one end of the corridor. Turning away, he saw two doors lined the wall to his right. A rectangular shaft of light spilled from one of the doors into the hallway, flagging Bolan it was open. The second door was closed. At the other end of the hallway was another door to Bolan's left. He guessed it led back into the kitchen.

Gliding along the wall, the soldier slipped into the nearest room. A couple of desks—each topped with a computer monitor and stray papers—stood in the room, along with rolling chairs and short filing cabinets. He found no people.

The soldier stepped back into the hallway. His nose wrinkled involuntarily and he noticed the smell of the cologne had grown stronger. He moved to the second door and tried the handle, but found it locked. The soldier switched out the SCAR for the Desert Eagle, aimed at the lock and squeezed the trigger. The Desert Eagle's blast filled the cramped hallway.

The boattail slug punched through the lock. The door trembled, but the ragged lock held until Bolan drove a booted foot into it.

The door rocketed inward. Bolan threw himself to one side of the entrance just as autofire erupted from within the room and streams of bullets sliced into the hallway. Slugs hammered into the wall opposite the door, chewed into plaster and began to choke the air with dust. The soldier dropped to one knee and snagged a grenade from his web gear. Bullets had begun to pierce the wall at his back, showering him with dust. Fortunately the shooters were aiming high, peppering the wall several feet up from the floor. Bolan guessed that would change in another second or two.

The soldier pulled the pin from the grenade and tossed the deadly egg around the door jamb and darted to his right. With the wall at his back shredded, Bolan couldn't be sure how well it would contain the grenade's shrapnel.

A second later the gunfire stopped and an instant after that a roar swelled up from inside the room. The blast from the grenade caused the wall to bow out. Bolan rose, the Desert Eagle in one hand, and went through the door in a crouch. Two men were sprawled on the floor of what turned out to be a garage, their flesh and clothes rent by the blast. Bits of razor-sharp metal had burrowed into the walls. Smoke wafted in the air.

The soldier moved up on the remains and studied them. Both had been clad in blue jeans; one wore tennis shoes, the other brown loafers.

From the flashes Bolan had caught of Vogelsgang, he'd been wearing dress pants and a white shirt.

Bolan had taken down two more gunners, but the head guy still was at large. On the run, but running out of places to go.

The Executioner gave the garage a closer look. A workbench ran the length of one wall in the windowless room. A rectangular seam in the floor outlined the top of the car elevator. A steel electrical box, bunches of frayed wires sticking out from the back, lay on the floor. The soldier guessed it was the controls for the car lift. It had been located a dozen or so feet from the blast, so Bolan guessed Vogelsgang's guards had ripped it from the wall before the grenade had exploded.

If Bolan was going into the underground garage, he was going to need the stairs. Just as he turned, two more shooters darted into the garage. One surged toward Bolan. He was swinging the muzzle of his SMG at Bolan while the second guard was running for the stairs. The Desert Eagle bucked in Bolan's grip. A Magnum slug punched into the guy's center mass. The impact shoved him backward. His finger tightened on the trigger in a final death spasm and the small, black SMG he held rattled a fast burst that missed Bolan by several inches.

The other guard stopped running for the stairs and wheeled toward the soldier, trying to bring his pistol into target acquisition.

The Desert Eagle roared twice more and the punch of the bullets thrust Bolan's opponent down the stairs. An instant later an explosion pealed from within the stairs, reverberating for a moment before it diminished.

The soldier rolled over and cast his gaze on the stairwell. Gray smoke rolled upward and spread through the garage. Bolan headed to the stairway door. Smoke stinging his eyes, he peered into the passage and saw the guard's limp form sprawled below, his legs turned at unnatural angles. One arm, encased in fabric, blackened by fire and smeared with blood, had been separated from the guy's shoulder. It lay, bent at a 45-degree angle, silver watch still wound around the wrist, on the top step.

His eyes lighting on the area around the second step from the bottom, Bolan saw where a portion of paneled wall had been torn away. The edges around the hole were blackened.

A constellation of pockmarks covered the walls and other surfaces of the enclosed staircase. Bolan guessed whatever explosive device had been planted in the wall had been packed with ball bearings for maximum killing power. The explosion had ripped away the carpeting on the stairs, exposing a metal pressure plate on the second step from the bottom.

Given his options, the soldier had to assume Vogelsgang was in the basement. He had no other way into the
lowest level. No other pressure plates were visible on the
stairs, but Bolan still stepped gingerly onto the first step
as he began his descent.

TREMORS OF ANTICIPATION raced through Vogelsgang as he
crept toward the stairs just seconds after the explosion
tore through it.

The industrialist had the H&K pointed ahead of him,
the buttstock pressed against his shoulder. Even before he
reached the stairs, he could see crimson smeared over the
walls, and saw a limp hand, fingers curled inward, resting on one of the steps. A thin smile spread over his lips.
He'd gotten the son of a bitch. Of course he had, he told
himself. For all the American's training and skills, Vogelsgang still was superior. Physically and mentally he
was more capable than most other men in the world. He
guessed Cooper was the best America had to send. He'd
killed America's best.

It would only be the beginning, he told himself.

After another couple of steps he could see a leg clad in
tattered gray slacks. The calf jutted back at an impossible
angle, the foot was missing.

Vogelsgang's blood ran cold.

He recognized the dead man as one of his own mercenaries, not Cooper.

His gaze flicked up to the head of the stairs.

He spotted a grim-faced man, clad in black, standing
on the top step.

Vogelsgang took in the pistol barrel pointed at him, then
the ice-blue eyes trained on him.

Cooper.

Move! Vogelsgang's mind screamed. He swung up the
H&K's barrel and stroked the trigger.

BOLAN DOUBLE TAPPED the Desert Eagle's trigger. The rounds pounded into Vogelsgang's face, one through the mouth, a second into the bridge of the guy's nose before punching through the back of his skull, reducing it to a fine mist. The German's body went limp and collapsed to the floor in a crumpled heap.

The soldier stared at him for a second and thought about the destruction he'd caused. His actions had left many dead. Putting him down probably wouldn't put their souls at rest, but it at least would give them a measure of justice. And by destroying Vogelsgang's network, he'd also garnered his country a measure of security, no matter how fleeting.

His mission complete, Bolan plucked an incendiary grenade from his combat webbing, pulled the pin and tossed the grenade down the stairs. Spinning on his heel, he sprinted for the nearest door wanting to put some distance between him and the hellstorm about to rip through the underground cavity.

* * * * *